A COMFORTING KISS

"My poor girl." Mark pulled Sophia into his arms and held her tight, wishing desperately that he could say something that would lift her spirits during what was bound to be a lonely journey to a place where she knew no one. "I wish I could help."

"You have." She smiled tremulously. "Just knowing that I have you as a friend . . ."

"A friend you may always call upon if you need him." Mark bent his head to press his lips to hers. He had meant the kiss to seal his pledge of friendship, but as his lips touched hers, something happened. He became acutely aware of the softness of her skin, the delicate scent of lavender, the slenderness of her waist beneath his hands, the long, slim line of her thigh pressed against his, and he found himself kissing her hungrily, desperately, fueled by a desire he had not thought possible. . . .

Lord Harry's
Daughter

Evelyn Richardson

A SIGNET BOOK

SIGNET
Published by New American Library, a division of
Penguin Putnam Inc., 375 Hudson Street,
New York, New York 10014, U.S.A.
Penguin Books Ltd, 27 Wrights Lane,
London W8 5TZ, England
Penguin Books Australia Ltd, Ringwood,
Victoria, Australia
Penguin Books Canada Ltd, 10 Alcorn Avenue,
Toronto, Ontario, Canada M4V 3B2
Penguin Books (N.Z.) Ltd, 182–190 Wairau Road,
Auckland 10, New Zealand

Penguin Books Ltd, Registered Offices:
Harmondsworth, Middlesex, England

First published by Signet, an imprint of New American Library,
a division of Penguin Putnam Inc.

First Printing, January 2001
10 9 8 7 6 5 4 3 2 1

PUBLISHER'S NOTE
This is a work of fiction. Names, characters, places, and incidents either are the
product of the author's imagination or are used fictitiously, and any resemblance
to actual persons, living or dead, business establishments, events or locales is
entirely coincidental.

BOOKS ARE AVAILABLE AT QUANTITY DISCOUNTS WHEN USED TO PROMOTE PROD-
UCTS OR SERVICES. FOR INFORMATION PLEASE WRITE TO PREMIUM MARKETING DIVI-
SION, PENGUIN PUTNAM INC., 375 HUDSON STREET, NEW YORK, NEW YORK 10014.

If you purchased this book without a cover you should be aware that this book
is stolen property. It was reported as "unsold and destroyed" to the publisher
and neither the author nor the publisher has received any payment for this
"stripped book."

To Poni and Bob

Chapter 1

Major Lord Mark Adair swept the horizon with his spy-glass one last time before closing it and sliding it back in his saddlebag. Then mounting a powerful chestnut horse who had been waiting patiently while his master surveyed the fortress below, he galloped back up the headland over-looking San Sebastian and headed back toward headquarters.

Lesaca was some ten miles away, and having spent the better part of the day in the hot July sun, observing and sketching possible approaches to the fortified city on the isthmus that connected the fort to the shore, the major was looking forward to a drink and a meal. He leaned over his horse's neck, urging it to a gallop. Caesar, who had spent his day standing quietly while his master worked, was only too happy to oblige, and they thundered along the rough road, leaving a trail of dust in their wake.

At last, as the sun was beginning its slow descent, they climbed their final hill before headquarters and, reaching the top, pulled up in astonishment, for there, not twenty yards away, as unconcerned as if she were on her family estate instead of the middle of a field between two oppos-ing armies, sat a young woman, leaning forward as she ex-amined the easel in front of her and then reached up with her brush to apply a few careful strokes. She paused, her brush in midair as she surveyed the scene in front of her, selected another color, and added a few more strokes to the picture.

Curiosity overcame his astonishment. Mark dismounted and walked toward the artist, who seemed blissfully un-aware that she had taken her seat and set up her easel in the middle of a war. *"Buenos días, señorita,"* he began courteously.

The young woman whirled around, her large hazel eyes, shaded by the brim of a straw-colored satin bonnet, were wide with surprise. In one glance she took in the dragoon's uniform, the dusty but superbly constructed boots, the unmistakably English horse, and let out a gentle sigh. "Good day, Major."

"You are English?" It was astounding enough to discover a woman in such surroundings, but to come across an Englishwoman was even more incredible. What sort of woman would sit so calmly in a field where soldiers from the Spanish, French, Portuguese, or British armies, not to mention guerillas of all sorts, could happen upon her. For a moment, Lord Mark was too nonplussed to respond. "My dear young woman, what on earth can have possessed you to wander off alone in such a manner? Do you have no idea . . ."

"That there is a war on? Of course I do, and I would venture to say that I have been aware of it longer than you have." Observing that the major was still having difficulty with the entire concept of her presence, the young woman took pity on him. Her expression of haughty annoyance softened a little. "I *do* have a groom with me." She nodded toward a lone tree several yards away where a man was sitting in the shade, a rifle in his lap and pistols in his belt, his gaze sweeping the countryside. Next to him stood two horses, one of which appeared to have another musket secured to its saddle.

"Well that is something at least, but one could hardly say that this is the proper place, or even a safe one, for a young lady."

"I appreciate your concern, Major." There was no mistaking the sarcastic tone of her voice. "But I have lived among soldiers my entire life and in the middle of the war for the past four years. I assure you, I am well aware of the state of affairs here in the Peninsula. Now if you will excuse me, the light is beginning to fade." She dabbed her brush in another color of paint and turned back to her easel.

It was a clear dismissal, but he was not about to accept it. No woman ever before had ignored Lord Mark Adair, second son of the Duke of Cranleigh. Ever since he had kissed his first tavern wench outside the taproom of the

King's Head in Cranleigh, Lord Mark had been the object of female attention, from the fluttering eyelashes of well brought-up young ladies to the more frankly appreciative smiles of opera dancers and Cyprians of all types. While he did not necessarily share their view of him as a wealthy and attractive prize worthy of capture, he was not accustomed to being dismissed so summarily. Actually, he was more intrigued by her obvious lack of interest in him than he was by her abrupt dismissal.

Ignoring her clear desire for his departure, he strode closer to get a better look at her work. The power of her picture took him by surprise. It was the scene in front of him, golden hills rolling off into the distance dotted by the occasional tree—yet it was not the same scene. She had invested it with all the passion of the wild blasts of wind that swept down from the Pyrenees and the restless energy that one felt under the broad expanse of the bright blue sky. It was a picture of the Spanish landscape, but it was more than that; it was a portrait of freedom itself, and it quite took his breath away.

"It is superb." The comment was wrenched out of him before he could even think of what he wanted to say.

"You are too kind." It was obvious from the ironic note in her voice that she had heard similar remarks countless times before.

"I am sure that more than one admiring officer has compared your style to Turner's, but in some ways I prefer yours. It is cleaner, without sacrificing the intensity. To achieve that effect in watercolors rather than oil must take a good deal of skill, not to mention years of practice."

That caught her attention. In fact, no one ever *had* compared her to Turner, and she would have been willing to bet that not many of the officers who, in their attempts to win her attention, told her how talented she was would have been able to name one painter born after Michelangelo. She turned to observe the officer more closely. Surprisingly enough, there was not a hint of guile in his dark eyes or the thin well-shaped lips. In fact, looking at the painting more closely, he seemed to have forgotten her entirely. Strolling over to the easel he tilted his head to one side and then the other, examining it carefully. Then he gazed off into the distance and back again at the picture.

So, he truly had meant what he said. A man bent on flattery would have been studying the artist rather than the picture, gauging the effect of his compliments on her and taking advantage of that effect rather than appreciating the finer points of her technique. This man, however, studied her picture with the intensity and concentration of a connoisseur and she could not help being intrigued by his indifference to her.

All her life Sophia Featherstonaugh, the darling of her father's regiment, had been surrounded by men, and she was more than accustomed to being the object of their attention. As the daughter of Lord Harry Featherstonaugh, one of England's most attractive wastrels, a daughter whose hopes had been continually raised and then just as regularly dashed by a man who promised everything and gave nothing, Sophia had become immune to masculine charm at a very tender age, having learned when she was very young, just how deceptive flattery could be.

Cocking her head to one side she studied the officer carefully as he continued to examine her work. As an artist she had trained herself to observe closely, to read the personality in the features. But there was no need for close observation here; everything about the man spoke of an energy and determination, not to mention courage, from the white line of a scar across his temple to the powerful shoulders, slim hips, and strong, lean hands of a cavalry officer. The tanned angular face with its high cheekbones and long narrow nose wore the expression of a man accustomed to dominating every situation, and there was an intensity of purpose in the dark brown eyes that was almost palpable. Only the mouth was at odds with this impression. The finely sculpted lips belied an elusive sensitivity that was so well hidden it might have been missed by the ordinary observer, but not by Sophia. She not only saw it, she sensed it in the way he looked at her picture, focusing all of his attention on it as though he were committing it to memory.

At last he sighed and stepped back. "Amazing what a sense of force a few well-delivered brush strokes can convey. You have captured the twists in that wind-blasted tree exactly, though how you can tell it from here I can not fathom. I passed it so I know, but you . . ."

"I have been training myself to observe everything for

years, to remember the touch and feel of it all so I can capture it later."

"You not only capture it, you invest it with a life of its own. Tell me, can you do the same thing if someone only describes it to you instead of your seeing it for yourself?"

"I . . . well, I can not say. I have never tried it before. I am not an imaginative painter; I do not create pictures in my mind before I put them on paper. I am merely an illustrator, painting what I see—people, horses, the countryside around me."

"This"—he waved a hand toward her picture—"is no mere faithful representation of a scene. It is passion itself. It shows the forces of nature at work. It makes the observer feel the wind in his face and the sun beating down upon his back."

"Why thank you." Sophia was pleased in spite of herself. Ordinarily she did not like to discuss her pictures with anyone, for they were too personal, too much a part of her to share with strangers who, more often than not, were more likely to base their comments on the way they felt toward the artist than the way they reacted to the picture. This man was different. It was clear that at this moment, he was far more interested in the painting that in its painter and Sophia did not know whether to feel flattered or insulted.

"Do you think if I described something to you, you could draw it?"

"I could try." She sounded doubtful.

"I have been reconnoitering over by San Sebastian and I have drawn a rough map of the area, but if I had a picture to show the men leading the attack it would make it all much clearer to them. Here." He pulled a crumpled piece of paper from his pocket and held it out to her.

Sophia studied it for a moment and then reached for her sketchbook, rifling through it in search of a blank sheet of paper.

"Wait a minute." Lord Mark put his hand out to stop her as he caught sight of a sketch of Wellington in laughing conversation with his secretary, Lord Fitzroy Somerset. "This is wonderful! So very like him, yet unlike any of the formal portraits which always portray him as a stern visionary. You show a side of him that anyone who spends time in his company sees. And Somerset, here, is given the importance he deserves for, in my opinion, he is a man whose value is severely underestimated. Both of them are as real as if they were sitting right here in front of us. You must know them well. Is your father attached to headquarters then?"

"It is nothing"—Sophia hastily flipped over the paper to a blank sheet—"just a rough impression I happened to do one evening after dinner. Now what did you wish me to draw?"

Mark looked at her curiously for a moment. Ordinarily young ladies were more than eager to show off their accomplishments to admiring gentlemen, but this one, who actually possessed considerable talent, appeared to wish to keep it hidden. "Ah, yes, the fortifications around San Sebastian. Now you see from the map I drew how they are laid out, but I also wish to convey the difficulty of the terrain, which poses a significant challenge. The castle is on the promontory in the sea and the town itself is at its foot and almost completely surrounded by water. It is only connected to the mainland by a low, sandy isthmus which, naturally enough, is heavily fortified. The mouth of the Urumea River is on the eastern side of the isthmus and at low tide it is possible to ford it, but it will be tough going. All around the mouth of the river are sand hills that will afford an excellent position to set up batteries, but will make it difficult for troops to climb down, for they will be extremely vulnerable to the French artillery, and then the stretch of sand and the shallow water our troops will be forced to cross to reach the town is nearly two hundred yards. The tide is such that the entire operation will have to be accomplished in broad daylight and without support from our navy."

Sophia began sketching slowly as he spoke, using his maps as an outline and adding detail as he pointed out a ridge here, a grassy slope there, and a seawall there, and the expanse of sandy soil that could be easily dug for trenches. At last they were done and Mark gazed at the picture with satisfaction. "Excellent. That is very like it and it will make my task of reporting it a great deal easier. I thank you. But now"—he glanced off to the west, where the sun was beginning to slip behind the rugged hills—"I fear that not only is the light fading, but I have taken up so much of your time that soon there will be very little of it left at all. May I help you gather up your things by way of an apology and escort you back to . . ."

"Thank you, no. I mean, that is very kind of you, but I would like to add one or two more touches."

He had never known a woman so eager to be rid of him, or to be so closemouthed about herself. Usually, given half a chance, every female of his acquaintance would have prattled on about her pictures, her friends, her family, and her admirers until he knew more than he cared to about every detail of her existence. As it was, he did not even know where this woman had come from; she had completely ignored his attempt to discover that as well as the identity of her father. "Well, good evening, then. And thank you, for your assistance."

Throwing himself on Caesar's back he rode off toward headquarters, leaving her there in the middle of the field, her easel in front of her, knowing no more about her than if she had sprung up from the every earth where he had found her, nothing, that was, except that she was a very powerful and talented artist.

Chapter 2

Sophia gave a few desultory dabs to her picture as the sound of hooves receded into the distance. Then she sat back and gazed out over the landscape until she was sure the rider was long gone. All of her life she had been surrounded by soldiers, cavalry officers in general, but this particular officer had had an unusually strong effect on her and she wanted to be alone to sort out her thoughts before returning to the small house on the outskirts of Lesaca where her mother and her stepfather, General Sir Thornton Curtis, were quartered.

Watching the sky as it turned from azure to pink and gold, she straightened up with a start as she realized that she did not even know the officer's name. In fact, she really knew nothing about him except that he was a cavalry officer who rode a magnificent piece of horseflesh extremely well. But that could have described any number of cavalry officers, most of them, in fact. Why then did she feel, after only the briefest of exchanges, as though she had learned enough about the man to want to know more, a great deal more, about him?

It was not his dashing good looks, for Sophia, constantly surrounded by gallant men in uniform, was inured to those. As the daughter of a man who had used his charm to its best advantage, she was fare more likely to mistrust a pleasing countenance than she was to be attracted to it. And as she mentally analyzed the major's features, she decided that they were too irregular to be thought of as classically handsome—the cheekbones were too high, the nose and the dark brows too prominent to be considered pleasing—but it was a face with character, a face that one would not easily forget and, in Sophia's case, a face that drew her to the man. The eyes, keen as a hawk's, had swept over her and scrutinized her with an intensity that was almost palpable, as though the man were trying to read her mind and her soul as well as remember her face.

Slowly Sophia gathered her things and put them in a satchel. She would have to ask her stepfather's batman about the major. Speen knew everything there was to know about everyone, or if he didn't, he could be counted on to find out, though it might be rather difficult with no name to go by. She could hardly expect Speen to know or discover anything about a man whose only definitive characteristics were that he rode like the devil, intruded into people's private moments, and analyzed their paintings with a skill and sensitivity beyond the grasp of almost anyone she had ever known.

Sophia thought back over their encounter, trying to recall other details that might identify this particular officer. He had been mapping the fortifications at San Sebastian, so it was clear that he was someone important enough to be trusted with a reconnaissance mission, which only narrowed the field to a choice of a hundred or so. And what reason was she going to offer Speen, who would naturally be suspicious, of her sudden interest in a man whose name she did not even know?

"The senhorita is ready to go now?" Luis sprang to his feet to take Sophia's satchel and help her onto Atalanta's back. The bay mare pricked up her ears and snorted in eagerness to gallop after her afternoon of inactivity. Sophia trotted her through the tall grass to the rough road down which the major had disappeared. "Now, my girl, let us show anyone who cares to see us that the major and his horse are not the only ones who can raise a cloud of dust." She touched the horse's flank with her heels and they flew off down the road with Luis following at a more rational pace.

"The senhorita will get herself killed one day riding like that. It is not normal. If the Good Lord had wanted man to fly he would have given him wings instead of legs," the servant muttered to himself as, trying to keep his mistress in sight, he urged his own mount to greater speed.

Oblivious to Luis's efforts to keep up with her, Sophia leaned over Atalanta's neck, glorying in the speed and the sense of freedom she always felt with the wind in her hair.

Now that the sun was setting she had removed her bonnet, tying its ribbons securely around her neck so that it bounced on her back as she rode, adding to the sensation of having cast off all restraints, for the moment at least. Once they came in sight of the pickets she would slow to a more sedate trot, replace the bonnet on her head, and conduct herself like a properly brought-up young lady and the stepdaughter of General Sir Thornton Curtis, but for now, she wanted to stretch her cramped muscles and loosen up after the hours of concentration in front of the easel. She wanted to revel in the wind and the sky and become part of the restless energy she had been trying to capture in her picture.

The road widened and its surface became somewhat smoother. Up ahead Sophia caught sight of an oxcart, laden with provisions, lumbering toward Lesaca. Pulling on the reins, she halted Atalanta, adjusted her bonnet, and then urged her into a ladylike trot. Glancing behind her, she could just make out the dark speck that was Luis. Poor Luis. Sophia grinned. She knew she was a constant trial to him, and she did feel sorry for the worry he suffered. She had told him times out of mind that he had no cause for concern, for she had practically been born on the back of a horse.

One of the few times that Lord Harry Featherstonaugh had paid attention to his infant daughter was the day when in a fit of desperation, he had taken her—a screaming, squalling bundle that refused to sleep—and trotted off down a country road so that her mother could get some rest. The motion of the horse had lulled Sophia into slumber almost immediately and won for her her father's respect, if not his continued attention.

After that, whenever Lord Harry could stop his gambling, drinking, and wenching long enough to remember his family, it was to make sure that his little girl grew up into a bruising rider capable of handling any horse that her father could put her on. By the time he had been killed in a futilely reckless charge across a ditch at Talavera, Lord Harry had at least succeeded in doing that for her, though he had given her very little else except an extreme reluctance to rely on any man for anything and a healthy cynicism where dashing men of wit and charm were concerned.

Fortunately for Sophia, before she had become a complete misanthrope, her mother had met and married Sir Thornton Curtis, a man as different from the rash and irresponsible Lord Harry as water was from wine. Where Lord Harry had charmed with clever conversation and empty promises, Sir Thornton won with practical sympathy and solid support, and the wife who had never known where her irrepressible first husband was to be found, or in what condition, now discovered the joys of a husband who preferred his own fireside to any tavern and the company of his own wife to the charms of any of the fascinating courtesans that walked the streets or graced the brothels of Lisbon.

This new matrimonial bliss was hard won and therefore doubly appreciated by the new Lady Curtis. The former Maria Edgehill had suffered much and for many years since she had first encountered the devastatingly handsome Lord Harry at a Harrogate assembly seventeen years before.

The only daughter in a strict Methodist household, the young Maria had longed for the wit and gaiety of society, something that was almost nonexistent in the wilds of Yorkshire. It was only by her mother's forcible representations to her father of the expense of supporting a grown-up daughter that Maria had been allowed to visit an aunt in Harrogate long enough to attend the assemblies and find a suitable husband to take her off her father's hands.

One dance with Lord Harry Featherstonaugh, the handsome younger son of the Duke of Broughton, had been sufficient to make her forget all her logical reasons for wishing to marry and Maria fell immediately and totally in love with the dashing scapegrace.

And, to do him justice, Lord Harry had fallen in love with her too. The young Maria with her glossy dark hair, pure white and rose complexion, and dark blue eyes was extraordinarily beautiful; furthermore she worshiped him. To Harry, accustomed to being the despair of his family, her admiration was balm to a wounded soul and he pursued her with all the ardor of a young man who had always been given anything he desired except love and admiration.

However, despite the Duke of Broughton's loud and repeated declarations that by buying his son a commission in the cavalry he had washed his hands of the young man and

his ruinous way of life, he had not washed his hands sufficiently not to be utterly horrified with the news that his
son wished to marry a provincial nobody.

Oddly enough, Maria's parents were no more enthusiastic than the duke over their daughter's engagement to a
wild and spendthrift young nobleman and they expressed
their displeasure as forcibly as the Duke of Broughton had.
Both families threatened to cut off their offspring without
a farthing if the match were brought forward, but Maria
and Harry were deaf to the dire threats of poverty and loss
of familial support and one glorious day in October of 1792
they eloped to Gretna Green.

By the time Sophia was born in August of the next year
a good deal of the romance had already gone out of the
marriage and Lord Harry was beginning to discover that
his ladylove could be just as annoyed by his unsteadiness
and his reckless disregard for anyone but himself as his
family had been.

To her credit, the new Lady Harry never voiced the
slightest criticism of her husband's callous behavior; however, it was hard to be trapped at home with only a small
baby for companionship while her husband was off enjoying himself and losing the money he might be using to
make his family's life more comfortable.

In the end, Maria bore her husband's neglect without
complaint, quietly dedicating herself to her little daughter
and to creating a home that was welcoming whenever her
husband saw fit to grace it with his presence. Her forbear-
ance, while it did not recapture the ardent affection of their
first infatuation, at least won Lord Harry's gratitude and
the dubious pleasure of being called his *good little puss* as
he kissed her good-bye before embarking on another evening of revelry.

When Lord Harry's regiment had been ordered to the
Peninsula, Maria and the baby, not having anywhere else
to go, had followed along and, oddly enough, things had
improved for a while. There had been too much real soldiering to be done for Lord Harry to find time to get into
trouble, and the qualities that had made him such a
wretched husband and father—his recklessness, his thirst
for excitement, and his craving for attention—made him a
soldier to be reckoned with. While no sane commander was

willing to risk a large body of men by putting them under Lord Harry's leadership, everyone acknowledged that if there was a dangerous mission to be accomplished or a charge to be led, Lord Harry was the man to do it.

Lord Harry's wife had also taken to life in the Peninsula, where she found herself making a home for more than just her own family. The men of Harry's regiment, longing for the families they had left behind, naturally gravitated toward the Featherstonaughs' quarters whether they were in a peasant hut or apartments in some provincial capital.

While Lady Harry might not have the companionship of her own husband, she could always count on being the center of a little group of officers who looked forward to an evening of quiet conversation in front of the fire.

Following the drum was an unusual upbringing for a child, but Sophia, who had never known any other sort of life, enjoyed it thoroughly, for there was always someone to talk to or to teach her something. Her eagerness to learn was totally disarming and young officers who had begrudged every minute spent poring over their Greek or Latin now found themselves wishing they had paid more attention as they struggled to recall what their masters at Eton or Harrow had taught them so they could explain things to Lord Harry's daughter.

Brothers who had refused to allow their sisters to tag along now found themselves falling over one another to teach her to fence, and shoot. But no one except Lord Harry was allowed to teach her to ride, for the very simple reason that he was clearly the best there was, no matter the horse, no matter the terrain. And his daughter took after him.

By the time she was ten, there was hardly a horse in the regiment she was not capable of handling. And when her father did take the time to pay attention to her, he would allow as how she was a natural horsewoman. "It is the Featherstonaugh blood," he would say, "and believe you me, it is the only damned thing you will ever inherit from them—not that you would want anything else from them— a pack of stiff-rumps the lot of them."

But by the time she was old enough to understand such a remark, Sophia was also old enough to know that there were two sides to every issue, and she had seen enough of her father's unreliable nature to suspect that the Featherstonaughs he criticized so harshly might seem considerably less rigid to a normal person. However, she did not regret the lack of relatives, for she had the entire regiment to look after her.

Indeed, when her father had been killed leading the men across the treacherous ditch at Talavera, she hardly missed him. Lord Harry had been such an infrequent presence at their meals or around their quarters that Sophia and her mother hardly noticed his absence.

The army moved to quarters in Lisbon and it was there that Lady Harry had decided to settle. She had no family in England to return to, and both the climate and the companionship were far more welcoming in Portugal than they would have been in England. It was in Lisbon that she became reacquainted with General Sir Thornton Curtis, one of Wellington's quartermasters who was helping to oversee the construction of fortifications for the city.

Sir Thornton's first wife had died in childbirth and, having no children of his own, he gravitated toward everyone else's. It had been Sir Thornton and not Lord Harry who remembered Sophia's birthdays and saw that the Featherstonaughs were made comfortable if he happened to be in the regiment's vicinity. Thus it was only natural for him to reestablish their friendship when he discovered that Maria and her daughter had set up house in Lisbon. And it was only natural that after years of looking out for them whenever he could, that he would make this attention official by making Lady Harry, Lady Curtis. Sophia's mother had blossomed as the general's wife. The lines of worry on her lovely face had been smoothed away by a solicitous husband who returned to his fireside at regular hours.

The fortification of Lisbon had been completed and Sophia and her mother had moved into Spain with Sir Thornton and the rest of the army. The general was a congenial and popular commander, which meant that their quarters, wherever they might be, were always a center for officers who sought a good dinner and a homelike atmosphere, two things that Sophia and her mother were more than happy to provide.

With the arrival of Sir Thornton had come the happiest period in Sophia's life. Even if she had not been fond of the bluff old soldier she could never be grateful enough for all he had done to make them comfortable and secure. Now every evening she could look forward to companionship and conversation instead of tense hours waiting for Lord Harry to return, wondering what condition he would be in.

Arriving at the modest half-timbered dwelling that was their home in Lesaca, Sophia dismounted and led Atalanta to the stable, reflecting as she did so on the good fortune that had brought the general to them in their bleakest period.

Sophia poured oats into the feed trough and then, with a final pat, bid Atalanta good night before turning to thank Luis for his escort. "I know it is a trial and that you disapprove of it thoroughly, but thank you just the same."

The servant grinned, his teeth gleaming white in his swarthy face. He shrugged and lifted his hands in humorous resignation. "What else am I to do? The senhorita will go on these rides so I go too. But the senhorita should not be tending to her horse. That is a job for Luis not for Senhorita Featherstonaugh."

"I know, I know. We have been through this a hundred times before. I like to do it, and Papa, who never exerted himself in his life, always said the best way to know a horse and win its respect is to take care of it."

Luis nodded. "The poor Lord Harry, he did know his horses." But, his tone implied, he had known very little about anything else.

"That he did." Nodding back at the groom, Sophia gathered her things and headed off in search of Speen. At this hour the batman was likely to be seeing to the buttons and gold braid on his master's uniform for the review the next morning. It was an ideal time to discover what, if anything, he knew about a tall dark-haired major who rode a magnificent chestnut on reconnaissance missions.

Chapter 3

Mark was not at quite such a disadvantage as Sophia in his quest to discover more about the artist he had encountered that afternoon, for there were not nearly so many gently brought-up young ladies attached to the army in the Peninsula as there were cavalry officers. In fact, there were so few young ladies with the army that until that morning Mark had not been aware of the existence of any.

Arriving back in Lesaca, he found Wellington and his aides-de-camp seated around a table in the house that served as headquarters. The commander was surveying a map in front of him. "We shall have to spread ourselves very thin to accomplish both the blockade of Pamplona and the siege of San Sebastian. I do not like it for we will not be so strong in either place as we ought to be, but there is nothing for it. I have sent Cole to Pamplona and the Fourth Division is covering Roncesvalles. Though I hardly expect that Soult would try to take thirty thousand men through the mountain passes, we can not be certain that he will not. At the moment he could strike for either Pamplona or San Sebastian. Ah, here is Adair. What have you found out about San Sebastian, Major?"

Mark laid his own map and Sophia's drawings in front of the duke. "Here is the layout of the fortifications for the town and the isthmus. Besides reconnoitering at San Sebastian I have found out that the French have stored materials for two pontoon bridges near the lower end of the Bidassoa and there is a concentration of their troops nearby that appears to be poised to cross the river and come to the aid of San Sebastian should they need to."

Wellington leaned over the maps and pictures, frowning in concentration. For a few minutes he was silent, lost in thought, then he looked up. "These pictures are quite good, Adair. I had no notion you were an artist."

"I am not, sir. They were drawn for me by an English young lady I happened to encounter on my way back to Lesaca."

"An English young lady?"

"Yes, sir. She was off in a field painting as cool as you please, and when I ventured to express my fears as to her safety she informed me in no-uncertain terms that she was very well aware of the danger since she had been here for four years. She even hazarded a guess that she had been here longer than I had. Certainly she acted as condescending toward me as if I had just stepped off the boat from England."

"And what would you guess to be the young lady's age?" A voice at the other end of the table spoke up. It was Fitzroy Somerset.

Mark turned to the duke's secretary. "I should say she must be somewhere between eighteen and twenty."

"With dark hair and an independent air?"

"*Most* independent."

"That would be Sophia Featherstonaugh, Curtis's step-daughter."

"You know her, then?" Mark asked, forgetting entirely that he had just seen an excellent portrait of Somerset done by the young lady in question.

"Anyone who has spent any time in Lisbon knows Sophia and her mother," another aide-de-camp broke in. "Her father was Lord Harry of the Twenty-third, and a more harum-scarum lad you could never hope to meet— devil of a husband for Lady Harry, who never knew what scrape he would fall into next. Come to think of it, he was probably the devil of a father as well. He was too hot-headed for command, but ripe for any skirmish, and a damn fine rider—a regular centaur—and his daughter is just as good as he was. You will never meet a better horsewoman."

"Or a better artist. I saw a sketch she did of Somerset here and His Grace that were so like them they practically breathed."

"She has a gift, that one." Colin Campbell, the headquarters camp commandant nodded in agreement. "But it is

more than just artistic talent; she sees things in people that
no one else can." He turned to the duke. "Do you remember, sir, the young lady who insisted that Ponsonby's batman was innocent because he had too honest a face to steal
anything? She came right up to you and told you straight
out that you ought not to allow him to be punished."

"Ah, *that* young lady!" Enlightenment dawned. "She was
not about to let me make a mistake like that even if she
had to call on me herself—a lot of pluck that girl." The
duke smiled reminiscently. "As I recall, it was Ponsonby's
clerk, not his batman, who was doing the stealing."

"But no one else had even considered the possibility.
Miss Featherstonaugh was absolutely convinced that Biggle
was not the thief, and then when everyone was gathering
for the inquiry, she took one look at Waters and said to
you, *That is your man.*" Campbell turned to Mark. "Never
saw anything like it before in my life. It was truly remarkable. Of course we were not about to take the word of a
slip of a girl so we conducted a very thorough investigation
into the affair, but in the end, after all was said and done,
we discovered that she had been right all along. Of course
we learned more about the details, but as far as the guilt
of the party went, she had picked the man out long before
any of the rest of us. She can read people like a Gypsy
fortune-teller. And you are right, she is a fair hand at drawing portraits."

"And landscapes." Mark agreed. "She was working on
one this afternoon that quite took my breath away. And
there she was, sitting in the middle of a field without the
least concern for the ruffians that might be about."

Campbell splashed some more wine into his glass. "I dare
say, though, that the faithful Luis was not far away and
that he was armed to the teeth." Mark's answering grin
confirmed this speculation. "He does look a bit of a bandit
though, does he not? One of the few responsible things
Lord Harry ever did was to find a servant who could protect his wife and child as well as act as a groom and coachman. It was not like him to worry about their welfare, but
in a fit of conscience he sought out Luis in Lisbon and the
man has been devoted to them ever since. However, I
would hazard a guess that Sophia had her own pistol hidden somewhere among her paints."

"Pistol?"

"Yes. Harry might be the only one allowed to teach her to ride, but the boys in the Twenty-third would not let her grow up without knowing how to fence and shoot as well as the rest of them. Of course it amused them to teach her, but they also knew what an independent thing she is and they wanted her to be able to defend herself in any situation. From what I have heard, they did a remarkably thorough job of it."

Mark was silent for a moment, trying to reconcile the picture of a young woman who rode, shot, and fenced like a cavalry officer with the sensitive, perceptive artist who saw things in people that others could not and captured them on paper with a skill that rivaled any of the portraits he had seen exhibited at the Royal Academy. "She appears to be a lady of many talents."

"That she is, and well beloved by everyone here. You might think that a young woman who has been so much indulged by young men missing their mothers, sisters, and sweethearts would be inclined to be spoilt, but she has not got an ounce of vice in her. I fancy one can see the influence of Lady Harry there, or I should say, Lady Curtis. She was bound and determined that no matter how wild and unreliable her husband was, or how unconventional their existence, her daughter would have a proper upbringing. As soon as Sophia was old enough to hold a book she was taught to read and do her sums. Fortunately, Briscall, the chaplain attached to headquarters, was only too happy to continue her education where her mother left off so I fancy she is as well read, if not better, than most of the officers you will find here."

"But who taught her to paint? Surely not a chaplain."

But Campbell was unable to answer that question. As far back as he could remember, Lord Harry's daughter had always carried a sketchbook and pencils, and later paints. She was never without something to draw on and had obliged a great many of her self-styled fencing masters and marksmanship tutors by providing them with portraits for them to send back to their loved ones.

"Excellent work, Adair." The duke, who had returned to his frowning contemplation of the maps and drawings, looked up. "Now if you could do the same for me in regards to Pamplona, Roncesvalles, and the Maya Pass I shall be satisfied. We should familiarize ourselves with the terrain so that we shall be prepared no matter what direction moves his forces. I shall expect reports from you on those within the week."

"And my regiment, sir?"

"Will just have to do without you."

"Very good, sir." Mark turned to go, hoping that his frustration and disappointment did not show. But, he told himself bitterly, it was highly unlikely they would, for it was his ability to conceal his emotions and assume a variety of almost impenetrable disguises that had gotten him this job in the first place. Before the duke had taken advantage of his services, these disguises had mostly been adopted to hoodwink jealous husbands. It was not until Mark had been captured by the French and managed to scape by disguising himself as a Spanish mule-driver that his skill, coupled with his flawless Spanish, had drawn him to Wellington's attention.

The duke had not been surprised by the young officer's reluctance for reconnaissance missions. "It does rather seem like spying, sir," was all that Lord Mark had said when the duke first approached him with the idea, but that was all he had needed to say.

"Perhaps. And every young man joins the cavalry to lead a victorious charge against the enemy, but cavalry charges and the like can be a disastrous waste of time and lives if one does not know what one is charging into," the duke had replied, not unkindly. "But with your dark complexion and the Spanish you learned from your mother, in addition to the quick-wittedness and skill you demonstrated in deceiving the French, you are worth a hundred gallant cavalry officers to me, and far more difficult to find among those serving under my command."

So, reluctantly, Mark had agreed to become one of Wellington's trusted exploring officers, and along with Sir John Waters and Colquhoun Grant, had regularly fed Wellington with reports on terrain, troop movements, and enemy fortifications.

"I shall ride out tomorrow, sir, to see what I can learn about the French positions around Pamplona and discover what I can about Soult's most recent movements."

"Good. What I also need is an accurate report on the roads. On a map a goat track can look like a main road and if we can force the French to travel on goat tracks while we march on roads, so much the better. That means a very thorough reconnaissance on your part, but I have every confidence in you. Not only do you speak Spanish, but you look like the Basques, who are some of the most infernally proud and independent people it has ever been my pleasure to meet. But if you win their trust, by God, then the Pyrenees are practically ours. Soult can not afford to march around these mountains forever. The most he can hope to carry with him is a few days' rations and then he will have to go back to Bayonne to feed his army. The more we wear him out by forcing him to march over difficult terrain, the better it is for us. Now go to it, lad."

"Yes, sir." Though he had a cavalry officer's natural distaste for an activity as devious as spying, and though all the tenets of his aristocratic heritage made him long to confront the enemy in a fair and open fight where honor was the chief ingredient, Mark recognized the accuracy of his superior's thinking. Distasteful as his role of exploring officer might be to him, he had to accept the fact that Arthur Wellesley, who had enjoyed the same aristocratic upbringing as he had, deemed his role and this mission important to the success of the British forces in the Peninsula. So he was left to console himself with the belief that honor lay in carrying out his general's orders to the best of his ability, whether it meant charging at the enemy head-on or ferreting out his weaknesses, using deception and disguise.

Chapter 4

Thus it was that several days later, as Sophia was painting the rugged landscape that rose on both sides of the Bidassoa River, she was greeted in a friendly fashion by a Basque shepherd driving his flock before him. "Buenos dias, Señorita." The man touched his forehead in a respectful manner, but the look he directed at her was decidedly familiar. She was just about to turn away with haughty disdain when she stopped. There was something about the set of the peasant's shoulders, which were unusually broad for a man who spent his life tending sheep, that made her turn back to get a second look.

Her eyes narrowed as she took in the long, angular face and the dark, straight brows that almost met across the high-bridged nose. Cocking her head to one side, she frowned suspiciously and then grinned. "Surely it is not the inquisitive major doing reconnaissance again? It is hardly necessary for you to go to such lengths, sir. If you wished to see more of my work you had only to ask instead of sneaking up on me in this havey cavey manner."

The answering crack of laughter proved her to be correct in her suspicions. "Very good. You certainly have an eye for what is beneath a disguise, which makes you a very dangerous young lady indeed." Despite his rough clothes, Mark sketched a bow as elegant and practiced as if he were greeting her at Almack's.

"I would not say that *dangerous* is precisely the word, but certainly *undeceived*." Sophia regarded him curiously. There was no doubt that the major was both amused and intrigued by her penetration of his disguise, but there was some other emotion, something deeper there, that she could not quite identify. Though he had laughed at her sally, there had been something else, a shadow that had crossed his face ever so briefly when she had accused him of sneaking up on her. The expression had disappeared in an instant. In fact, if she had not spent years training herself to observe, identify, and record every flicker of an eyelash, every flaring of a nostril or tightening of a lip, she might not even have noticed it, but she had, and it made her more curious than ever about the man.

Keeping an eye on his flock, Mark strolled over to look at the picture. "Most impressive, but not, I think, as good as the one I first saw you working on. This is picturesque, but it lacks the power of the other even though the landscape you are painting here is far more sublime."

"It is almost too sublime. The scenery itself is so overwhelming that I can not quite get a feel for the place."

"Perhaps you do not feel comfortable enough yourself in such a landscape to be able to read its secrets and interpret them."

Sophia, who had been gazing absently at the rocks on the other side of the river while he was speaking, turned around to stare at him, her hazel eyes wide with astonishment. "Yes, that is what it is. That is precisely what it is, but how did you know?"

"Because I, too, am an observer of sorts, though not so talented as you, nor do I paint beautiful pictures." Again the shadow crossed his face and an ironic, almost bitter note crept into his voice.

Sophia recalled the reconnaissance mission that occasioned their first meeting. "Oh, so then you must be . . ." She paused, struggling to remember the precise term Speen had used. When she had described the officer she had met to her stepfather's batman, she had told him that the major seemed to have been observing the fortifications at San Sebastian. *Ah, one of the duke's exploring officers, I expect,* Speen had replied. As she questioned him further he had elaborated. *The duke has a group of men upon whom he relies to find out information about everything—French troops, the roads, who among the locals can be trusted and who would sell him out for a few pieces of silver. They are all under the direction of the quartermaster general and the ones I know of, Sir John Waters, Colquhoun Grant, are exceptionally brave and talented men, as clever at disguising themselves as they are quick at seeing a thing and remember-*

*ing it. They are as bold and resourceful as any man you
could hope to meet because they always work alone. But
neither Grant nor Waters looks like the man you describe.*

"An exploring officer?" Mark supplied dryly. "Yes, I am
one of those fellows who skulk around finding out what he
can so the rest of the lads know what to expect when they
ride into battle."

"Oh, you must not say it like that. Speen, my stepfather's
batman, says that men like you are excessively ingenious
and brave."

"And brave." A mocking smile twisted his lips. "But
otherwise, mostly ingenious and . . . deceptive."

That was it. Now she understood the shadow. He was
ashamed of being thought of as a spy. "Ingenious, yes, deceptive, perhaps, but certainly perceptive as well, and no
less important than the men who drink and gamble all night
and then die a hero's death the next day because they were
too befuddled or too stupid to notice the ditch in front of
them, a ditch that, if they were sober, would have embar-
rassed them even to give it a second thought."

"So *that* is how the dashing Lord Harry died."

Sophia whirled to face him again, but this time the hazel
eyes were dark with anger. "How dare you, sir! You have
known all along who I was and yet you did not have the
grace to in . . ."

"Introduce myself? I apologize. I have been a spy too
long and I have forgotten the niceties of civility, is that
what you mean to say? That will not fadge. You would
have done the same to me if you had known my identity,
but your resources were not so good as mine."

Sophia bit her lip. "And who were yours, sir? Who was
telling you tales about Lord Harry Featherstonaugh and
his daughter?"

"Fitzroy Somerset and, ah, the duke."

"Oh." She was silent for a moment, somewhat mollified.
"Still you had no right to go asking around about me."

"No right? I find a woman, an Englishwoman, in the
middle of a field, in the middle of a war in Spain, and I
ask the commanding officer about her because I want to
know the name of someone who happens to be the most
superb artist I have seen in some time, not to mention that
I was concerned for the safety of a young woman who

wanders a countryside that is teeming with guerrillas, ban-
dits, and soldiers of all types, and you take offense. Yet
you who asked your stepfather's batman about me, tell me
I have no right to ask such questions. I must take exception
to such unequal treatment."

"I beg your pardon. It was rather high-handed of me."

"High-handed!" Mark was about to favor her with his
full opinion of people who gossiped about other people
when he paused. After all, she had apologized. She had
looked him straight in the eye and offered her apology and,
her expression told him, she still offered it. In all his years
of dalliance, he had never known a woman to admit she
was in the wrong, and he could not for the life of him
remember when one had looked him full in the face with
no dissembling, no coy smile, no pouting lips, just frankly
and apologetically. It was completely and totally disarming.
"Well yes it was high-handed of you, but understandable,
given the circumstances."

"Thank you."

Oddly enough, she truly did sound relieved. Most women
would not have given a second thought to what some exploring officer thought of them, but she really did seem to
care for his good opinion.

Baaaa. Mark was suddenly recalled to his responsibilities
toward his flock and he turned around just in time to catch
one of its members in the act of breaking away toward a
promising patch of greenery. "If you will excuse me, I must
look after my charges. When one of them takes it in his
head to go another direction, the rest soon follow, and I
promised Jose that I would return them all safe and
sound."

He had just stepped out from behind the herd to go
retrieve the stray when Sophia, applying one last touch of
paint, turned to protest. "You still have me at a disadvantage, Major."

"A disadvantage?"

He looked so blank that she could not help laughing.
"Yes. You seem to know who I am, but as you pointed
out, my, er, *sources,* were not so forthcoming as yours."

"Oh. I am Adair. Major Lord Mark Adair. It must be these
clothes, they have made me positively rag-mannered." He

hastily sketched another bow and charged after the errant sheep.

Sophia chuckled as she turned back to her painting. At least she had a name now, and with a name she could find out as much about him as he had found out about her. She might be able to dispense with Speen, who had become rather suspicious of her sudden interest in one particular officer. Instead, she could ask Andrew Leith Hay, an exploring officer in his own right, and aide-de-camp to his uncle, Major General James Leith, a friend of her stepfather's and a frequent dinner guest.

Andrew, who was a competent artist himself, had admired her pictures one evening when he had accompanied his uncle to dinner and he and Sophia had fallen into a discussion of all the picturesque opportunities offered by the Spanish countryside and bemoaned the difficulty of obtaining artistic supplies in a war-torn foreign country. Surely he could tell her something more about the major. Sophia was not about to remain at a disadvantage. For the moment, the major might possess more information about her than she did about him, but the situation would not remain that way for long.

Having settled that in her mind, she returned to her painting. What she did not admit to herself was that Speen, ordinarily the most incurious of individuals, had been entirely correct in the suspicions he had voiced when she had questioned him about the major's identity. "Seems to me you be mortal interested in this major fellow, Miss Sophia. That is not like you." The batman had stopped brushing her stepfather's uniform long enough to fix her with an inquisitive stare.

"It is just that I do not like discussing my work with unknown critics," she had replied airily. But Speen had not been fooled. He knew that it went deeper than that. There were hundreds of cavalry officers in the Peninsula to whom she had not given a second thought. What was it about this one that piqued her interest so?

If she had allowed herself to think about it, which she would not, Sophia would have had to admit that after this second encounter she was even more intrigued by the major than she had been after the first. Most cavalry officers were bluff, hearty men, dashing perhaps, but basically they were just splendid horsemen in search of excitement, and that was the extent of it. Everything about them could be learned in the course of one conversation and Sophia had met scores of them over the years.

Like all of them, this man was dashing and a splendid horseman, but there were hidden depths. He seemed to read her pictures in a way very few people had been able to. The comments he offered were not the standard admiring kind. They were thoughtful and insightful, and they revealed not only an observant eye, but a sensitive mind at work. Then there was his obvious discomfort over the role he was forced to play as an exploring officer. Most of the men she knew would have thoroughly enjoyed the intrigue and the adventure. They would have revealed in the unique trust that Wellington placed in them. But this man was clearly unhappy about the level of deception he was required to adopt, and this unhappiness hinted at a nature that was more reflective than most. Yet in spite of this, he had an air of insouciance, even bravado, that was at odds with this sensitivity, and that made him dangerously attractive, even to a woman who had spent her life among men noted for their bravado.

Chapter 5

While Sophia was rather unwillingly occupied with these reflections on Major Lord Mark Adair, the major himself had little time to reflect on anything but returning Jose's flock to him in one piece. It was not until after he had seen them safely penned behind Jose's simple hut, had changed back into his own clothes, and was making his way back to headquarters when he was struck with a thought. *How in thunder did she recognize me? Surely my disguise was better than that.*

The question plagued him during maneuvers all the next day, and it was still bothering him the day after that when donning a monk's robe, he went to visit the sympathetic *alcalde* of Ostiz, whose position gave him ample opportunity to observe the French troop movements. The pretext of consulting with the mayor on a civic matter also gave Mark the opportunity to meet with other citizens who furnished useful information.

He spent a long, hot day riding from to Lesaca to Ostiz and back on the back of an exceedingly bony and recalcitrant donkey and by the time he had reached the outskirts of Lesaca again, he was tired, thirsty, and his patience had been tried to the utmost by the stubborn behavior of his mount. They were just approaching the first house in the village when the donkey, his interest seemingly caught by something at the side of the road, came to a complete halt and refused to budge.

Growling with exasperation, Mark slid off and cautiously raised the cowl he had pulled down to cover his face. Glancing around, he tried to discover what had caught the beast's attention. Off to the right was a small but exquisite shrine and there, in the sheltering shade of a gnarled tree, sat Sophia with her easel. "I do not blame you for being curious," Mark muttered to his mount as, pulling the donkey's reins, he advanced toward the shrine, with as reverent an air as it was possible to adopt towing a reluctant animal, as though he intended to offer up a prayer to the saint of the shrine.

Tugging the cowl back down over his face he approached Sophia. *"Buenos días, señorita."* He kept his voice low and gravelly this time.

Sophia glanced up and nodded abstractedly. *"Buenos días, padre."* She turned back to her work, then paused, her brush hovering in midair of the easel as she directed a penetrating stare at the monk.

Blast! She had recognized him again. How in the devil's name had she done that? Still, Mark maintained his reverential pose, hoping against hope that he was wrong.

"Good day, Major." Her voice was amused. "This certainly *is* a most uncharacteristic role for you."

Mark shoved the cowl back so he could see her eyes dancing and the dimple at the corner of her mouth. "And just what is it about me that allows you to see through my disguises so effortlessly?"

Sophia could not help chuckling at the utter frustration in his voice. "My lord, you are far too . . ." She stopped and flushed as she realized the implications of what she had been about to say. Spanish peasants and Spanish priests did not have the broad shoulders and magnificent athletic physique of British cavalry officers. And even though it was mostly obscured by robes, Lord Mark's physical presence was still a powerful one. But a young lady, even one raised in army camps, could not allude to such a thing.

"Far too . . ." he prompted, relishing her momentary confusion. He was enjoying her discomfiture. After all, she had certainly discomfited him, recognizing him as quickly as she had, and she knew she had discomfited him. "Ahem, now what were you saying?" He grinned and waited expectantly while she wrestled with the answer.

"I was about to say that Spanish peasants and Spanish priests are not so . . . I mean they do not have . . . well, in general they are not so *well nourished* as cavalry officers," Sophia finished lamely.

So that was it. He as rather flattered, in an odd sort of way, that she found it difficult to acknowledge to him that it was his physique that had given him away. During their previous encounters she had been so coolly self-possessed, so eager to get back to her painting that it had appeared she saw him as an interruption rather than as a man—an attitude that had caused him to stop and reassess himself.

All of his adult life, women had been as attracted to Mark as he had been to them. He had become accustomed to seeing a certain appreciative sparkle in their eyes when they looked at him, detecting a certain coyness in their smiles, and hearing a certain breathlessness in their voices. None of this had been present in Sophia. Both of their previous encounters had left him with the uneasy suspicion that he was not as interesting as he had previously assumed. Each time he had parted from her he could not help wondering if he had become such a coxcomb that he expected every woman to be intrigued by him, and when one was not, he found it not only disconcerting, but difficult to accept. So now it gave him more satisfaction than he cared to admit to discover that Miss Featherstonaugh did see him as a man after all.

"I shall have to make sure that I stoop after this, hunch my shoulders, and perhaps shuffle just a bit so I look a little less *well nourished,* as you put it." He was being deliberately provocative and it gave him a great degree of satisfaction to watch another faint tinge of pink wash over her face. "It is to be hoped that the average French soldier is a good deal less acute than you are."

"I expect they are. And besides, they are men."

"Men? Of course they are, but what does that have to do with anything?"

"Well, it seems to me that in general men tend to be more preoccupied with themselves than women are and therefore are less likely to pay attention to others around them. Women, on the other hand, are brought up to care for their husbands and look out for the welfare of their children and servants so they are naturally more aware of everyone around them."

Mark was about to launch into a fierce rebuttal of this poor opinion of his sex when he realized that it was largely true. It was his mother, for the short time she had been alive, who had listened to his childish joys and woes while his father had remained distant and uninvolved. He was the authority who commanded awe and respect from his sons but had very little interaction with them. Certainly the women Mark had enjoyed during his adult life had made a habit of studying the likes and dislikes of their men, catering to them with such determination and skill that he had never been entirely sure of what they wanted or enjoyed in life except for him. "You may be in the right of it," he agreed slowly. "And it has also been my experience that women are far better at dissembling than men so it would seem that a woman would be much better equipped for identifying dissembling and deception in others."

"You are a misogynist indeed, sir." Sophia could not help wondering which particular woman in the major's life had been responsible for the ironic note in his voice and the cynical twist of his lips.

"Not at all. I am a great admirer of the fair sex, especially those who are talented as well as beautiful." The mocking expression became an admiring one as he watched the color rise again in her cheeks. She was not what the fashionable world would call a classic beauty, for her mouth was too wide, generous, he would call it, and her cheekbones were a little too pronounced for a world that liked its women to be decorative rather than determined. But the eyes made one forget about everything else. They were large and expressive, fringed with thick, dark lashes and their hazel depths mirrored every thought. No, she was not precisely beautiful, but she was striking in a way that instantly captured attention and made one want to learn more about her.

At the moment her eyes gleamed a wicked green as she surveyed his rough habit. "And what were you able to learn today, Father? Surely you discovered more than the few small sins of some poor villager who works too hard even to think about transgressing."

"They may be too busy to stray from the paths of righteousness, but they are not too busy to notice French troops marching by their fields or bivouacked outside their villages. And some of them understand enough French to be able to listen to conversations as they wait upon the officers. All of this they report to a few trusted alcaldes who in turn unburden themselves to their trusted confessor"— with a wave of his hand he pointed to his robes—"who listens most carefully and sympathetically to all their problems and then offers them advice that has more to do with survival in this world than advancement in the next."

"And how is it that you are able to converse with these people? Surely they do not speak English, and their language more closely resembles Gascon than Spanish."

"My mother was Spanish, from this area of the country. And yes," he responded to her inquisitive look, "I inherited her looks." My father met her at the Spanish embassy in London. Her father was part of the Spanish delegation. Spanish was in fact my first language because she always used to sing to me and tell me stories in her own language and my nurse, who had been her nurse, spoke the dialect of this area.

"My father little thought when he married her that he would be responsible for creating one of Wellington's most adaptable spies. Unlike many of the exploring officers, I can be depended upon to respond in Spanish even if I am caught unawares or awakened from a deep sleep, something that even our most accomplished linguists cannot be counted on to do because English is their mother tongue. However, my father was ignorant of my spying activities— I spared him the shame I have brought on our name—and he lived with the happy deception that his second son was honorably employed in winning the war as a major in the Fourth Dragoons.

The bleak expression in his eyes and the bitter note in his voice made Sophia want to reach out and smooth away the angry lines that wrinkled his forehead and twisted his lips into a self-mocking smile. "And what of your mother? Surely she must be proud of what you are doing to help her homeland?" Sophia could not think why it was so important to reassure him about the value of what he was doing, but it was.

"She is dead."

"Oh. I am sorry." Her portraitist's intuition told her that there was more to it than this. Behind the ironic self-deprecation lay a hurt so deep that it had never been addressed, a hurt that had remained, covered over, perhaps, but never healed.

"At any rate, now you see why I am so good at what I do, and why no one, with the exception of a suspiciously sharp-eyed artist, questions my identity, whether I am a shepherd or a priest. Now if you will excuse me, I shall be on my way. The duke needs his information before nightfall and the way this contrary beast moves"—he gestured disparagingly at his donkey, who was quietly munching a vicious-looking thistle—"I shall barely make it."

"Very well. I shall not detain you, Major." Sophia returned to her painting, but her brush hovered ineffectually over her paper as she puzzled over the torment she sensed in the soul of Major Lord Mark Adair. What was it about him that made him so savagely ironic when he spoke of his role as an exploring officer? Certainly Andrew Leith Hay did not appear to suffer a similar distaste for the role or for himself. She would just have to ask him what he knew about the duties of exploring officers in general and Major Lord Mark Adair in particular, when he returned. She had not seen him for some months, not since they had been quartered in Frenada. A few days after they left Frenada she had heard that he had been captured by the French. Sophia herself had been too busy packing and repacking as they followed the army across the Ebro to discover any further details until after the battle at Vitoria when she heard that he had been released *en parole* in exchange for a French officer, a Captain Cheville, who was being held prisoner in England.

Chapter 6

Sophia did not have to wait long for the opportunity to speak to Andrew Leith Hay, for when she arrived later that afternoon at their modest house just down the street from headquarters, it was to discover her mother bustling about with more than her usual energy as she directed two girls from the village. "Ah, Sophia, I am glad that you are returned. Sir Thornton has invited several officers for dinner and, as luck would have it, Andrew Leith Hay has just arrived. Now if you will see to it that Teresa and Maria finish with the cleaning, I shall go to speak to Jorge about dinner.

Removing the apron she had been wearing during the vigorous dusting, Lady Curtis went off to the kitchen, where the sound of banging pans and voices shouting in Spanish suggested that once again Jorge was finding the local kitchen help to be greatly inferior to what he had been accustomed to in Lisbon.

"Senhora, it is impossible . . ."

Lady Curtis held up her hand to stem the flow of objections. "I know, I know. Preparing a dinner worthy of your reputation is impossible in these trying circumstances, Jorge, but consider that the gentlemen who will be dining with us tonight are already familiar with the superb cuisine you are capable of preparing and will make every allowance for the crudeness of our quarters."

The beleaguered cook sighed dramatically. "Very well, senhora, but I make no promises."

"Thank you, Jorge. I know you will produce something exquisite as always. Remember that these gentlemen have been constantly on the move and living on very poor rations, so that even a warm meal will be a luxury to them, and fresh fish from Passages with a shrimp sauce and roast tongue will be beyond all their expectations."

A gloomy shake of the head was Jorge's only reply as he returned to chopping onions after frowning ferociously at the girl washing pans.

In point of fact, she need not have worried, for Andrew Leith Hay, Lieutenant Colonel Colin Campbell, General Pakenham, and Captain Fitzroy Somerset were so delighted to spend an evening in the congenial society of Sir Thornton, his wife, and his stepdaughter that they paid very little attention to the food that was set before them.

A good deal of the conversation centered around Andrew Leith Hay's sojourn with the French Army. "At first, I was treated very well indeed and was invited to dine with General Maransin at the archbishop's palace in Toledo. He discussed most frankly and openly with me the sufferings of the Grand Army in Russia, even their difficulties in the Peninsula. But then I was turned over to General Soult, a man of most inferior appearance and not to be compared with his brother the marshal. Hoping to be able to effect my escape, I refused to give my parole. They were a good deal more watchful after that, and ultimately, after a very unpleasant interrogation by General Leval I was sent to the dungeons of the Retero in Madrid. Naturally, I protested and eventually I was moved to another prison which was gloomy enough, but a considerable improvement over the dungeons. When we moved to Breviesca, I was summoned before General La Martinière, who informed me that his superior, General Gazan, desired that I be exchanged for a captain of the French artillery captured at Badajoz. Knowing I was going to be offered in exchange for another French officer, I gave my parole and was treated most cordially. When we reached Vitoria I was handed over to Captain Owen of the Eighteenth Hussars. He took me to Sir Lowry Cole, and the rest you know as well as I."

"Were you not worried that they would kill you?"

The captain smiled at his hostess. "Not greatly, for as a British officer I was far more useful alive than dead. Other exploring officers, however, have not been so lucky. Anyone caught in disguise is treated as a spy and disposed of as quickly as possible. Indeed, Major Adair of the Fourth

Dragoons had a very close call last year before Salamanca. He was traveling behind enemy lines dressed as a monk when he was captured by two dragoons on patrol. They had no idea that he was a British soldier and were simply responding to a report that a local priest was passing on information about French troop movements. They bound him and threw him on a horse to take him to headquarters, but believing him to be a man of the cloth, they were not so careful as they might have been. As they traveled, he struggled to get his hands free and waited until they stopped at an inn for dinner. They dismounted and were about to dismount him when, much to their chagrin, he dug his heels into his own horse, grabbed the reins of both of theirs, and rode off."

"Yes, Adair is one of the best," Colin Campbell agreed. "He speaks Spanish like a native and can adopt whatever accent he pleases, the plodding Asturian peasant, a fierce Andalusian guerrilla, or he can discuss the works of Calderon in the purest Castilian. Not only that, but he can speak French and German with only the faintest of accents so that the man from Paris thinks he is a Gascon, the Gascon thinks he is a Breton. He is an absolute master of disguise. The stage lost a fine actor in Adair."

Not to be outdone, Fitzroy Somerset took up the narrative. "I remember the time when two of the men in Adair's regiment were captured. Without even telling his colonel, he took it upon himself to discover the inn where they were being held, scaled a tree and dropped onto the roof of the house next door, leapt onto the roof of the inn, and scrambled across the tiles. Tying a rope around the chimney, he hung down over the edge and climbed into the room where they were being held, freed the men, and then using the rope, got them down and over the wall without anyone being the wiser. He is a good man in a tight spot, is Adair, a quick thinker and fearless as a lion. I do not think the man has a nerve in his body. He is as cool on the battlefield as he would be in your mother's drawing room."

"I believe I must have met this Major Adair of yours once not long ago when he was returning from San Sebastian. He is certainly an excellent horseman, if nothing else." Sophia could not say quite why she was so reluctant to admit to the other two encounters with him. Actually, she had not intended to admit to meeting him at all, but she did want to hear more about him, and the conversation had appeared to be drawing to a close.

"Aha!" Fitzroy Somerset shot a teasing smile in her direction. "Now that I think of it, he did mention encountering a demented young lady who was out painting in a field without the least regard for roving French soldiers or fierce Spanish guerrillas."

Sophia felt the heat rising in her cheeks and hoped desperately that the candlelight was too dim for anyone to see her blush, though why she should be doing so she had no idea.

"Have care, Sophia." Colin Campbell wagged an admonitory finger at her. "He is the very devil with the fair sex and has broken hearts from here to Lisbon. He charms the ladies by concentrating all his admiring attentions on them one day, and then on the next he will ride off without so much as a by-your-leave. And it is well known that he treasures his bachelor status."

"Sophia is far too levelheaded to waste a second thought on a fellow like that." Andrew Leith Hay came to her defense. "Besides she has lived among such fellows all her life. Why should she be in any more danger from Mark Adair than she is from all the rest of us?" He winked broadly at her.

Why indeed? Sophia had asked herself that very question more than once in the past few days. Why had she even spared a passing thought for Major Adair?

"Sophia knows all you military men too well to have her head turned by any one of you. She does not want a man who will forget her very existence the moment he gets a whiff of grapeshot." General Curtis turned to smile at his stepdaughter. "And I promise her that the moment the war is over we shall return to London where she can meet a steady young man instead of you harum-scarum lads. Now tell me, Andrew, did the French look to be well supplied?"

Glad to have the conversation turn to more general topics, Sophia heaved a sigh of relief and directed a grateful glance at the general. One of the things she loved most about him was his kindness. For a man who had spent the better part of his life in the rough and tumble existence of military camps, he was very sensitive to the feelings of others, especially those who were close to him.

"Well, sir, before Vitoria, I would have said yes they are. Before the battle on the outskirts of the city I saw in the army's reserve parks more pieces of field artillery lined up than I have ever seen before—rows and rows of them beautifully arranged. But after the battle, those same fields were littered with overturned gun carriages and abandoned cannon. It appeared as though in their flight the French had left everything behind. One hardly knows what they now have left to defend themselves."

"We need not congratulate ourselves on that score," Fitzroy Somerset concluded grimly. "Adair reported enough artillery at San Sebastian and Pamplona to cause a great deal of damage."

"But what is the terrain like? If our troops are crossing the beach to reach the fortress at San Sebastian we may be able to come in under their guns. If I were not under this infernal parole I could make a sketch of the place and then we should have an accurate idea of what we are up against."

"Relax, Andrew." Colin Campbell laid a hand on his shoulder. "Sophia, here, has already drawn us an admirable picture of the place."

"Sophia?"

Despite her best efforts, Sophia could not help sounding just the slightest bit self-conscious as she replied. "Yes. Major Adair asked me to draw him a picture while the details of it were fresh in his mind."

"Ah." Andrew said nothing more, but his expression betrayed his thoughts. How had Sophia, who ordinarily did not share her pictures with most of her friends, come to show them to a perfect stranger? It was obvious from the look on her face that Sophia was not about to answer these questions, and Andrew was certainly not going to ask.

Chapter 7

The next few days Sophia and her mother saw very little of the general or anyone else as all of Wellington's staff were occupied with the plans to storm San Sebastian. Sir Thornton spent his entire day at headquarters or riding to inspect the troops and their supplies at Irun, Vera, and Echelar, returning home only to sleep.

Sophia continued to go out on sketching expeditions, but she remained within the limits of the village, satisfying herself with pictures of the sturdy Basque peasants at work in their daily tasks or vistas of the distant mountains as seen from the windows at the back of their house. On the one day she had planned to get out early to take advantage of the softened tints of early morning light, she awoke to the sound of shutters banging in the wind and the distant sound of thunder. Peering out the window, she could see the storm clouds approaching from the coast, but it took a few minutes more to realize that the ominous rumbling came from cannon fire and not from thunder.

Hastily pulling on a plain cambric morning dress and sturdy half boots, she hurried down the steep stairs to the parlor just in time to witness the general kissing her mother good-bye.

"Ah, Sophia, you heard the cannon. Graham has attacked San Sebastian. At the moment the duke is prepared to leave the attack to him, but I must be in readiness to send forth fresh troops and supplies." He glanced at the worried faces of the two women. "Both of you should be safe enough here. You are close to headquarters and a good distance from any possibility of fighting."

"We are not thinking of ourselves, my dear." Sophia's mother spoke for both of them. "Do take care."

"You need have no fear on that head. I am but a quarter-master, a provisioner, not a fighter."

Lady Curtis smiled and shook her head. "A provisioner who is so zealous in his duties that he rides to the front in order to assure himself that all he has ordered forward has arrived according to his instructions. I know you too well, sir."

"That you do, Lady Curtis, that you do. Now I must go." And with a jaunty wave he strode out to join Speen, who was holding his restive horse.

"Well, Sophia, there is nothing to do but occupy our-selves as usefully as we can until we hear further news." Lady Curtis sat down in a chair near the window, pulled out her workbasket, and calmly took up her needlework.

"I know, Mama, but it is so tedious just waiting. I wish I could do something." Sophia paced restlessly for a few minutes, then went to the window to watch officers assem-bling down in front of headquarters. "I am hopeless at nee-dlework and I shall not be able to concentrate on anything I read."

"There is always your sketchbook, my love."

"I know, but I detest still lifes and there is nothing else to do for I can not go outside; I shall merely be in the way. I wish I were a man, then I would be able to do something to help win this wretched war."

"There will be wounded to tend to soon enough, and we do a great deal to help win this *wretched war* by insuring that there is a comfortable house and a good meal to return to after the exertions of the day."

"I know, Mama, I know." Sophia had heard it all many times before, but she was sick and tired of waiting patiently for men to return home after they had been out doing exciting things. She had spent her entire life waiting, it seemed. Her mother was kind and patient and well suited to the task. No matter how late her husband returned or how worried she had been, she was always ready with a warm smile of welcome and a hot meal. *It is no small ac-complishment to provide a home for a man when one is following the drum*, she had told her daughter over and over again. And Sophia agreed. She was well acquainted with the effort that went into running a household smoothly in a foreign land where supplies were uncertain and where one never knew where one would be laying one's head next. But she was not her mother. She was not content to sit quietly by while someone else was out doing things, accomplishing things.

The rest of the morning Sophia and her mother occupied themselves around the house as best they could, straining their ears to determine if the booming was coming from San Sebastian or somewhere else, and how the British troops were faring in the attack, but it was impossible to tell. Nor could they get any clues from the activity in the village itself. Officers were coming and going in all directions. Finally, just before noon, Lady Curtis looked up from her needlework. Head tilted to one side, she listened intently for a moment.

"What is it, Mama?"

"Hush, listen."

"I hear nothing."

"That is just it. The cannonading has ceased."

"Then they have succeeded."

But Lady Curtis shook her head. "No, did you not hear Thornton say how massive the walls of San Sebastian are and how impregnable the city is? This is far too short a time . . ."

Her words were cut off by another muffled boom sounding in the distance.

"There, Mama, they have started again."

"No. That is in another direction."

"So it is." Sophia crossed over to the window and looked out, but the scene remained unchanged. Then came another low rumbling. "It is coming from our right. I wonder . . ."

But further speculation was cut off by a banging close by. Both ladies jumped and looked anxiously at one another. It was a full minute before either one of them realized that the banging was at their own front door.

"If you please, senora." One of the maids ran in.

"I am coming, Maria." Lady Curtis rose to follow her but was forestalled by the appearance of a tall officer, his uniform covered with dust.

"What can I do for you, Major . . ."

"Adair, Major Adair, ma'am. And if you please, I have come to see if I might borrow your daughter."

"Borrow my daughter?" Lady Curtis stole a quick glance

at Sophia. Major Adair—so this was the officer whose name had come up at dinner the night Andrew Leith Hay had joined them. This was the officer whose name had made her ordinarily self-possessed daughter flush self-consciously. He was certainly an impressive-looking man even in his travel-stained uniform. But Sophia had been surrounded by such men all her life. What was it that was so unusual about this particular man?

"Well, not your daughter precisely, but her talent."

"Oh." This explanation did nothing to clarify the situation for Lady Curtis.

By this time Sophia had come forward to join her mother. "How may I help you, Major?"

"I have two peasants over at headquarters. They were both waiting for me when I returned from San Sebastian. Each one carries a tale of massive French troop movements; however, one tells me that a large French force is marching toward the Maya pass on our right and that there are rumors another force of equal size is on its way to the pass at Roncesvalles. The other, who claims to be with the Mina, insists that they are massing to cross the Bidassoa and preparing to strike for San Sebastian. Now I have met Mina himself and I could probably test the truth of this man's story by asking him to take me to the guerrillas' stronghold, but I do not have time. General Curtis"—Mark nodded at Sophia's mother—"has the Seventh and the Light divisions held in reserve and needs to know whether to send them to help Graham at San Sebastian, Stewart at Maya, or Cole at Roncesvalles. I need to know immediately which man to believe. I recall hearing that Miss Featherstonaugh, with her skill at reading character, was once able to tell that Ponsonby's batman was innocent of a crime everyone else thought him guilty of. I need someone like that now, someone who can tell me which man to trust."

Mark moved over to smile down at Sophia. "From what I have seen of your portraits you are able to see through to a man's very soul. Can you do that now for me?"

"I do not know. I do not think . . ." Sophia looked up into the dark eyes. There was a warmth in them that almost seemed like admiration, a special expression meant only for her, an expression that only she could understand. He needed her. He needed her skill, a skill that no one else possessed. She drew a deep breath. "Very well, I shall try, but . . ."

"Thank you. I *know* you can do it." It was almost a whisper, soft and intimate, as though no one else were in the room.

She stood for a moment, transfixed by the look in his eyes and the current of understanding that seemed to run between them, a current so strong it was almost visible. A warm tide of happiness swept over her. She was needed after all. There was something she could do at last after all these years of waiting helplessly among men who marched and suffered and died for their country. Now she could do something for her country, too. This man had seen it. He had appreciated it. He had given her a chance. "Just let me get my shawl and my things. I shall not be a minute." Sophia hurried out of the room.

"May I get you some refreshment, Major?"

"What? Oh, ah, no thank you. I am fine, thank you."

Lady Curtis smiled. She had spoken more out of a desire to discover the major's state of mind than to offer him her hospitality. It had seemed to her, watching her daughter and the major out of the corner of her eyes, that this soldier affected Sophia strongly. She had never seen her daughter respond to anyone quite this way before and she was curious to see whether or not the encounter had the same effect on the gentleman as it had on the lady. Where she was breathless, he seemed abstracted. Where she flushed and smiled self-consciously, he seemed to retreat into his own world, and after their discussion, he had been surprised to discover that Lady Curtis was still in the same room with him. But no matter how dissimilar their reactions might be, they led this particular observer to the same conclusion—there was some special bond that drew these two together, some secret understanding that only the two of them shared.

Mark recovered quickly. "I beg your pardon, Lady Curtis. It is these two men. I can not for the life of me decide which one to believe." He flashed an apologetic smile that did not fool Sophia's mother in the least. He had no more been thinking of the men than he had been of flying. She had seen the look in his eyes as they had followed her daughter out of the room.

"I understand, Major. I am sure Sophia can help. Ever since she was a little girl she has had an extraordinary ability to see beneath the surfaces people adopt to cover their true feelings. It is a rare talent, but it can be most disconcerting at times."

That caught his attention. "Yes, I expect it can." For the first time since his arrival he really looked at Sophia's mother. She was still a lovely woman, with the same lively intelligence in her eyes—blue eyes rather than Sophia's smoky hazel ones—and they were observing him closely now with a knowing expression and a sparkle of humor. She had seen Sophia's effect on him and she was not fooled in the least by his excuse.

Mark raised a rueful eyebrow and sat in the chair she pointed to. This was a woman who had listened to Lord Harry's excuses for years; she was not going to be deceived by Mark Adair. "One has only to glance at her portraits to realize that she sees a great deal more than the rest of us and . . ."

"Here I am at last. I do apologize for taking so long, but I have everything I need now. Shall we go, Major?" Sophia hurried back into the room clutching her satchel and pulling on her shawl.

Mark rose and held out a hand to take the bag containing her sketchbook and pencils, then bowed to Lady Curtis. "I appreciate your letting your daughter help me. I promise I shall take good care of her."

"I am sure you will."

But they were already halfway out the door and too intent on their mission to hear Lady Curtis's reply, much less detect the wealth of meaning in her voice.

Chapter 8

It was no more than a few steps down the street and across to headquarters where the two peasants under guard were seated in chairs at one end of the main room far away from any doors and windows. The two men glanced uneasily around them, but their faces lightened when Mark reappeared.

"Separate these men." Mark spoke to the sergeant standing guard over the two of them. "I shall speak to them individually. I have brought Miss Featherstonaugh here to draw maps of what they tell me about roads and troop movements and supplies. That way I can concentrate on the interrogation." He turned to explain in Spanish to the two peasants before the sergeant escorted one of them from the room.

Mark pulled up a chair for Sophia. "I have told the men that you will be drawing the maps and that I will have to stop and translate for you every once in a while."

"Very good. I shall make it appear that I am following your instructions then."

"Clever girl."

Sophia was surprised at how much his glance of approval meant to her. She pulled out her sketchbook and pencil.

"Let us get this man something to drink." Mark sent another soldier out to get refreshments then sat down at a table in front of the peasant. "Now, tell me your name."

"I am Pablo, sir. I am a shepherd tending flocks up near the Maya Pass and I have seen many French troops marching toward that area. Other troops seem to be moving toward St. Jean Pied-de-Port. I have spoken with other shepherds though who say that most of the French are heading toward the pass at Roncesvalles—about forty thousand of them, while twenty thousand are at the Maya."

"And San Sebastian? Are any of the troops making for San Sebastian?"

"Not that I could tell, sir. They all seem to be going inland and moving in the direction of Pamplona."

The soldier brought a bottle of wine and two glasses. Mark poured a glass and handed it to the shepherd, who drank it gratefully. "That is good. Thank you, Pablo. You are a credit to your country and most helpful to mine. We shall make sure we are ready to meet them. If you discover anything further, let me know. I am Major Adair."

The shepherd rose and bobbed his head toward Mark. The angular planes of his face softened into the hint of a smile. "I shall, Señor Adair. Now I must get back to my sheep."

The second man looked very similar to Pablo, with the same weather-beaten face that spoke of a life spent out-of-doors, the same straight dark brows, proud nose, and high cheekbones, but while the expression on Pablo's face had been one of the natural wariness of any native toward a foreigner, a shepherd toward an army officer, this man seemed sullen and suspicious rather than cautious.

"Do sit down and have something to drink." Mark greeted him with the same courtesy as he had the shepherd before him. "Now what is your name and what do you have of interest to tell me?"

"I am Miguel. I fish from the port at Passages and I sometimes go as far up as where the Bidassoa River enters the sea. There I have seen that the French are massing for an attack across the river. I have seen them gathering in Hendaye and then they will capture Irun and march down the coast to San Sebastian."

"How many are there?"

"Many. But of course I did not get close enough to see and it would have been very dangerous. Those French *diablos,* they would shoot a poor fisherman as soon as look at him. They come into our country, steal our food . . ."

"I know, I know. Calm yourself, Miguel. We shall do what we can to drive them back. Now about how many men would you say there are?"

"Oh very many regiments, all prepared to attack."

"At Hendaye, you say, and then Irun? Excuse me, I must

convey this information to the young lady drawing the map."

Mark turned to Sophia. "Do you have that?"

"Yes. I have everything."

"Are you certain?"

"Quite certain."

"Very well." Mark turned back to the fisherman. "I thank you for helping your country and mine. We shall make sure our troops are ready for them and if you learn anything more, let me know. I am Major Adair."

"Yes." The fisherman was glad to leave and hurried out.

Mark strolled over to Sophia, who was putting a few final touches to Miguel's portrait. "So which one of them is giving me the correct information? We do not have enough troops to reinforce both Graham at San Sebastian and the others guarding the passes on our right. I have allowed each peasant to believe that I am going to act on his information even though we can only afford to act on one of their stories, but whose story do I believe?"

"Oh Pablo is the one to believe."

"Then we shall reinforce the passes. But the French do have the material for pontoon bridges to cross the Bidassoa. I have seen that myself."

"Perhaps, but Miguel had no notion of the number of troops."

"True, but Miguel would have had to observe from a less protected position; he is a fisherman and can not stray too far from the ocean without looking suspicious."

"Miguel is no more a fisherman than I am."

"What? How can you possibly know that?"

"Did you see his hands? They were the hands of a peasant, roughened by work, yes, but they were not the hands of a fisherman, hardened by years of hauling in nets. I have seen the hands of fishermen and sailors and Miguel's were soft in comparison."

"Oh." Mark could not disguise the chagrin in his voice.

Bending quickly over her sketch, Sophia did her best to hide the superior little smile that tugged at the corners of her mouth before handing it to Mark. "Here, see for yourself what you think."

He took the two sketches and studied them carefully. "Yes." He let out a slow sigh. "You are right. There is really no doubt about it. Not only is Miguel imprecise, he is lying. I can see that now. One has only to look at the eyes and the hands. They tell it all, do they not?"

"Usually." Sophia put her pencil in her satchel and rose to leave.

"How could I have missed it?" He shook his head in disgust as he handed her back her sketchbook and escorted her to the door.

"You were listening to what the men were saying. You had to concentrate on the information they were giving you and evaluate it in terms of what you yourself have discovered. You could not pay attention to their facial expressions and their hands as well."

"You are being kind. Thank you, though. You do see a great deal in people that the rest of the world does not. What do you see in me, I wonder?" Mark opened the door for her and accompanied her down the steps and into the street.

"I see a man—a proud man, a man who knows he can rely on his strength and his resourcefulness to take care of himself in any situation. But I also see a troubled man."

"Troubled? What would there be to trouble me, pray tell, other than the usual killing and death that is part of war?"

"I do not know yet. But it is more than the usual dangers and discomforts that are every soldier's lot. It is a deeper sadness, I think." She was treading on dangerous ground. She could see it in the tension around his mouth and the whiteness of his knuckles as his hands clenched at his sides. "But I am an artist and in addition to depicting landscapes and faces faithfully, I try to invest them with drama and passion. You have said so yourself, I believe, or at least you have implied it. Perhaps I sometimes see drama where there is none."

"So I have," he responded lightly, relieved that she had let it go at that. Sophia Featherstonaugh saw a great deal and understood even more. Sometimes it was too much for him to deal with, and certainly more than he wished her to see. "But now I must take you home so that I can get word to your stepfather as to where he should send his reserves."

"And will you join your regiment if there is to be a major battle?"

"I sincerely hope so. What you heard today was a little more on the order of major skirmishing, but as you can see, the French have still not committed the bulk of their forces. If we are to drive them back into France we must seize the opportunity to strike at the major body of their troops and force them back across the Pyrenees before the weather becomes too cold. Even now I have heard that it can snow in some of the higher passes. If we do not push them beyond the Pyrenees then we shall have to spend another winter in Spain."

"Yes, that is what Sir Thornton says. Well, Mama and I are always ready to move at a moment's notice, though I have enjoyed it here. Everyone complains about the fleas, but it is pretty here and the people are interesting, strong, and self-reliant. It is a place full of possibilities for an artist."

"But a rather rough one for a young lady. Do you not long for more society, the balls and soirées, the dancing and flirting that are the main preoccupations of every well brought-up young woman I have ever known?"

They had crossed the street and walked down it until they were standing under the wooden balcony over the door of Sophia's quarters.

"But I am not a well brought-up young lady, Major. I have spent my life in the rough and tumble of army camps. I do not have much use for balls and parties."

"Surely you must wish for something more than traipsing after one army officer or another, setting up a household in one place only to tear it down and move on?"

"I do."

"So you admit it. You do long for a life more suited to a young lady, one that is filled with the comforts of ball-rooms, drawing rooms, parks, and gardens,"

"I did not say that. I merely said that I wished for something more than *traipsing after one army officer or another,* as you put it. But I do not necessarily wish for the life of elegance and ease you are so quick to imagine."

"Then what *do* you wish for?" He had moved quite close to her now so she could almost feel his breath on her face and the warmth from his body.

"I wish . . . I wish to make a contribution, to be useful in the way that you are useful, to *do* something."

"And so you have. You did something very useful today. No, it was more than useful, it was crucial. And now, in order not to diminish the usefulness of what you have done, I must go and get word to Wellington and the others. In fact I have tarried too long already. But I do not forget what you did for me and our country. Thank you." With that he was gone, striding back to headquarters, eager to climb in the saddle, to be off, joining in the action.

Sophia remained standing in front of her door, watching him go, thinking about the look in his eyes as he said, *You did something very useful today. No, it was more than useful, it was crucial.* He had understood her. And that look of understanding had been as intimate and as meaningful to her as a kiss.

A blast of wind, brisk and cold from the mountains, swept down the street, whirling clouds of dust as it passed. She pulled her shawl tightly around her and opened the door.

Lady Curtis was precisely where her daughter had left her, calmly doing her needlework, waiting for whatever news there was to hear of her husband. "And were you able to assist the major?"

"I hope that I . . ." Sophia paused and smiled as she recalled his words of thanks. "Yes, I was."

"I am glad." Her mother snipped a thread and turned to her workbasket to select another color; as though she had not observed the flush in her daughter's cheeks or the special sparkle in her eyes, but she had. It would be most interesting to see what developed. Lady Curtis felt certain that they would be seeing more, much more, of Major Lord Mark Adair.

Chapter 9

But it was some time before the major reappeared in their lives. Sir Thornton arrived home that evening exhausted and ravenous, but in between bites of a roasted chicken he was able to thank his stepdaughter for her part in the day's proceedings. "I understand that it was your decision that I send reinforcements to help Cole, Stewart, and Hill defend the passes to our right instead of concentrating them on San Sebastian."

"My decision? I merely drew a portrait of two men to enable Major Adair decide which one was telling the truth."

"Well you drew wisely. When Wellington returned this evening from San Sebastian there was a message from Cole telling him that they had been attacked at Roncesvalles. Of course I could not order the troops to march to Cole's rescue without the duke's authorization, but I was able to prepare them to head in that direction and to show them the maps your Major Adair had drawn."

"He is not *my* Major Adair."

"From what I hear, you are his *eyes,* as he called it, and he credits you with the accuracy of his prediction that the bulk of the French forces will attack on our right instead of our left."

"That is very kind of him, but I only drew pictures; he made the decision." Though she might demur in front of her stepfather, Sophia went to bed that night feeling immensely gratified. Not only had she actually been able to do something, but she had been given credit for it. How many other men in a similar situation would have even respected a woman's judgment enough to ask her advice—very few, if any. And she could not imagine a one that having asked a woman's advice would have taken it and then given her credit for it.

The next day the general rode off to Ostiz to direct the reserve troops marching to reinforce Cole's and Picton's men at Sorauren and was gone all night, prevented from returning home by a fierce thunderstorm. The ladies waited up anxiously, but finally, comforting themselves with the thought that the ferocity of the storm would make it impossible for anyone to fight, they went to bed.

When Sir Thornton at last returned he was exhausted, but jubilant. "Soult is back on French soil. With the exception of the garrisons at Pamplona and San Sebastian, we have driven the French out of Spain!" He turned to Sophia and raised the restorative glass of Madeira his wife had pressed into his hand. "And your drawings helped us do it. If we had believed the other peasant we should have sent our reinforcements to San Sebastian, our forces would have been pushed towards the sea, and it would have taken many more weeks and many more lives to regain our position."

"Thank you, sir." Sophia smiled gratefully at him. The general understood, better than her mother, how much she longed to contribute and how much she chafed at the inactivity. "I was thinking, sir . . ."

"Yes?"

She hesitated. When the idea had come to her in the middle of the night it had seemed so logical, but now that she was about to articulate it she was not so sure that it did not sound rather farfetched. "I can ride, observe, and draw as well as any man. I could do many of the things the exploring officers do. I could survey French positions and movements, count troops, and no one would suspect me of doing anything more than sketching. If I were to do that, it would free one of the exploring officers to fight with their regiments."

"Hmmm." The general rubbed his chin thoughtfully. "It is an idea, but I do not think it would work. You are a woman."

"But I can ride, and even shoot as well, if not better, than most men."

"Steady, lass. I am not doubting your abilities or your courage in the least. In fact I would rather have you under my command than some of my officers. All I mean is that ladies are in short supply in this part of the world. The French would remember seeing you more readily than they would some man and it would not take long for them to put it all together. Men, on the other hand, are everywhere and it is difficult to be certain that the man one sees at one particular moment is the man one saw at another particular moment."

Sophia nodded slowly. "Yes I see what you mean, sir."

But she did not give up on the idea and several days later she posed the question to one of the exploring officers himself. She was sitting sketching the sixteenth century church of St. Martin when Mark crossed the churchyard on his way to headquarters.

"Good afternoon, Miss Featherstonaugh."

"Good afternoon, Major." With a few deft strokes Sophia sketched in the lines of the church's slender bell tower.

"I am glad to see that you have found a more appropriate subject for your artistic talents than spies and informers."

"In the middle of a war I find spies and informers more appropriate subjects than churches and landscapes."

"Then undoubtedly you must look forward to a time when landscapes and churches are appropriate, when the majors you meet ask you to dance rather than identify traitors."

"I have already told you how I feel about balls and parties. I enjoy meeting majors who are doing something besides thinking up meaningless phrases to flatter their dance partners, spending their days with their tailors, or losing their fortunes at play."

"But a good deal safer."

"Oh, safe." Sophia snorted in a most unladylike manner. "Besides, I told you I wish to do something useful with my life rather than waste it dressing for balls or rides in the park. In fact, I was thinking of becoming an exploring officer myself."

"You what?" The major's expression of horror was as unflattering as it as ludicrous.

"I do not see anything so very surprising about that. I think it is a good idea. I daresay that I am just as familiar with the situation as you are. I have probably been in the

Peninsula as long, if not longer than you have. As an artist I have trained myself to observe closely. You yourself admitted that I see more than you do. I can certainly draw as well as any exploring officer, and I am a woman. No one would suspect a woman of spy . . . er . . . *observing*. With my sketchbook I have a perfect excuse for being anywhere, and anyone who comes upon me will see that I am working on a landscape. No one will realize that I am also observing troop movements. I will re-create all these observations when I have returned home." Her haughty tone and flashing eyes dared him to find fault with her scheme.

"I have never heard of anything so preposterous. A female exploring officer!" Mark snorted.

"And why not, may I ask?" If Sophia's voice had been haughty before, it was absolutely frigid now. "What is it that makes it so impossible to conceive? What can you do that I can not?"

"What can I do? I can ride, for one thing, and I can defend myself."

"So can I."

Her calm assurance infuriated him. "Even at twenty paces I never miss my mark," he replied through gritted teeth.

"Nor do I. And with a rifle it is at least a hundred yards."

"With a what?"

Sophia smiled grimly at his astonishment. "With a rifle. You forget, my lord, that I have been with the army *all* my life while you have been in it only since you left university."

It was more than Mark could stand. "Very well, then. We shall just have to prove it."

"Whenever and wherever you like, I shall be happy to meet you."

"Let us say tomorrow at ten by the shrine where I saw you sketching. We can use my pistol, but I shall have to procure a rifle."

"I shall bring my own, thank you," Sophia assured him tranquilly, then bent her head to hide a smile as he stomped off in disgust. Let him laugh at her aspirations, she would show him how badly he had underestimated her.

But the more she considered it, the less she was amused by his obvious incredulity. She had thought, after their last conversation, that he would understand that she was motivated by the same things that motivated him and everyone else who was fighting against the French—a belief in her country, the desire to stop Napoleon from conquering all of Europe, the wish to free the Spanish from French tyranny. She had thought, after their last conversation, that he considered her as capable of helping in this struggle as anyone else stationed in the Peninsula, but she had been wrong.

Though Major Adair had been grateful for her assistance, had even admired her perspicacity and her talent for portraiture, it was obvious that he still thought of her as a woman who, given half a chance, would choose a ballroom over a bivouac, an assembly over an army camp, and a life of frivolous amusement over a life of contribution and service. Too discouraged to do anything further on the picture she had begun, Sophia gathered up her pencils and returned her sketchbook to its case.

As she trudged home through the narrow cobbled streets, she took herself to task for allowing herself to be so affected by one man's opinion. All her life she had lived in such unconventional surroundings that she had become accustomed to thinking and acting for herself. And growing up in an atmosphere where actions were honored more than words, she usually worried very little about what anyone thought of her, if she considered it at all. But now one man's opinion had suddenly become very important to her, important enough to make her feel alive with happiness when he understood and appreciated her and annoyed and self-doubting when he did not. Why was that, and how had it happened?

Sophia lifted the latch on the door and glanced quickly around before entering their house. In her present unsettled mood she did not wish to encounter anyone. Hearing Jorge's and her mother's voices in the kitchen and Maria and Theresa chattering over the laundry in the small yard in the back, she heaved a sigh of relief and stole upstairs to her tiny bedchamber, laid her satchel on the little table she used as a desk, poured some water into a basin, and scrubbed her face vigorously.

Feeling somewhat refreshed, and resolving to push all thoughts of the major out of her mind until their meeting the next morning, she returned downstairs to help her mother.

While Sophia was able to restore her equanimity by plunging into household chores, Mark was having less success at putting the entire discussion out of his mind. In fact, the more he thought about it, the more he disliked his role in their entire dialogue.

From the very beginning of their acquaintance he had been impressed by Sophia's talent, her obvious intelligence, and her wide-ranging interests—characteristics that set her apart from most of the women he had ever known, who were more than satisfied to be decorative objects in some man's life, and to spend his money improving their decorativeness. It was Sophia's difference from these other women that attracted him so strongly to her. He had never thought that a woman could be a friend to him in the same way that a man could until he had met Sophia. With her he found it as easy to relax and enjoy a conversation about shared interests as he would have with any brother officer, and the novelty of such a relationship made it even more intriguing.

But now that she was being different enough from other women to challenge him in his own areas of expertise he did not find it quite so intriguing, and he was not reacting to her as he would to a brother officer. If another officer had made the same claims about his marksmanship that Sophia had, Mark would probably have accepted it as a matter of course instead of patently disbelieving it.

After growing up with a rigidly disapproving father who worshipped the tradition that had kept the Dukes of Cranleigh as lords of the land since the Tudors, and a brother who was equally as devoted to the proprieties, Mark had sworn never to judge people by their ranks or their outward appearances alone, but solely on their own individual merits and accomplishments. Until this moment he had been able to live by that principle and it had won him the respect and love of the troops that had served under him. But now he was acting as conventional and as blindly judgmental as his father and his brother. He knew it. He had seen it in the angry sparkle of Sophia's eyes and the furious compression of her lips. He was not proud of this, but he was powerless to help himself. For some reason, the idea of her engaging in dangerous activities was extremely upsetting to him. He told himself it was because she was an artist and an artist's mission was to create, to inspire, not to destroy or to participate in the ugliness of war, but deep in his heart, he knew it was because she was a woman, a woman who had come very quickly to mean a great deal to him.

Chapter 10

The next morning Sophia rose earlier than usual to make sure that her rifle and her pistol were clean. She smiled grimly as she wiped the barrel of her rifle. If Major Lord Mark Adair was surprised at her owning such a weapon, he would certainly have been astounded to learn that she cleaned and loaded it herself as Sergeant Mapplethorpe had taught her to do many years ago. He had been concerned for the safety of Lord Harry's wife and daughter and made sure that Sophia at least knew how to protect them. She wished for the sergeant now, but he had returned to England with the Twenty-third Hussars soon after her father's death.

"Are you ready, miss?"

Sophia whirled around to see Speen standing in the doorway, his hand held out to take the gun she had just finished cleaning.

"Yes, thank you, Speen." Sophia picked up her hat and crop and, clutching the skirt of her riding habit in one hand, followed him to the stables. To her great relief they encountered no one. The general had gone to headquarters early that morning to plan the final assault on San Sebastian and her mother, from the sound of it, was directing the maids in the airing out of the bedding.

Sophia breathed more easily. If asked, she would say that she and Speen were going out for target practice, which would not be precisely a lie, but it would not be the truth either. As it was, she had been reluctant to reveal her plans to her stepfather's batman, but she had had no choice in the matter. Luis would have flatly refused to accompany her in such an outrageous endeavor, and he would have felt it incumbent upon him to report it. Speen, though he might be critical of her actions, knew that with or without him she would keep her appointment with the major. Initially he had been reluctant to help her and it had taken some convincing on her part.

"I do not know about this, Miss Sophia. I can not think that your mother or the general would approve of such a thing."

"Perhaps not, but what could I do? My honor, the family's honor, was at stake." Sophia had been somewhat daunted by the skeptical expression on the batman's face, but not to the point of giving in. "Speen, you would not want it noised about that anyone in this household was so weak as to back out of such a challenge. It would never do to have it thought that General Curtis's stepdaughter was not a woman of her word."

Speen had read the determination in the hazel eyes fixed so steadily on him and in the stubborn set of her jaw and he had given in. After all, it was better to go along with her so that he could at least keep an eye on her. Silently consigning all headstrong young women to perdition, he had agreed to act as a judge at her upcoming contest. "But when it is discovered what you have done, and you know it will come out, Miss Sophia, I will not have said I approved of such behavior, for you know I do not."

She had smiled gratefully. "Of course not, Speen. I shall take all the blame."

"Humph. Much good that will do me when the general gives me a dressing down."

"You are a true friend, Speen, and I know you would not have me back down on my word."

"No, Miss Sophia, I would not." Only slightly mollified, he sighed heavily, then his bright blue eyes twinkled. "Is the major aware of the competition he is facing?"

"I warned him, but I do not think he took my warnings too seriously." There was an answering twinkle in Sophia's eyes. She had won him over as she had known she would. Speen might act disapproving, but in truth he was as proud of her prowess as he would have been of any young officer who was his protégé.

They arrived at the designated meeting place to find the major and his batman pacing out the field behind the shrine. The field had been allowed to run fallow and thus offered a fairly smooth and level area. "I have been considering another contest along with marksmanship." Mark greeted her. "After all, as you said yourself, being able to ride as well as defend oneself is critical for anyone aspiring to be an exploring officer; therefore Finbury and I have marked out a racecourse for us." He gestured to some sticks stuck in the ground to form a rough oval.

"Very well." Sophia slid off Atalanta's back and reached for the rifle that Speen handed her. "And where are the targets?"

"They will come later. First the race."

"But that makes no sense. Riding a horse is sure to tire one's arms and affect one's aim."

"I thought you wished to prove yourself worthy of being an exploring officer."

"I did, but . . ."

"And exploring officers rarely, if ever, have the choice of riding first or shooting first."

"Very well." Ignoring Speen, who came to help her re-mount, Sophia hoisted herself back into the saddle. "I am ready."

"Good. The start as well as the finish is here." The major pointed to a rough line in the dust drawn between two twisted apple trees. "On the count of three Finbury will fire the starting shot and we shall go once around the course."

Sophia walked Atalanta over to the line and gathered the reins tightly in her hands. The more clipped and busi-nesslike the major's accents had become, the more she re-solved to beat him or perish in the attempt. She stole a glance over at Speen, who nodded encouragingly, and then focused her attention on Finbury.

Gun pointed skyward, the batman intoned, "One, two, three." The pistol cracked and Sophia dug her heels into Atalanta and bent low over the mare's neck. She knew the major was a bruising rider and there was no doubt he was splendidly mounted. On a horse two hands higher than Atalanta, he had a distinct advantage despite his weight. She would just have to make up for it by skillful riding.

He rounded the first stake half a length ahead of her, the second by only a little less, for Atalanta's nose now was at Caesar's hindquarters. By the third post they had gained so much that Atalanta's nose was at Caesar's shoul-der, and at the fourth it was equal with his neck, but in spite of all she did, Sophia was a nose behind as she pounded across the finish line.

If Sophia was less than pleased with her performance, Mark was nothing short of astounded. Accustomed to besting most of his fellow officers in such contests, he had expected to win easily. Ordinarily in such an unequal contest he would have taken his time, but annoyed by Sophia's delusion that she could shoot and ride well enough to do his job, he had resolved, at least at the beginning of the race, to push as hard as he would against the most challenging of opponents, promising himself that once he had established a respectable lead he would back off to give Caesar a rest and keep him from completely destroying her illusions. He was still a gentleman, after all, no matter how unladylike his opponent's behavior might be. But that respectable lead never came.

"That were as magnificent a race as I ever did see. You are a fair rider yourself, miss, for I never saw anyone nearly overtake his lordship the way you did. Another few lengths and you might have won." Finbury's obvious admiration for Sophia did not improve his master's temper one whit.

"Thank you." Pushing a stray tendril of hair back under her hat, Sophia leaned over Atalanta's neck and held out her hand. "A wonderful race, Major. I can not think when I have been so well matched." Her eyes sparkled with exhilaration and her gentlemanlike behavior only made Mark feel all the more churlish.

Trying to regain control of himself and of the situation, he dismounted and strolled over to help her down. "And now what will it be, pistols or rifles?"

"Oh pistols, I should think. Let us give ourselves some time to catch our breaths before attempting to do anything truly challenging."

"Very well." Mark nodded to Finbury, who affixed a wafer to one of the stakes that had marked the racecourse, and all of them paced off twenty paces. "As the loser in the last competition and since you are unfamiliar with my pistol it is your right to have a practice shot." Mark handed his pistol to Speen, who handed it to Sophia.

"Thank you." Sophia grasped it, hefted it to get a sense of its weight, and then, aiming at an apple hanging from a nearby tree, fired. "It does throw a little to the left, does it not?"

"It does," Mark responded, grimly watching her as she reloaded.

Sophia drew several deep breaths. She could tell from her opponent's barely suppressed annoyance that he had not expected her to do as well as she had thus far and it made her all the more determined to show him up. Grasping her lower lip in her teeth, she held her breath, sighted carefully, and squeezed the trigger. The stake shook, but the wafer remained in place.

Nicked it, Mark thought and allowed himself a superior grin while Speen, glancing over his shoulder at Sophia, winked broadly.

"Right in the center, hole clean through, a perfect shot," Finbury declared as he retrieved the wafer.

Grinding his teeth, Mark took the pistol from Sophia, reloaded it, aimed it, and fired. The wafer fluttered to the ground. "Nicked it, by God," he muttered under his breath.

This time it was Speen who retrieved the wafer. "Well, you *did* hit the edge of it, sir." The general's batman did not bother to hide the jubilant note in his voice. "Now let us pace off for the rifle. A hundred yards, did you say, Miss Sophia?"

"Yes, a hundred yards, and this time it is the major who may have a practice shot and the first shot."

After picking up Mark's wafer and affixing a fresh target, a larger one this time, pulled from Sophia's sketchbook, Speen returned to the group, handed the rifle to the major, and they paced off the distance again.

Declining to take a practice shot, Mark raised the gun to his shoulder and sighted even more carefully this time. Holding his breath, he fired, praying that his bullet would land squarely in the center of the target.

"A capital shot, sir," Speen remarked as he retrieved the piece of paper that sported a neat hole on the ring surrounding the bull's-eye in the center.

A good shot, but will it be good enough, Mark wondered as he handed the rifle back to Speen. He had seen enough now to be less certain of his prowess than he had been, and it did not improve his temper any to see Speen hand Sophia the rifle for her to reload herself.

Some of Sophia's nervousness had worn off now that she had bested the major in at least one contest and she was calmer this time as she raised the rifle and fired.

"Well, I'll be blowed!" Finbury held up the target to gaze in astonishment at the bullet hole fixed squarely in the center of the target.

"She is an angel with a gun, she is," Speen declared proudly. "There is not a man in any regiment that can get the best of Lord Harry's daughter."

"It is a question of observation," Sophia amended modestly. The ferocious scowl on her opponent's face was all the satisfaction she needed. There would be no more aspersions cast on her ability to defend herself after this.

"Oh naturally." The major did not look particularly enlightened.

"As an artist I have trained myself to see to a degree of accuracy that the ordinary person does not."

"It is also a matter of control which you also possess to a remarkable degree." The tone of his voice made it clear that the major did not necessarily consider this to be a particularly admirable trait.

"Of course it is a matter of control. It is one's control in any area of endeavor that gives one the degree of mastery it takes to excel at anything." Sophia could not say why she felt so defensive except that her opponent had made control seem like a defect instead of a virtue.

Mark ground his teeth for the second time that day. The lady was speaking as though everyone who did not exert this iron control over themselves and their lives was a rash and impetuous thrill seeker who could not be depended upon to carry out any task in a responsible manner. "Except when control becomes so rigid that it stifles creativity and impedes action, which it frequently does. In fact, you will find that most soldiers do not make good exploring officers because they are so accustomed to following orders and acting in an orderly fashion they can not think for themselves in difficult situations that require the ingenuity, resourcefulness, and courage that are the distinguishing characteristics of the exploring officer."

"And therefore, even though I have beaten you on two of the three tests you gave me you still disapprove of my notion to become an exploring officer." Sophia spoke calmly enough, but there was a dangerous sparkle in her eyes. "If I were a commanding officer, forced to depend on information furnished to me by someone else, I would want that someone to be reliable rather than reckless, but I see that you do not agree with me. I thank you, Major, for a most interesting morning and I bid you good day." And with that parting shot, Sophia handed the rifle back to Speen, grabbed Atalanta's reins, threw herself into the saddle, and headed back to Lesaca without so much as a backward glance.

Chapter 11

Left behind in ignominious defeat, Mark walked slowly over to Caesar and mounted. He did not head toward Lesaca, however, but turned instead off across the field toward the Bidassoa. He needed time alone to think, and the wild beauty of the rocky heights above the river was exactly suited to the tumult of his disordered thoughts.

At the outset he had challenged Sophia to their contest out of sheer annoyance at the absurdity of her ridiculous notion of becoming an exploring officer and out of a desire to prove to her just how farfetched and impractical such an idea was. Not only had she ended up testing him formidably in one event, but she had beaten him soundly in the other two, and her parting remark had seriously shaken his self-image. Was he a rash and reckless thrill seeker after all? Certainly he had heard others criticize the exploring officers as men too headstrong and too independent to follow the orders of their regimental commanders and too ready to court danger to be in charge of other men, but he had always prided himself on being the exception. He was daring, yes, but all the risks he took were calculated. They were carefully thought out and weighed in balance against the importance of the information he would gain by taking them.

He did not do his job for the sheer glory of being an exploring officer; in fact he longed to be returned to his cavalry regiment. He was only an exploring officer because the information he was able to unearth could only be gotten by someone acting alone, someone who was able to move quickly and change his course of action in an instant if circumstances demanded it. However, he was never rash. He never lost sight of the main objective, which was to find something out, to stay alive, and to evade capture long enough to report it back to his superiors. Actually, Mark attributed his phenomenal success to the very care he took not to get caught or wounded. Now, in one brief moment Sophia had called all that into question by implying that it was a lack of control on his part that had allowed her to beat him.

His entire life, Mark had been the adventurous one in his family. His father and his brother were forever pointing out to him his many lapses in respectability. It was not that he deliberately flouted the traditions they held dear, he merely required a good reason to believe in them, and both his father and his brother viewed his attempts to develop his own values as out-and-out rebellion.

But now he wondered. A young woman, who was nothing if not unconventional herself, appeared to have arrived at much the same conclusions as his hidebound relatives. Was he so reckless, undisciplined, and lacking in control after all? Did Wellington see that in him, too, and was that why he had taken him from a cavalry command and made him into an exploring officer instead?

Mark stared down into the water swirling around the rocks below him. In all his life he could never remember doubting himself. When his father had lectured him or his brother had disparaged what he called Mark's harum-scarum life, Mark had been sure in his own heart that he was right. He might not demonstrate his duty to his family, but he showed it to his country. He might not abide by the rules of the *ton,* but he abided by the army's code of honor.

No matter how much anyone had criticized him, no one had made Lord Mark Adair question himself until this slip of a girl had appeared and forced him to question everything: his skill, his motivation, the very essence of who he was.

Mark returned to headquarters in a somber mood to be greeted by the news that the storming of San Sebastian had begun. "I still say it is the greatest of pities that the tide makes it necessary to attack in broad daylight," the duke remarked as Mark joined the group of officers gathered around the large map that had been drawn from Sophia's sketches of the area. "Those poor fellows have to cross the beach in full view of everyone. Adair, be a good lad and find out from Graham how the attack is proceeding. An hour ago he asked for volunteers to help the Fifth Division storm the breach in the fortifications. They seem to be having a most difficult time of it."

Action was the perfect antidote to his black mood, and accepting his orders with some relief, Mark mounted Caesar and tore off in the direction of San Sebastian.

He found General Graham and a crowd of grim-faced officers clustered on the sand hills overlooking the broad expanse of beach that was the mouth of the Urumea River. As Mark approached, the general turned to his artillery commander. "Well, Dickson, you are in the right of it; the only way to stop those lads from throwing their lives away is to make an opening in the wall large enough for them to get through, but I do not like it. I do not like it at all." He shook his head unhappily. "And there is no way to let them know what we are about."

"Very good, sir." Colonel Dickson left to relay the command to his troops. His departure was soon followed by a deafening boom as the batteries on the sand hills opened fire on the ramparts of San Sebastian. As the smoke cleared, Mark watched the wavering column of red that had been huddled against the wall begin to pour over the rubble that had been laid by the cannonfire.

"I think it is ours at last." General Graham wiped his brow and let out a sigh of relief. "It was a dangerous thing to do, but I do believe it has done the trick. The lads will be able to take it now, not immediately of course, but we have tipped the balance in their favor."

These were the only words Mark needed to hear, and offering his congratulations to the general, he threw himself on Caesar and galloped back toward Lesaca.

As he came up over the hill before Lesaca, he caught sight of the twisted tree where he had first seen Sophia sketching and he slowed for just a moment. He had the oddest urge to ride directly to General Curtis's quarters to tell her that the attack her drawings had helped them plan appeared to be successfully underway. But the happy memory of their first encounter was quickly succeeded by the recollection of their last meeting and her scornful parting words. *If I were a commanding officer forced to depend on information furnished to me by someone else, I would want that something to be reliable rather than reckless.* Gritting his

teeth, he dug his heels into Caesar's flanks, forcing all
thoughts of Sophia Featherstonaugh and her condescending
criticisms from his mind.

It might have given Mark some consolation had he known
that the young lady causing such an orgy of self-reflection in
him was subjecting herself to the same self-scrutiny and finding herself no more pleased with herself than he had been.

After besting the major on the shooting range, Sophia
tried to assuage her annoyance with him by riding Atalanta
at a furious gallop along the dusty road home. Her anger
had not abated one bit by the time she reached the village,
so she continued on past it for several miles until her horse,
already having had a more than sufficient workout during
the race, showed signs of tiring. "Forgive me, Atalanta."
Sophia leaned forward to pat the sleek bay neck now dark
with sweat. "I am forgetting that you have already had a
great deal of exercise today. I shall just have to work off
my ill humor some other way. Perhaps I shall return to the
river and work on my painting."

But even after stabling her horse, peeling off the riding
habit that was now sticking to her own sweaty body, splash-
ing her face with cold water, and changing into a walking
dress of lilac muslin, she remained furious.

As she made her way toward the river she discovered
that she was still too upset to paint. However, as she
walked, she gradually realized that what was bothering her
was not the major's lack of confidence in her abilities, but
his implication that she was a rigid person, and as she set
up her easel overlooking the river, she struggled to identify
precisely what it was about this implication that upset her.

From the time Sophia had been a little girl, old enough to
worry when her father did not come home, and young enough
to be frightened by his loud, boisterous good humor after an
evening of carousing, she had vowed that she would never
allow herself to become such a ridiculous figure. When his
gambling debts swallowed up his promises of new clothes,
when he came home smelling of another woman's perfume,
she swore she would never let anyone down as her father
had let them down. She would always be dependable, someone who could be counted on no matter what. And the erratic
nature of their slender income had taught both Sophia and
her mother to scrimp and save, and plan. She had witnessed

all too often how an impulsive burst of generosity on her father's part would affect the quality of their meals for months afterward, not to mention lessening the number of rooms that could be warmed by a welcoming fire.

Until this moment, Sophia had always thought that the discipline she had acquired over herself and her emotions, her skill at organizing and planning, were good things. But now she began to wonder. Had she missed something by always thinking before she responded? Had she sacrificed her enjoyment of life by trying to avoid its excesses? Could it be that what she considered to be her responsible, dependable nature was in fact cold and calculating, and that in seeking to be serious and trustworthy she had succeeded only in being less lovable and less creative?

Certainly Lord Harry Featherstonaugh had been a trial to his wife and daughter, but to the rest of the world, the world that did not depend on him for food, clothing, or support, he was the best of good fellows. As far back as Sophia could remember he had been a universal favorite, and the men in his regiment were forever bragging to their brothers-in-arms of Captain Lord Harry's incredible feats of horsemanship, his bravery, and the crazy risks he took in order to be the first into battle, to push the furthest into the French defenses. No one Sophia could think of would understand that for his wife and daughter at least, life was a good deal calmer and less upsetting without the wild Lord Harry, who was genuinely missed by his comrades in the Twenty-third.

Sighing, Sophia picked up her brush, hoping to push all these disturbing thoughts from her mind as she concentrated on her painting, but she was only partially successful. Every once in a while the thought would intrude that maybe if she were not so aware of the time and not so busy helping her mother with household tasks she would paint better and more easily; she would be able to express the wild beauty of the scene instead of the pale imitation she seemed to be producing now.

At last she gave up in disgust and, packing up away her supplies, trudged slowly homeward, still asking herself if the major's comments were really true or if they had been inspired by his frustration at having been beaten by a woman.

Chapter 12

Sophia was left to ponder this problem on and off for several days as Mark, busy carrying messages to and from the besiegers of San Sebastian, had no thought for anything except accomplishing his mission until General Graham remarked late one evening as he unfolded Wellington's latest instructions, "The duke is fortunate to have you as his messenger, Adair, for there is not a better or faster horseman to be had in the Peninsula."

Even as he thanked the general and turned Caesar around toward Lesaca, Mark pictured a slim figure in a slate-colored riding habit bent over the long slender neck of a swift bay mare. What would the outcome of the race have been if their course had been a few hundred yards longer? Who was the better rider? Sophia's slow start was a natural consequence of her horse's lack of stature, but her catching up to him so quickly was ample proof of her skill. And he had rather churlishly refused to acknowledge that skill. Would he have been such a dog-in-the-manger if he had been competing against a fellow officer? Mark snorted in self-derision as he bent over Caesar's neck and galloped along in the waning twilight. No. He would have scorned to demonstrate such a paltry attitude to another officer, and he would have been punctilious if not genuinely admiring, in expressing his admiration for such superb horsemanship and such skill with firearms. Why then had he not acted that way with a woman?

Now that he had recovered from his annoyance at Sophia's suggestion that he was reckless and unreliable, Mark admitted that he was not proud of the way he had conducted himself, and he resolved to apologize handsomely at the first opportunity.

The opportunity presented itself rather sooner than he

expected, for much to his surprise, after having given Graham's dispatch to Wellington, and returning to his own quarters as he mounted the massive stone steps of the ancient stone bastion where the officers had their quarters, who should be coming down them tying the strings of her bonnet, but the young lady herself.

"Miss Featherstonaugh, what on earth are you doing here?"

Sophia looked up, and recognizing the major, raised her eyebrows in some surprise. Most of the men were so accustomed to seeing her about that it would never have occurred to any one of them to question her. Controlling her annoyance, she responded as mildly as she could, "Colonel Taylor appears to have contracted a fever, and as the surgeons are entirely occupied with the wounded just now, Mama and I are nursing him."

Mark bit his lip. "I beg your pardon. I did not mean to speak to you in such a peremptory manner. It was just that I had been thinking of you, and then at that very moment, you appeared."

"Thinking of me?"

"Yes." He smiled apologetically. "I realize that I behaved rather badly the last time I saw you.

Sophia opened her mouth to reply, but he held up one hand to forestall her. "No, let me apologize. You rode magnificently and you are clearly a superior shot and I failed to congratulate you on either count."

"Why thank you, Major, but you have no need to apologize for failing to compliment me." But, Sophia thought, even as she accepted the apology, you still have not admitted to the original point of discussion, which was the question of my becoming an exploring officer.

"But I do." Somewhat disconcerted by her coolly gracious acceptance of his apology, Mark followed her down the steps. "Not only did I not acknowledge your unquestionable skill, but I also was not, er, ah, entirely complimentary."

Sophia turned to look at hm. He was being genuine. The sheepish note in his voice and the awkward way he held himself betrayed his discomfort. Good. A little reflection might have a salutary effect on the boldly confident Major Lord Mark Adair.

"You see," he continued, "I had not expected to do so poorly. Though it does sound rather puffed up to say so, I am accustomed to winning such contests, even against my fellow officers. To lose a shooting match and nearly lose a race is no small thing, and losing to a young woman is even harder on my self-esteem. I am afraid I wanted to diminish your accomplishments by implying that you were rigid and controlling."

"Think nothing of it, Major. Being told that one is rigid is hardly the incalculable insult you make it out to be. And you may be right; I may very well be rigid and controlling."

"Oh no, you are not. You could not paint half so well if that were true. It is just that I . . ." He paused, trying to frame his thoughts.

"You?" By now Sophia was truly puzzled. The look in his eyes and the bitter twist of his mouth made her realize that there was more at stake here than a horse race and a shooting match.

"I was thoroughly shown up, and the only way to justify that to myself was to make you out to be the sort of person I would never want to be, the sort of person I would scorn to be. And rigid, controlling people are the sorts of people I scorn the most. In fact, it was to avoid people such as that that I joined the army and left England."

"What people are they?"

Mark grimaced. She was far too astute to be fobbed off by a mere generalization. "My father and my brother. All my life they tried to mold me into something I am not, to make me live by the long list of rules and traditions that form the very core of their existence, but I have always refused. I have seen how blind devotion to duty and propriety can stifle warmth, an enjoyment of life, even humanity, in a man, and I will never let myself become that sort of person."

"Surely you exaggerate. Surely they were not entirely cold and without feeling. What of your mother? Did her presence not soften their attitudes?"

"My mother?" The bitterness in his voice grew even more pronounced. "She was the chief victim of it. All the warmth and love that were so much a part of her passionate nature were frozen by their constant disapproval of her emotional responses to things. *Do not spoil them,* she was always being told whenever she was generous to the servants or when she sympathized with my childish woes. She was forever being criticized for not acting like a duchess, for not being distant enough, and stately enough. In the end, she was slowly forced to withdraw from everyone except the few people my father considered to be worthy of her attention. She lost her health and she died from the loneliness of it all."

"How very sad." Sophia laid a comforting hand on his sleeve. "I am so sorry."

He covered her hand with his own, marveling at how much sympathy even the lightest touch could convey. Gently he clasped the long slender fingers and raised them to his lips. "Thank you for understanding. No one else seems to. They blamed it on the climate and accused me of dramatizing it all, but . . ."

"But if that is what you sensed as a loving son, then you are right. Too often people seek out coldly rational explanations for things at the expense of the real truth. We British in particular are guilty of this for we do not like to express or examine our emotions and as a result we miss a great deal."

Again his clasp tightened on hers. "You, however, do not. You see the inner emotional life hidden beneath the physical exterior and you capture it in such a way that it permeates the picture you are creating. You are well aware how powerfully emotions can affect a person's character."

"Only too well." It was Sophia's turn to sound bitter now. "I have seen how self-indulgence can lead to a selfishness and a reckless abandon that can be as destructive to other people, if not more so, than ignoring them completely." She gazed unseeingly into the darkness that lay beyond the glow of the windows from the staff quarters, but Mark saw the slight tremor of her lower lip and the flutter of the thick, dark lashes as though she were blinking away unwelcome tears.

How she must have suffered from Lord Harry's thoughtlessness. As a child she must have adored a father whose charm was as legendary as his unreliability, and she must have felt betrayed countless times when he failed to return home or remember a promise. Cold and distant as Mark's father had been, at least he had been predictable, and in that predictability Mark had found security if not love. It was a security so strong that he had confused it with love for years until he had been old enough to recognize the difference. Sophia had not even been given that by her father. "Enjoying life and indulging in it to the fullest degree can make a person so self-centered that he appears even colder and less feeling than someone who sacrifices his humanity to duty, for at least a person such as that pays attention to others out of a sense of noblesse oblige." Mark felt the fingers on his arm clutch at it involuntarily.

Sophia no longer gazed off in the distance now, but surveyed him curiously, her eyes wide and questioning.

Mark could not help smiling, ever so slightly, at the surprise he read in them. "I am not entirely devoid of the powers of observation, you know."

It was not until she let out a deep sigh that Sophia realized she had been holding her breath for quite some time. "No. I know that. You could not be an exploring officer if you did not possess them. It is just . . ." She paused and a faint flush, barely visible in the dim light form the windows, rose in her cheeks. "It is just that I did not expect you to be so . . . so understanding."

"Believe me, I do understand. And if I could make it up to you, I would." Again he brushed her hand with his lips, but this time they lingered there a fraction of a moment longer.

She stood, mesmerized by the look in his eyes, the warmth of his lips on her hand, and by a host of feelings, impossible to define or describe. It was almost as though no one had ever understood her before this moment and now this man whom she barely knew saw into and sympathized with the deepest parts of her soul. It was wonderful, but it was frightening to be understood so well. "I . . . I must go." Sophia retrieved her hand. Even to her, her voice sounded breathless and unsure. "Mother will be wondering what has become of me." She turned and hurried down the steps so fast that it almost appeared as if she were running away from him.

Mark could not help grinning as he continued up the steps. So he had made the coolly self-reliant Sophia Featherstonaugh uneasy at last. The threat of enemy soldiers and Spanish guerrillas left her unmoved, but sympathy, understanding, and the intimacy they led to, were quite another thing.

Over the years Mark had known many women, enough of them to recognize the signs—the widened eyes, slightly trembling fingers, the flushed cheeks—that told him Sophia was not accustomed to being affected by a man in this particular way and she found it disconcerting. Good. He paused on the top step and turned to catch a glimpse of her as she hurried down the street. He was glad that he had been able to get beneath that self-assured exterior, for she had certainly gotten beneath his, and he did not relish being at such a disadvantage with a mere chit of a girl.

It was bad enough that she had bested him at a shooting match and very nearly a horse race as well, but that she should be able to read his innermost feelings was most unnerving, if not completely unacceptable. Or was it? Mark stepped back into the sheltering columns that supported the porch of the staff quarters. Propping his shoulder against a rough stone column, he pulled out a cigar, lit it, and puffed on it thoughtfully for a moment. Actually it had been rather a relief to unburden himself to someone who grasped so quickly all the implications from his sketchy description of his family.

In the few minutes it had taken for him to present a picture of his father and his brother, Sophia had been able to absorb it and interpret to the degree that she could put her finger on the crux of the matter—his mother—the beautiful, passionate, and loving Isabella, Duchess of Cranleigh, who had been slowly, inexorably deprived of every opportunity to express that loving nature until it eventually had killed her.

With a muttered oath Mark tossed the cigar on the ground and crushed it beneath his boot. He had not wanted to remember all those things—the old hurts and sorrows, his own helplessness to change the situation. For years he had forced it out of his consciousness where he had not had to think about it, but now she had made him recall it, examine it, and suffer all over again. But this time he had not suffered alone. There had been someone to share his suffering, someone who had been equally hurt and equally helpless, someone who could sympathize, who, with a single compassionate touch on his arm, and the warmth of understanding in her eyes, could soften the painfully ragged edges of those memories and reduce them to a dull ache. And for the first time he felt he could actually examine those memories without being overwhelmed by them. Giving a final twist to the cigar under his boot, he strode back inside and went in search of a good bottle of Madeira.

Chapter 13

Sophia quietly shut the door behind her and, observing her mother and stepfather in front of the fire in the sitting room, deep in conversation, hurried up the stairs, not even bothering to light a candle. Agitated as she was, she welcomed the darkness and the privacy of her own bedchamber.

Removing her bonnet and the Pomona green cossack mantle she had tossed over her shoulders to protect her from the damp night air, she hung them on a peg on the back of the door and sank onto the chair by the window. The cool breeze felt good on her flushed cheeks and the light from a crescent moon visible from her window made the view across tiled rooftops seem peaceful in contrast to the tumult of her own emotions. The hardworking citizens of Lesaca went to bed early and there were few lights or sounds to break the stillness that had settled over the little town.

Sophia breathed deeply, trying to inhale and absorb the serenity of the scene before her, but it did not the slightest bit of good. Her pulses were pounding, she felt weak in her knees, and there was a strange fluttery sensation in the pit of her stomach. She could not think what was wrong with her. What was it about her encounter with Major Adair that had affected her so strongly? It was not as though she was not used to sharing her thoughts with men, for she was actually more accustomed to male companions than she was to female ones, but no one had ever caused her to feel as she felt now. The way he had looked at her, the way he had seemed to read her thoughts and feelings— feelings that she was only vaguely aware she possessed— was both comforting and frightening. His wryly sympathetic smile had warmed her, but at the same time the depth of his understanding frightened her. Even she had not realized the extent of her anger at her father until the major had pointed it out to her. It was wonderful to have a person know one so well that one hardly had to speak, but it was also unnerving to be known that well.

The sympathy that she had read in the major's eyes and heard in his voice had been as intimate as an embrace. She sighed as she recalled the strength in the comforting hand that had clasped hers and the flood of warmth that the touch of his lips had sent from her fingers, through her arm, through her entire body. It had been infinitely consoling, but at the same time, she acknowledged reluctantly to herself, there had been another feeling that had not been consoling in the least. There had been an ache, a longing that she had never before experienced, a longing that was both delicious and upsetting because she did not know, did not want to guess what would satisfy it.

Sophia rose and slowly began to undress, telling herself that it would be best to put such troubling thoughts completely out of her mind, but in truth she did not really wish to. She wanted to linger on each moment of their interlude, to savor the closeness, to recapture the concern she had read in his eyes and the tenderness she had felt in his touch.

Shaking her head at her own weakness, she crossed over to her washstand, poured water into the basin, and splashed it on her face. It was not just that Major Adair was understanding; after all, she and Andrew Leith Hay had known one another longer and shared more interests in common. They both sketched and painted constantly, everything from the mundane aspects of campaign life to the most sublime landscapes, yet she did not find herself drawn to him as she did to the major. She did not feel breathless in his presence, nor did she suffer from that odd sensation in the pit of her stomach that seemed to overcome her every time Major Lord Mark Adair smiled at her.

Sophia lay down on her bed and pulled the covers over her. It had been a long day. Perhaps she as just tired. Perhaps the trembly feeling that overwhelmed her at the memory of his lips on her skin was purely and simply fatigue and nothing more.

Yes, that was it, she was tired. She would put herself to sleep as she always did by thinking of the pictures she would sketch tomorrow. If she could only fall asleep she would wake up refreshed and her usual cool and competent self.

Sophia was not the only one in General Curtis's household who went to bed with questions on her mind. Though Lady Curtis spoke nothing of it to her husband, she was rather surprised that, upon her return, Sophia went immediately to her bedchamber. Sophia always came to wish her good night and usually stayed to talk over the events of the day or discuss plans for the next one. It was not like her to go to bed without a word, but as Lady Curtis heard the slight creek of the floorboards above them, she decided that was just what her daughter had done.

Lady Curtis respected her daughter's obvious wish for privacy, but she was concerned enough to tap gently on Sophia's door sometime later when she and her husband were retiring for the night. There was no response so she opened it gently to peer in at her daughter. In the faint moonlight she could just make out Sophia's sleeping form, and the steadiness of her breathing reassured her mother that whatever thoughts her daughter had wished to keep to herself, they were not so upsetting as to keep her awake. Softly she closed the door and, returning to her own chamber, undressed and climbed into bed with her husband.

Though Sophia had fallen asleep, her mother lay awake for some time, turning over the day in her mind, trying to come up with some idea of what might have occurred to cause her daughter's unexpected behavior. The only slight variation in their routine had been that Sophia had gone to sit with Colonel Taylor that evening after supper, but there had been nothing so unusual in that, for she and her mother often visited the sick and the wounded, and while they would never become accustomed to the pain and the suffering, there was very little they had not seen. If something particularly upsetting had occurred, Sophia was more likely to share it with her mother than keep it to herself. No, something else must have happened, but Lady Curtis could not imagine what it might be. Sophia had led a life of such constant change and uncomfortable conditions that she adapted quite readily to almost anything. The more she considered it, the more Lady Curtis was certain that whatever had occurred must somehow be connected to Sophia's visit to Colonel Taylor, for all the rest of the day she had gone about her daily routine with her usual calmness, neither seeking nor avoiding conversation with anyone.

Sophia and her mother had lived on their own so long and in such isolated situations, relying on one another for solace and companionship, that there was very little that one did not know about the other, and this made Sophia's avoidance of conversation even more puzzling. As she finally drifted off to sleep, Lady Curtis resolved to keep a closer eye on her daughter.

During the ensuing days it did appear to Lady Curtis that Sophia was more reflective than usual. She would often look over to see her daughter's hand hovering over her sketchbook while she stared at some invisible point in space, her forehead wrinkled in thought. And occasionally Sophia would break off from the task at hand, whatever it was, to gaze out a window or a door, but her mother could see that she remained oblivious to whatever view lay beyond.

At last Lady Curtis could refrain no longer from comment and one morning as they were mending sheets and she had noticed that ten minutes had passed without Sophia's sewing a single stitch, she turned to her daughter. "Sophia?"

Sophia started and plunged her needle into the linen so vigorously that she pricked her finger. "Yes, Mama?"

"Is anything amiss? It seems to me that you have been rather distracted of late."

"Distracted? Me? No, Mama, nothing is amiss." The delicate pink that tinged her cheeks, however, belied her assertion, and she kept her eyes firmly fixed on the work in front of her.

"I am relieved to hear that." Lady Curtis was forced to be content with her answer, but it strengthened her resolve to keep an eye on her daughter. In all her life Sophia had never lied; she had never even prevaricated, until now. Her mother could not guess what possibly could cause her to do so now, but she knew that, whatever it was, it was significant.

Chapter 14

During the next few days, however, no one, especially Lady Curtis and her daughter, had time or energy to spare on reflections of any sort, for the army had begun its move across the Pyrenees toward France. General Curtis debated in vain with his wife. "My dear, you and Sophia are comfortable here in Lesaca, not to mention safe. We shall, if we are lucky, just be able to make it into France before the weather turns bad and we are forced into winter quarters. Why not remain here until spring to avoid all the discomfort and confusion of moving a household across the mountains in weather that is bound to be unpredictable at best?"

"And when have safety and comfort been more important to us than the people we love? The weather, as you say, is beginning to turn. If we remain here any longer it will prevent us from joining you for some time. Sophia and I are coming with you, sir, and that is that!" Lady Curtis looked to her daughter for confirmation.

Sophia nodded vigorously. "I agree with Mama and besides, I have quite run out of subjects to sketch around here."

General Curtis smiled ruefully. "I knew I stood very little chance of convincing you ladies, fire eaters that you are. Very well, but mind you, you are to promise me that you will remain safely in the rear, well out of the way of any fighting."

"We shall." Sophia's mother spoke for both of them.

"Just the way you did at Vitoria, I suppose." There was no mistaking the irony in the general's tone. "The wounded barely had time to fall before the two of you were out there offering them aid and comfort."

Sophia and her mother said nothing, but the expressions on their faces were answer enough.

"Was there ever a man plagued with two more strong-minded females than I?" The general chuckled. "You may come along and help us over the rough spots; I know you will anyway no matter what I say. I wonder that I even waste my breath trying to convince you to think of your own safety."

Following the general was more easily said than done, for the bridge at Vera, the only bridge across the Bidassoa that had not been destroyed by the French, led directly to the heavily defended heights of the mountains separating France and Spain.

"You must wait until the fortifications have been captured and the surrounding countryside subdued," the general instructed his wife. "But even when the French no longer pose a threat, the terrain may prove too much for the carriage. If the bridge at Behobie had not been burnt, you could follow easily enough on the road that leads from Irun to Bayonne, for it is excellent, but it will be some time before it will be rebuilt. It might be the wisest thing, though, to wait until it has been repaired."

Hearing this, Sophia and her mother were somewhat daunted. The prospect of spending the winter as the only English in a small village in Spain was not a particularly pleasant one. Sophia said as much to Mark one morning when she encountered him in the street outside headquarters.

"Good morning, Miss Featherstonaugh." Mark could not help feeling pleased as he observed the conscious look in the hazel eyes and the faintest color in her cheeks. He had been thinking far too much about her since their last encounter and it was gratifying to see from her reaction that she had apparently felt much the same way. "What, no sketchbook, no satchel full of pencils and paints? What has come over you?"

"I am too busy at the moment to paint. There are too many things to attend to, for Mama and I are to leave soon." The defiant tilt of her head and the obstinate compression of her lips suggested that the proposed move was a sore point.

"I can certainly understand your not wanting to leave

the place where you have established yourselves so comfortably."

"On the contrary"—Sophia fixed him with a scornful glance—"we are quite as anxious to go into France as the rest of the army, but the general tells Mama that the only bridge left standing leads to a road no carriage could possibly travel. It is not for myself that I am worried, for I rarely travel in the carriage, but Mama does need one."

"I see." Mark was silent for a moment as he debated with himself as to whether he should interfere. Since it would quickly become obvious that there were other ways to cross the Bidassoa, Sophia would find out sooner or later on her own. It was a question of angering General Curtis or Sophia. "I myself have recently received intelligence on that very topic." He grinned as her expression changed in an instant from scornful to pleading.

"You have? Is there another way for us to travel into France? Mama is a trooper, but she does fret when she and the general are separated for very long."

Mark was somewhat surprised at the wistful note he heard in her voice. If he had the time to think about it, he might have wondered if Sophia were just the tiniest bit envious of her mother's newfound domestic happiness, but he was too busy thinking of how he was going to defend himself against General Curtis's wrath when he discovered Sophia and his wife were part of the British invasion of France. There was only one way to avoid it and that was to offer to look after the two of them himself.

The previous evening Wellington had delighted Mark by dispensing with his services for the moment. *You look too much of the Spaniard for you to do me much good in France, Adair. You will have to stay in uniform or you will be shot for a guerrilla for sure. No*—correctly interpreting the cavalry officer's hopeful expression, the duke had hastened to disabuse him of any notion that he might be returned to his cavalry duties—*I am not going to waste your talents by returning you to your regiment. Once we get into France I shall need your skill at reconnaissance, but you will just have to do it without relying on disguises. For the moment that means staying with us and seeing to it that we get smoothly across this damn river.*

"You were saying, Major." Sophia recalled his attention to the present problem.

"Oh, yes. I have it on the best authority of the local fishermen, and not false fishermen such as Pablo, but real ones, that it is possible to ford the Bidassoa River in several places at low tide."

"But I thought it was very swift and very deep."

"So it is, but several fishermen have reassured me that when the tide is at its lowest ebb the river falls as much as sixteen feet. I should be happy to see to it that you get safely across once the First and the Fifth divisions have secured the other bank."

"You would? But surely you have much more important things to do?"

"Wellington will not need my services until we are established in France and helping you and your mother is the most important thing I could be doing."

"Oh, thank you. Thank you so much."

He could not help smiling at her eager gratitude. Every other woman he had ever met would be complaining of the loss of comfortable quarters while this one was thanking him for helping her to make a risky and no doubt uncomfortable journey into enemy territory. "The Fifth is to cross at about half past seven on the seventh when the tide will be at its lowest possible point. They will be camped at Fuenterrabia before that. I suggest you plan to arrive in Fuenterrabia in the evening after they have crossed. It is an easy distance from Lesaca and you should be able to find suitable accommodations after everyone has left."

Lady Curtis, however, was less enthusiastic than her daughter when she heard the news. "It sounds rather uncertain, counting on the tides in such a way. And I would not wish to cause the general any undue alarm."

"But, Mama, Major Adair has assured me that he will accompany us and assist us in crossing."

Lady Curtis laid down the sock she was darning and looked curiously at her daughter. "That is most gentlemanly of Major Adair, but surely he must have many more pressing duties than escorting two women across a river."

"He assures me that until the army has established itself in France, his services are not necessary."

"Very well, then." Lady Curtis did not discuss the issue further, but she had not missed the slight flush that stole across her daughter's face at the mention of Major Adair, a flush that was remarkably similar to the one she had seen when she had spoken to her daughter the morning after she had retired without saying good night. So that was how it was. Lady Curtis had been an officer's wife long enough to know that on the whole, men preferred to avoid the complication of ladies altogether, especially where any sort of tactical maneuver was concerned. And here was the major actually volunteering to take on the responsibility of the two of them, their baggage, servants, and all the attendant possibilities for disaster. She could only conclude, therefore, that some powerful motivating force was impelling him to tackle such an undertaking. Glancing once again at her daughter's face, she deduced that Sophia herself was the source of his inspiration.

Lady Curtis bent quickly back over her darning to hide the smile she was unable to suppress. She had wondered when, if ever, one of the daring young men who were their constant companions would make an impression on her daughter. Until now, she had been of the opinion that Sophia was so accustomed to military men that she looked upon anyone in a scarlet coat as a brother and nothing more, but the situation appeared to have changed somewhat. It would certainly bear watching at any rate.

Lady Curtis folded the sock with its mate and returned her needle and thread to her workbasket. "Then that is all the more reason to make sure that we are carefully packed and ready the minute we are called upon to move."

Chapter 15

On a gloomy morning several days later they finished supervising the loading of the household items into a second carriage, which left just enough room for Jorge to climb in and Luis to mount the box. They bade good-bye to a tearful Maria and Teresa, and were off, lumbering slowly down the road to Fuenterrabia, where Mark had agreed to meet them.

The sky grew more ominous as they neared their destination. Lightning crackled across the sky, and thunder echoed loudly among the mountaintops. Sophia, riding Atalanta, glanced up at the storm clouds racing overhead and resigned herself to being thoroughly soaked. She and her mother hoped against hope that they would reach Fuenterrabia before the roads became so muddy as to be impassable They had to reach the Bidassoa in the next day, when the tides at the mouth of the river were near their lowest, or it would be impossible to cross, and there was no telling how long it would take the Royal Engineers to establish a bridge over the river.

A crack of thunder more violent than the rest crashed directly overhead and the heavens opened. Rain poured down in such a torrent that Sophia could barely see the road in front of her.

Pushing down the carriage window, Lady Curtis stuck her head out. "Sophia, please come inside the carriage. You will catch your death of cold."

"It is only rain, Mama," Sophia shouted back between thunderclaps. "I won't melt, and besides, there is no room for me inside the carriage."

"We do not have to take everything with us. There are some things in here we could do without. I certainly have no need of the looking glass that is beside me here on the seat. We could strap it on the outside."

"We can not do that, it may break. It has been with us in all our lodgings since we left England."

"Then let Jorge sit on the box with Luis and you may ride inside the other carriage."

"I am far better suited to this than Jorge. His rheumatism bothers him enough already as it is."

Her mother closed the window. She had known at the outset that it would be useless to remonstrate with her daughter. Sophia was as stubborn as the mules that made up the army's supply trains, especially where her family was concerned. Lady Curtis comforted herself with the thought that perhaps maybe Major Adair might succeed in convincing her daughter where she had failed.

Certainly Mark was suitably horrified by Sophia's appearance as they entered the taproom of the Venta del Rey, a cozy inn nestled next to Charles V's imposing castle. "My poor girl, you are wet through!" He hurried forward to remove the soaking cloak that Sophia had grabbed and flung over her riding habit when the rain had first started. "Here, let me." Long fingers untied the strings of her hat which her hands were too stiff to manage.

"Whatever were you thinking to ride in a torrent such as this?" He pulled a handkerchief from his pocket and gently wiped the remaining raindrops from her face. "There. Now come sit by the fire." And taking her arm, he led her into a small private parlor while her mother looked on with a good deal of satisfaction. If the major was concerned enough over the condition of her daughter to forget the comfort of the mother completely, it was surely a sign that his interest in Sophia was as strong as her interest was in him.

"If you will excuse me, I took the liberty of ordering supper for you so that you would have something hot to eat when you arrived." Mark poked the logs in the fireplace into a warming blaze and then turned to nod at the innkeeper, who was hovering in the doorway. In no time at all the innkeeper's wife appeared bearing a platter of roast chicken while her daughters followed with wine and fresh bread.

It was not until she stretched her hands to the warmth

of the roaring fire in front of her or smelled the savory aroma of the chicken that Sophia realized quite how tired and hungry she was, so tired and hungry that she did not even change out of her damp clothes. She could do nothing but watch hungrily as Mark carved the chicken and then tuck into it eagerly as one of the innkeeper's daughters placed a heavily ladened plate in front of her. But she was not alone; both her mother and the major were equally famished, and silence reigned for some time after they had been served.

At last, mindful of her manners, Lady Curtis laid down her fork. "And was the attack across the river successful? I assume that it was as Fuenterrabia seems remarkably empty of soldiers."

Mark took a drink of wine. "Yes, it was most successful. At seven-thirty this morning the Fifth Division led the plunge into the river and by eight o'clock, when the rocket was shot from the church tower signaling the attack of the Fist Division, the Fifth had overrun Hendaye and were swarming up the slopes of Mount Calvaire."

Sophia laid down her own fork. "So the British Army is in France at last. How you must have longed to be part of the force that first established our foothold in Bonaparte's own territory. We are indeed honored that you volunteered to see to our welfare."

Mark examined Sophia's face suspiciously over the rim of his wineglass, but there was not an ounce of guile in it. She truly did understand what it had cost him not to be one of the first to set foot in France. Most women he knew would still be complaining about the unpleasantness of the journey, but this one, who had scorned even the dubious comforts of the carriage, was able to put aside her own concerns long enough to see things from his point of view. Her understanding was even more warming than the excellent Madeira whose heady fumes he inhaled appreciatively.

"Do tell us more about the attack, Major, Was the passage across the river very difficult? Will the tide remain low enough tomorrow for us to make it across?" Lady Curtis, less intensely aware of the major's state of mind than her daughter, was more interested in the practical aspects of the situation.

"I should think that the Bidassoa would pose no risk

were you to attempt to cross it tomorrow, but I still urge you to wait until the engineers have constructed a suitable bridge. We have a pontoon train with the army that only wants setting up now that we have secured the other side of the river. It should merely be a matter of days before you may cross safely without the risk of getting yourselves wet."

"If you think it possible for us to cross tomorrow, then I prefer to join my husband as soon as I can. And now, if you will excuse me, Major, my daughter and I are somewhat fatigued after our journey today and, with the prospect of a more arduous day tomorrow, must get some rest."

Mark rose as well and signaled to one of the girls who had reappeared with a fresh bottle of wine. "The landlord's daughter will show you to your room, which, I trust, will be to your satisfaction."

Lady Curtis managed a tired smile as they left the room. "I am sure they will. Thank you, Major, for looking after us."

"I am happy to do so, ma'am." He spoke to the mother, but his eyes were on the daughter, who looked worn out after her day in the saddle.

Mark poured himself another glass of wine and strolled over to the window. Darkness had fallen and the rain clouds blocked out stars and moon while a light rain still continued. He wondered how the troops across the river were faring. After the torrential rains, the banks of the river must have been murderously slippery. Certainly the cavalry would have been useless. But he did wish, as Sophia had so acutely suggested, that he had been among the first wave of British to cross into France. Well, there was no use repining. Wellington had made his duty clear to him. He had done it, and would continue to do it to the best of his ability, which meant that it was time for him to rest up for the journey tomorrow. But first, he would see to it that the horses had been taken care of. Setting down his glass and picking up a lantern hanging by the door, Mark crossed the courtyard to the stable.

As he entered the stable, he was somewhat surprised to see light from another lantern coming from one of the stalls and to hear the low murmur of a voice. Surely the servants had taken care of the horses long ago. Mark crept quietly toward the stall. Theoretically, he was in friendly territory, the British having pushed the enemy back into France, but one could never be too careful.

Cautiously he peered around the corner of the stall and there, still clad in her damp riding habit, was Sophia chatting with Atalanta as she inspected the mare's hooves and gave her a final pat on the neck. Then she moved over to the saddle and bridle hanging on the wall and carefully inspected them for signs of wear.

He watched in fascination. He had never seen a woman so at home in what was usually the realm of servants, male servants at that, nor had he ever observed a woman so enthralled by such a mundane task. There was something extraordinarily attractive in watching the slender, capable hands feeling every inch of bridle and testing every buckle.

At last she finished her task and restored the saddle and bridle to their places, but she did not leave. What else was there to be done? Mark could not imagine what she had in mind. He quickly withdrew into the empty stall next to Atalanta's as Sophia bade good night to the horse and, picking up the lantern, crossed to the stall just opposite, where she went through the same routine with the carriage horses.

Mark could stand it no longer. "Surely your coachman, if not the stable boys, could be counted upon to see to the horses?"

Sophia whirled around. "You! What are you doing here?"

"I?" He raised one eyebrow in faint surprise. "The same thing that you are, I expect, checking to see that Caesar is comfortably housed and fed."

Sophia bit her lip. Judging from his expression, the major was not accustomed to being addressed in such a peremptory fashion by a female. Undoubtedly most females were all smiles and fluttering eyelashes where he was concerned, but she had had an exhausting day and she did not relish being startled the way he had just startled her, or being observed unawares, as he had obviously been observing her. It made her feel vulnerable and most uncomfortable. "I beg your pardon. I expect it did sound rather rude of me. It is just that I had thought you already retired." Blast, her face grew hot as she realized how she must sound, as though she were watching every move he made. And the fact that she was constantly aware of his presence, especially now, with the light from his lantern emphasizing the angular planes of his face, the firm line of his jaw, and the deep-set eyes made her face grow even hotter. "I, er, you are correct, I did come to check on the horses. And yes, the coachman already checked on them, but I like to see to them myself."

"Ah."

"It is not because I am rigid or controlling," she began defensively.

"Now did I say that?"

"You did not have to." But Sophia could not suppress a tiny smile in response to the sly grin that tugged at one corner of his mouth. "But even Papa, who was so havey-cavey about everything else, always made sure that his cattle, at least, were well looked after."

Despite her obvious effort to sound offhanded, there was no mistaking the bitterness in her voice. Mark felt the oddest urge to pull her into his arms and reassure her that while he was her escort, her welfare, and that of her mother, would be his primary goal. But he resisted the urge. Sophia Featherstonaugh was not the sort of woman who asked for, or expected assistance in any way, and she might take such a gesture as a slur on her capability rather than an expression of concern. "Undoubtedly he assumed that you and your mother were more capable of looking after yourselves than his cattle was and left you to your own devices. I am sure you took care of yourselves admirably, proving his point and freeing him from any pangs of guilt that might have assailed him from time to time."

Sophia was silent, her head tilted thoughtfully. "You are quite clever, are you not? That is my father to perfection. Without even knowing him, you have captured his very essence."

"Perhaps it is because his daughter has portrayed his very essence to me." He had moved closer to her now so that she could feel the warmth of his breath on her cheek. "But just because he expected you to look after yourselves does not mean that every man who travels with you expects you to do so. As long as you are traveling with me, you are to let me worry about the details. No"—he held up his

hand to forestall the words of protest that rose to her lips—
"it will not inconvenience me, and yes, I am just as capable
of looking after things, if not more so, than you are. More
importantly, I wish to save you the effort. And furthermore"—this time he laid a finger on her lips as she opened
them to object—"it would do you good to relax and let
someone else take care of things for you. Now"—he gently
grasped her shoulders and turned her toward the door—"I
want you to march right out of here and back to your
chamber, where you can change into something dry and get
some rest."

Sophia turned around to face him. "But I can not let
you."

"And why ever not?" Mark's hands slid down from her
shoulders to her arms. "You are still quite damp, you know,
and we do not want you catching your death of cold when
the journey has only just begun."

"I . . . it . . . ." Intensely conscious of the warmth of his
hands through the damp fabric of her riding habit, Sophia
paused in some confusion. "It is not fair."

"Fair?" The air of mild amusement gave way to surprise.

"Yes. Fair. You have had as long and as tiring a day as
I have. Why should you look after the horses and carriages,
especially since they are our horses and our carriages?"

"Why indeed?" It was the major's turn to look bemused.
Never in his life had a woman, except for his mother, concerned herself with his welfare. It was a novel sensation
and he found it oddly touching. A slow smile spread across
his face. "So I have, but I am accustomed to such days."

"And so am I."

"You are incorrigible." He brushed away a dark curl that
clung to her forehead. "I begin to have a great deal of
sympathy for your servant, the one who was armed to the
teeth and watching over you the day I met you."

"Oh Luis." Sophia smiled guiltily. "Yes, I am afraid that
I am a bit of a trial to hm."

"Then it is time you learned to be less of a trial to those
who wish to look after you. Now come," he said and, taking
her by her shoulders, led her toward the door.

But as they reached the doorway, Sophia stopped and
turned to him. "I do not know why you exert yourself so
much on our behalf, but thank you."

Mark fought against the impulse to kiss the parted lips and tell her that he would do anything for her. Most of his women complained about his lack of gallantry. Paradoxically, he was discovering that the more this woman wished to do things for herself, the more he wished to do them for her. "Let us just say that I enjoy being of service to a lovely young woman."

It was the wrong thing to say. Her shoulders stiffened and the bemused, half-wondering expression on her face disappeared.

The intimacy of the moment vanished. Sophia regained her air of cool self-possession and the distance between them seemed to widen considerably. Any other woman would have moved closer to him to press her advantage. Not Sophia.

"I forget that you have been around cavalry officers too long to accept any Spanish coin they might offer you. The truth of the matter is that Wellington has dispensed with my services for the moment, and desperate for life-threatening adventure, I asked for the most dangerous assignment I could find, and here I am."

Sophia chuckled and Mark let out an inward sigh of relief as he opened the door for her. It had been a very near thing, but he had managed to retrieve his position with her.

They entered the inn and he paused at the bottom of the stairs. "Good night. We must leave early so that we are at the river when the tide will be at its lowest."

"But, Major, what about you? Are you not going to rest as well?"

"I shall keep an eye on things down here. Believe me, I am quite accustomed to sleeping any time anywhere. Do not concern yourself with me. Now get some rest."

"Very well. Good night then."

"Good night."

Chapter 16

Reluctantly, Sophia climbed the stairs to the bedchamber, where her mother, worn out by the day's exertions, was fast asleep. Sophia wished she had some plausible excuse to remain downstairs talking with the major, savoring the feeling of closeness. There had been something so solid and reassuring about the major's presence and his appreciation of what life had been like with Lord Harry. In fact, from the moment the major had gently wiped the rain from her face, all the discomforts of the journey had seemed to slip away. What was it he had said in the stable? *I wish to save you the effort.* Over the years men had offered her assistance, but they had always done so out of a conviction of their superior ability. Major Lord Mark Adair, on the other hand, had made it clear that he was doing it because he cared for her comfort, not because he doubted her capabilities.

She sighed as she undid the buttons of her riding habit. The major's care and concern for her had been palpable. She had felt it in the warmth of his hands as he had taken her cloak, in the strength of his arm around her shoulder as he had led her from the stable. She had read it in his eyes as they looked at her, searching for signs of cold and fatigue.

Sophia struggled out of the damp riding habit and hung it up carefully, hoping, not too optimistically, that it might be a little less damp by morning. It had felt so wonderful to have someone caring for her, just for her. General Curtis had made their lives much more happy and secure, but, though he had been kindness itself to Sophia, it was clear that all his concern was for her mother, and happy as she was to see this, Sophia felt just the tiniest bit left out. But this time someone had made her comfort and happiness his major concern.

As she put on her night robe and climbed into bed, she told herself that the major would probably have done as much for any, what was it he had called her, *lovely young woman.* Certainly his practiced response to her thanks indicated that he had been in many similar situations, and it behooved her not to put any store by the feelings he had inspired in her. Still, as she pulled the covers up to her chin, Sophia could not help hoping that she was not just any *lovely young woman* to him. No matter what her coolly rational self told her, she found her heart wanting to believe that all the major's solicitude had been because he cared. Surely he would not be able to read her thoughts and feelings with such uncanny ability if he did not care for her at least a little bit?

This was dangerous ground indeed, especially for one who knew only too well how charming gentlemen could lavish attention on their loved ones one day and forget their existence entirely the next. It was time she stopped entertaining such ridiculous notions and put her mind to the journey ahead of her.

Sophia and her mother rose before dawn the next day, but the major was already waiting for them in the parlor when they descended. "I took the liberty of ordering breakfast." He indicated pots of chocolate and baskets of crusty bread on the table in front of the fire. "I am afraid I can not give you too long to eat, however, as I have ordered the horses be harnessed and the carriages brought around. We should be at the ford well before the tide is fully out so that we may begin to cross at its lowest ebb."

His smile as he helped both ladies into their chairs at the table was warm, but there was none of the intimacy there had been the previous evening. Observing him under her lashes as she poured her chocolate, Sophia was glad she had talked herself out of assigning any special significance to his attentions the night before. Resolutely ignoring the strange effect this thought seemed to have on her stomach, she helped herself to a large chunk of bread.

It was a subdued and silent party that made its way through the narrow stone streets of Fuenterrabia. A few remaining troops were beginning to stir as they reached the broad meadow outside the city by the river and made their way toward the narrow opening in the earthworks that had protected the meadow from enemy fire across the river.

"See"—Mark pointed to the pontoons pulled up at the shoreline, to form the beginnings of a bridge—"if we had waited a few more days, we could cross high and dry."

"Yes, but a great deal may happen in a few days, Major. Sophia and I could never forgive ourselves if we did not make every effort to provide the general a warm fireplace and a good dinner as quickly as possible."

Mark grinned. "Spoken like a trooper. Very well, then, let us get on with it." And leaning over to seize the bridle of the lead carriage horse on the first carriage, he led it slowly into the swirling water. The animal snorted and rolled its eyes, but it followed Caesar's lead docilely enough.

For the first moments, Mark was too occupied with his own horse and the animals pulling the carriages to pay attention to Sophia. When he at last had the opportunity to glance back at her, she and Atalanta were well into the river. The water rose nearly to the mare's belly, but horse and rider moved as calmly and deliberately as though they were making a sedate appearance at the peak of the fashionable hour in Hyde Park.

Mark felt the oddest surge of pride as he watched them. The day before, many experienced cavalry officers had had difficulty convincing their mounts to enter the swiftly moving water in the first place, but Sophia never blinked an eye, and her calm demeanor was followed by Atalanta, who trudged across, ears pricked and eyes fixed steadily on the opposite shore.

At last, with a mighty heave, the first carriage horses clambered up the bank on the other side and drew to a halt, their shoulders steaming in the morning sun. The second carriage followed suit and they stood there catching their breaths, looking back at the river they had just pushed their way across. "France at last," Sophia exclaimed, riding up alongside the carriage. "Did you ever think you would see the day, Mama?"

"No, my dear, I did not." Lady Curtis leaned out of the carriage. "And a great deal of our successful arrival on French soil is owing to you, Major. I do thank you."

"Yes, thank you," Sophia, who had been observing the hive of activity on the other shore, added belatedly. Shading her eyes, she turned to survey the rugged slope in front of them. "And there, if I am not mistaken, appears to be a camp on the summit of that peak just ahead of us."

"Yes. It was abandoned yesterday quite hastily by the French and our fellows moved right in. I am told that it is extremely commodious and the view it commands of the Bay of Biscay is truly magnificent."

"Then what are we waiting for?" Sophia gathered up the reins, which had fallen slack while she had paused to catch her breath and reorient herself after fording the river.

"What indeed?" The major could not help shaking his head in amazement. Undaunted by the exertions of fighting the current and struggling to help her horse keep its footing in four feet of water, she was eager to tackle the rugged wooded ridge rising in front of them. Mark urged Caesar in front of the first carriage, and nodding to the coachman, led the way up the rough road that climbed up the ridge.

They progressed steadily, but slowly, plodding along in silence, animals and humans alike concentrating on their footing until at last they arrived at the top, where what appeared to be an entire village lay before them. Streets and squares were laid out with placards bearing the names dear to their former French occupants: RUE DE PARIS, RUE DE VERSAILLES, and the new British arrivals were making themselves comfortable in the abandoned huts.

Reining in Atalanta, Sophia halted and inhaled deeply the cool, fresh air, tangy with the scent of pines and campfires and the mouthwatering aroma of dinners simmering in pots throughout the camp. Soldiers were cleaning weapons, checking harnesses, and settling into their quarters as calmly as though they had been there for months instead of having forded the river and fought their way up the wooded slope a scant day before. Off in the distance, directly below them, lay the rich plain watered by the Nive and the Nivelle, and on the left, as the major had promised, the Bay of Biscay shimmered a deep blue in the autumn sunshine.

The moment they neared the camp, Mark had spoken to the coachman. "Remain here while I locate the general." And he had gone in search of General Curtis. He was away for some time and the horses were beginning to shift impatiently in their harnesses when at last the general came hurrying to greet his ladies.

"You made excellent time, my dear," he exclaimed, helping his wife descend from the carriage. "You had no trouble, I trust?"

"None at all. And our speed is due to the efforts of the major." Lady Curtis turned to acknowledge their guide, but he had turned to help Sophia dismount.

"I hope you do not think I am such a poor thing as to need any assistance." Ignoring the hands held out to help her, Sophia slid easily to the ground and, giving her skirt a twitch, strolled over to join the general and her mother.

There was nothing for Mark to do but swallow his chagrin and accept the thanks of the general. "I do appreciate your escorting the ladies, Major. It was a great relief to know that they were in excellent care and believe me, fighting our way across the Bidassoa was less strenuous than keeping an eye on these two strong-minded females. I am deeply in your debt." He winked at Mark sympathetically before turning back to his wife. "Come along, I must show you our quarters. They are extremely rudimentary, but Speen has positively transformed them. It is only a little larger than the soldiers' huts, but it does boast a fireplace and a solid roof. I trust that you will be comfortable, but you will recall that you *did* insist on coming, you know."

"I know." Lady Curtis smiled fondly at her husband as she allowed him to lead her down one of the makeshift streets.

Sophia was just about to follow them when her eye fell on the major as he untied Caesar's bridle from the tree. Something about the tired slump of his shoulders touched her in the oddest way. In the effort to keep Atalanta from losing her footing in the river and then on the tortuous path to the camp, concentrating on the road in front of her, she had almost forgotten the major. And if she was beginning to feel the waves of exhaustion roll over her, how much more must he be experiencing, he who had borne responsibility for leading their little expedition.

"Major?"

Mark turned in some surprise. From the disdainful way she had rejected his offer to help her dismount, he had deduced that she was more than anxious be rid of him. It had been abundantly clear from the beginning of the journey that there had really been no need for him to accompany them. Sophia Featherstonaugh was more than capable of managing such a journey on her own and though she had not spurned his assistance, she had certainly not requested it. And, strangely enough, he, who was less tolerant of helpless females than the average man, rather regretted that she had not asked more of him.

I can not thank you . . . No, that sounded horribly formal and priggish. *It was most kind of you . . .* That hardly sounded better. Sophia twisted her gloves in her hands as she tired to find just the words to let him know how reassuring it had been to know he was there watching over them at every moment of their journey especially when at the sight of the raging river or facing the steep, winding road she had felt her courage weaken.

Mark raised a quizzical eyebrow. It was not like the self-assured Sophia Featherstonaugh to be so ill at ease. "Yes?"

"I . . . ah, nothing. Thank you. I just want to thank you."

"For what? I did nothing that you were not completely capable of doing yourself, and completely prepared to accomplish on your own."

"I know." Sophia bit her lip. How odiously self-satisfied and arrogant that sounded. "I mean, yes, I could have, I suppose, but it was ever so much nicer knowing you were there."

Mark's lip quivered. Her words had come out all in a rush, tumbling over one another. It was blatantly obvious that Miss Featherstonaugh was not accustomed accepting assistance of any kind, and he could not help chuckling at her awkwardness. "Why thank you. Coming from someone as used to control, er, *arranging,* things to her own satisfaction, that is rare praise indeed."

Sophia stiffened. "I do not control . . ."

"Relax, Miss Featherstonaugh, I was only teasing you. You were having such difficulty thanking me for something I was happy to do, that I could not help teasing you."

"You were?" She wrinkled her brow in such a puzzled way that he burst out laughing. There was no doubt about it, amazingly, self-sufficient, yet charmingly naive at one and the same time, Sophia Featherstonaugh was an original. Certainly he had never encountered a woman so delightfully natural and unassuming in so many ways. "Believe me, I was only too happy to escort you. No, do not poker up at me. I am not offering you platitudes. To be brutally honest, I will tell you that if I had been asked to look after any other females but you and your mother I would have found some way to get out of it no matter who was asking. But I had seen enough of you to know that you would ask nothing of me, that you were entirely capable of making the journey on your own, and, oddly enough, that made me want to help you, not that I did."

"Oh but you did. Every step of the way I knew that if something happened to me, you were there to take care of things. I have never had anyone to take care of me before. Yes, I have Mama, but she does not know about horses and carriages. And yes, I have the general, but he has his own duties to look after. Luis and the others do their best, but they are not thinkers or planners. They only do what they are told to and though they are devoted and hardworking, they can not do anything they have not been instructed to do. It is simply not in their natures. You, on the other hand, have been dealing with dangerous situations, unexpected occurrences, for years. You have no notion what it is to be able to trust in someone else's abilities like that."

The big hazel eyes, dark with the intensity of her feelings, gazed up at him almost pleadingly, willing him to understand what it had meant to her. It was not until he exhaled that Mark realized he had been holding his breath, hoping that their trip, the moments of understanding and working together so smoothly without even having to talk to one another, had meant as much to her just as it had to him.

He clasped one of the hands that was still twisting the gloves and raised it to his lips. "I am glad you felt that way, because I felt that way about you, too. Even though I am surrounded by men who have, more or less, been trained to be soldiers, I find that there are very few of them I could truly count on in a tight spot as I can count on you. I am glad I was able to make you feel the same way." He pressed his mouth against the warm, smooth skin of her hand. Then, he sketched a playful bow and, mounting Caesar, headed off toward headquarters.

It was Sophia's turn to let out a long deep sigh. So he *did* understand what it was like to discover the rare person who could be trusted and counted upon in life's more challenging situations. What a miracle that sort of understanding was, and how rare, yet how wonderful when it happened. She could see it every time her mother and the general looked at one another and she envied it.

Mounting her own horse, who had been patiently waiting, Sophia rode off in the direction in which her mother and the general had disappeared.

Chapter 17

The next few days Sophia and her mother were so occupied in making a home out of the shepherd's hut that they had time for little else and they kept much to themselves while the rest of the army was very much occupied planning its next move. Wellington, his aides, and General Curtis spent a good deal of time in the saddle communicating with troops spread all along the ridge overlooking the plains of Gascony. Much to his delight, Mark was now ordered to take part in these plans as a cavalry officer once again and he reveled in casting off his role as an exploring officer.

He was soon so involved with preparations for an offensive against the French holding the port of Saint Jean de Luz and those manning the stone redoubts along the Nivelle that he hardly had a thought to spare for Sophia except for the occasional moment when he would look down from the wild heights of the ridge to the panorama below and think what a splendid subject it would make for someone who excelled in painting dramatic landscapes. Unconsciously he kept an eye out for a slender figure seated at an easel, but he looked in vain for Sophia never appeared.

The next time he encountered her, she was absorbed in her art, not capturing a magnificent vista spread before her but struggling in the dim light and fetid air of a field hospital.

Sophia had been chasing some determined spiders from the corners of their new quarters when Speen materialized beside her. She was accustomed to the batman's silent, efficient movements, but she had been so lost in her thoughts that she was unaware of his presence until he coughed politely. "Miss Sophia?"

"Oh!" She jumped, dropping the crude twig broom that

she had been using to mount her attack. "Speen, how you startled me."

"Begging your pardon, miss, but there's a young lad from the Sixtieth Foot who has been badly wounded. He was off where he should not have been and ran into a French foraging party. He is in mortal pain and Mr. Henry, the surgeon who looked at him, says there is nothing that can be done except to give him opium. But I thought, as he is so young, and far from home, that you might possibly visit him and be of some comfort to him."

Sophia smiled. "You have a soft heart under that ruthlessly efficient manner of yours, Speen."

"Perhaps, but this lad is no more than a boy."

"Very well." Sophia untied her apron, hung it on a hook, and, preparing herself for anything, grabbed her Bible and her sketching things. "I am ready. Take me to him."

Speen led her to another shepherd's hut, this one larger and with fewer window openings than theirs. These openings had been covered to keep in what little warmth came from the fireplaces at either end of the room. Cots were lined up along either wall, and except for the tortured breathing of several of the room's occupants and the occasional stifled moan, it was deathly silent.

The batman led her to the bed nearest the door and departed to continue with his duties. A young man, barely more than a boy, lay still as death, his hands clenched at his sides, his blond hair plastered across his ashen forehead. The blue eyes watching her approach were dull with pain and his breathing was ragged.

Sophia sank to a nearby stool and gently shook one of the clammy hands in hers. "I am Sophia. Speen told me that you were in a bad way and I came to see if there was anything I could do. Would you like me to read the Bible or write a letter for you?"

The boy shook his head ever so slightly. "I don't know no one who can read."

"Do you have any family?"

"Just me mum. She was powerful sad when I joined up." He gasped with the effort of speaking. "She were right, too."

"Then perhaps she would like a picture of you."

"A picture?" A faint spark of interest shone in his eyes.

"Yes. I brought my drawing things."

"But not like . . ."

"No, not the way you are now, but the way you were when you joined up."

"Yes." It was more a sigh than a response.

Gently disengaging her hands, Sophia pulled out her sketchbook and pencil and hastily roughed in the outline of the young soldier's head. She would have to work fast, breaking frequently to show him the progress of the portrait.

Except for the boy's labored breathing and the gentle swish of the pencil on the paper, silence reigned as she struggled to capture the essence of her subject in happier times. It was not easy and she had so little time. His breath was growing shallower by the minute.

"There." She straightened and held the pad out for him to see. "It is only the outline. What do you think? Will it do?"

A wan smile tugged at patient's lips. "Aye," he gasped.

Sophia bent over her work again. The young lad standing proudly in his regimentals, one hand resting on his musket with the ragged Pyrenees rising behind him made an impressive picture. She worked feverishly sketching in the details until a thought struck her. "I must know your name and your mother's and where we should send this to her."

"Billy, ma'am, Billy Barnes."

"And your mother?"

"Is Mrs. Barnes and she lives next to the tavern in Fingest."

"Very well. I shall see that this gets to her." Sophia again held the picture up for him to see.

"It's good, isn't it, ma'am? She'll like that. And now, if you please, I'll rest." The last words were scarcely a whisper.

Carefully, quietly, Sophia laid down her things and gently took one of his hands in hers and brushed the hair off his brow.

"Mum." The word was so faint she could barely hear it, but the mile that accompanied it as he turned his head toward her told her that she had accomplished all she had hoped to.

She sat for some time with the dead soldier's hand in

hers. Tears pricked her eyes, but she blinked them rapidly away. She could not think of the sadness or she would not be able to go on.

Sophia was not the only one whose eyes were clouded with tears. In the doorway, Mark had been a silent observer as she had tried to take the dying man's mind off his pain. He had come to check on one of Wellington's aides who had come down with a fever, but he had halted in the doorway, mesmerized by the sight of Sophia and her patient. At the moment, Mark would have given anything to be able to draw himself. She looked so beautiful, almost angelic, the faintest ray of light from the door lighting up her face in the faint gloom of the hospital. Despite all the death he had witnessed over the years, his own eyes filled with tears. A lump rose in his throat and he was overwhelmed by the strangest longing for his own mother. The thought was quickly replaced by the memory of his stern-faced father saying, *You cosset the boy so much that you will make an old woman out of him,* and of his mother struggling with her tears hastily banished from the sickroom. *No, Father,* he thought grimly, *it did not make an old woman out of me. I am unmoved by war or death, but tenderness and gentleness completely unman me.*

His reverie was broken as Sophia gently withdrew her hand from the dead soldier's grasp and placed his hands together on his chest. Blinking rapidly she gathered her things and made her way slowly to the door, not even noticing the major until he held out a hand to help her across the threshold. "Oh, is it you." She did not seem the least surprised to discover him there. In fact, she almost sounded as though she expected it.

Taking her arm in his, Mark led her to a clump of trees and rocks behind the hospital. Wordlessly he took her things and dusting off a large boulder, gently seated her. His hand still on her shoulder, he lowered himself next to her on the rock.

Chapter 18

They sat silently for some minutes until at last Sophia turned to him, her eyes brimming with tears. "Such a waste of so many fine young men. Does it ever go away, the helplessness one feels in the face of such death and destruction, the sadness?"

Mark shook his head slowly as images of his friends brought down by the enemy's fire and men under his command trampled beneath their horse's hooves rose before him. "No. It never really does. The first spurt of anger one feels at the sight of such things becomes a slow, steady burning and that is what keeps one fighting, courting one's own death and destruction."

"And do you ever ask what it is for?"

Gently he wiped away a tear that was beginning to trickle slowly down her cheek. "No. I know what it is for. It is to end all this so that people here can live in peace, can go back to their farms and their sheep without fearing that some Frenchman will take them all away." He would not allow himself to wonder what he would do with his own life once the conflict was over.

"You are fortunate to be able to do something about it."

Mark reached over and lifted one of the hands clenched tightly in her lap to his lips. "You, too, did something about it. My only recourse is to respond with more death and destruction, you offer comfort and creativity. Not only did you help that unfortunate lad endure the pain, you worked to keep his memory alive. You are the one with the real answers to all this, not I."

He pressed his lips against the back of her hand and the icy numbness that had taken hold of Sophia vanished. The warmth of Mark's kiss seemed to spread throughout her entire body, just as his words warmed her heart. For many yeas she had felt as though she were a mere hanger-on, while the soldiers surrounding here were accomplishing the real things in life, but this man had changed that. He made her feel that she had something of value to offer.

As if voicing her thoughts, he added, "Not only will you keep the lad's memory alive, your sketch has the makings of a very fine portrait as well as a generous gift."

"Thank you. I have often hoped . . ." Sophia paused. She had been about to confide her dearest wish to him, a wish she had shared with no one, not even her mother. But she paused to reconsider and, thinking better of it, stared off at the mountains in the distance. Just because someone offered sympathy at a particularly trying moment did not mean that that person would appreciate one's wildest dream.

"You had often hoped . . ." Mark watched the self-conscious flush rise in her cheeks and wondered what wish she treasured so dearly that she was uncomfortable confiding it to others.

Sophia ignored his prompting, continuing to stare off into space as though lost in some reverie until she felt firm hand grasping her chin, turning her face toward him, forcing her to look at him. His eyes were alight with interest and something else she could not quit fathom. All of a sudden it seemed rather paltry not to confide in someone who seemed to appreciate and understand her the way the major did.

Unable to bear his scrutiny, she avoided his eyes, concentrating instead on the circle she was drawing in the dust with her toe. "Ah, it is my hope to . . . well, to paint well enough so that I can make my own way in the world like Elisabeth Vigée Lebrun and Angelica Kauffmann." The words tumbled over one another as though she were afraid she would never utter them if she were to speak normally.

"You already do."

Sophia abandoned her circles in the dust to stare up at him in some surprise. For a moment she suspected him of teasing her, but his smile was reassuring and his eyes were warm with approval.

"I have seen several of Kauffmann's portraits—Frances Hoare, the Duchess of Richmond and her son, the Marchioness of Townsend—and I assure you that though they are exquisitely executed, they do not capture the personality of the subject nearly so well as you do, even in the crudest of sketches."

"Oh, surely not." Sophia stole another glance at him. "Do you truly think so?"

"I most assuredly do." Now why would he have such an overwhelming urge to kiss the soft, full lips that parted slightly as she drew in an eager breath? Mark could not explain it. Surely kissing Sophia Featherstonaugh would do nothing to convince her of the accuracy of his opinions. Quite the contrary, it would probably make her doubt them altogether. He remembered how she had seemed to draw back into herself when he had once called her a *lovely young woman*. Yet at this particular moment he ached to pull her to him, to feel the warmth of her in his arms, to caress the back of her neck where the dark curls clustered, and to crush her mouth under his until she was as breathless and lightheaded as he suddenly felt.

Mark drew a deep, steadying breath. He could not understand it. He liked his women to be stunningly beautiful, provocative, and sophisticated, but here was this young woman, no more than a girl really, who had not an ounce of coquetry in her, who seemed to see all men as friends and nothing else, and lately, he had been able to think of nothing but kissing her, of tracing the gentle curves of her slim figure with his hands. It must be his life, the military duties, that had kept him from having a female for so long. That was it. Ruthlessly he stifled the little voice in his head that reminded him of the invitation of the dark eyes of the innkeeper's daughter in Fuenterrabia or how she belt low to reveal an enticing bosom as she served him, or the suggestions dropped by the wife of the alcalde in Irun, who kept hinting to him that her husband was away from home most of the day. He would not listen to this little voice that told him he had had plenty of opportunities to have several women if he had really wanted them and that asked him why he wanted this one so badly now.

Sophia tilted her head quizzically, trying to fathom the expression on the major's face. He seemed to exude a suppressed energy all of a sudden. His eyes darkened and the tanned skin of his face tightened, revealing more than ever its sharp angles, the prominent cheekbones, the high, narrow bridge of the nose. This inexplicable energy drew her toward him like a magnet. Unable to stop herself she leaned toward him, laying one hand on his shoulder. "Thank you," she whispered.

"What?"

"Thank you." This time she managed to speak, though it was more a croak than anything else. "Thank you for having faith in my ability, for not laughing at my absurd ambitions."

"Ah." With an effort, Mark tore his eyes off the inviting lower lip, the gentle swell of her breasts under the lemon sarsenet of the closely fitting Cossack coat. Drawing another deep breath, he steadied himself. He had led her to the secluded grove to comfort her, not to ravish her. What was wrong with him? Never in his life had he been subjected to such a wide range of emotions in so short a space of time, from the ache of longing for his mother's tender reassuring touch to overwhelming pity for the dying solder and the sadness of the woman comforting him, to the desire that had suddenly taken possession of him when he had least expected it or wished for it. It was most disconcerting and exceedingly unwelcome. Bold and reckless he might be, but Major Lord Mark Adair had always remained in control of his emotions—until now, until he had met Sophia Featherstonaugh. And she, the very model of cool independence and self-sufficiency, had suddenly thrown him into a turmoil and confusion that he had not thought possible.

One more deep breath and he was himself again. "I am glad I was able to . . ." What had he done? Mark tried desperately to find the words, but looking again into the wide hazel eyes, he realized that no words were needed. "You do have talent, you know, and I am most fortunate, and most grateful that you have shared it with me. But anyone will tell you that you have a superior gift."

"Perhaps." She was almost somber now. "But acknowledgement is one, belief and confidence another. There are many who might say I have a knack for capturing likenesses, but few, if any, would have the insight or know what it means to suggest I might make a career of it. You understand the difference between a facility for something and a passion for it. One is born with a facility for something, but one dedicates one's life to a passion. You seem to understand the difference between the two."

Again he raised her hand to his lips. "I do, Miss Featherstonaugh, believe me, I do." Unable to bear the intensity of the moment any longer, Mark realized that he had two choices: to take her into his arms, or to leave her. At the mercy of his own uncertain feelings, he decided that the only thing to be done was to leave her before he became more deeply involved. He sensed that he was already in danger of becoming more involved with her than he had ever been with any woman, more deeply involved than he had sworn he ever would be.

Mark had believed in a woman the way he believed in Sophia only once before in his life, honored a woman that way only once before, and she had left him and, in his father's eyes, dishonored them all and turned out to be false. Even now, so many years after overhearing his father and mother in the library, he could still hear the exact tone in the Duke of Cranleigh's voice as he scornfully berated his wife for lavishing her affections on the homesick young secretary to Spain's new ambassador. He had heard his father's accusations of trysts in the rose garden, conversations by the ornamental water, and even though Mark knew his mother to be a virtuous woman, he also knew that all the meetings his father had accused her of were true.

He had screwed up all his courage and entered the library to speak in her defense, to swear that Señor Alvarez was a very nice man, and to tell his father how kind the señor had been. But even as he endured his father's scornful glare he had wondered if his father's accusations of infidelity were true. He had fled to his room in an agony of doubt and uncertainty, which had not been helped by his mother's sudden reclusiveness, her refusal to see anyone, and the slow decline that eventually had led to her death. He had not wanted to believe it, had waited for her to repudiate the awful accusations, but instead she had died—a seeming admission of her guilt—and left him all alone with no one to love him, no one to take his part or share his joys and sorrows, his hopes and fears. The memory of her had grown dim over the years, but the sense of loss and abandonment had not. He had sworn he would never trust another person again in his life, that when he married, as he knew he must, it would never be for love. But here he was, not only ready to believe in someone again, but actually longing to do so. It was time he stopped himself before it was too late.

"Now, if you will excuse me"—even to his own ears his voice sounded unnecessarily harsh— "the duke ordered me to return within the hour and I must not be late. As you well know, keeping Old Douro waiting is simply not done." A quick bow and he was gone, leaving Sophia to gather her wits as best she could.

Chapter 19

Slowly Sophia made her way back to their quarters, skirting the edge of the camp, but keeping well within the picket line. Such a wild confusion of thoughts and emotions were jostling with one another in her mind that she wanted to sort them out before encountering anyone. First and foremost was an odd kind of joy that bubbled up inside her as she kept hearing him say, *I am most fortunate and most grateful that you shared it with me, but anyone will tell you that you have a superior gift.* However, Sophia could not decide what affected her more, the sense he had conveyed that he treasured the fact that she trusted him enough to share her hopes for the future, or the fact that he had seemed to think she had the talent to be another Angelica Kauffmann.

Sophia paused to gaze out over the far-off Bay of Biscay. She could not say which she wanted more, to share a special intimacy with Major Lord Mark Adair, or to command his admiration. A delicious shiver ran through her as she recalled the way his eyes had lingered on her lips and then bored into hers with an intensity that was almost palpable. For a moment she had almost thought he might kiss her. Her cheeks grew hot at the thought, and even hotter as she admitted to herself that she wished he had. He had seemed so solid and so strong as he had led her to the clump of trees, his arm around her so comforting that she had wanted to throw herself against his chest and cling to him, absorbing all his vitality and wiping out the image of Billy Barnes's face gray and lined with pain.

But, and Sophia was ashamed to acknowledge such a thing even to herself, the image of Billy Barnes had quickly faded, and so had her need for solace. Something else in her had ached to have his arms around her and his lips on hers, something very different from comfort, that made her breathless at the very thought of it. Without even knowing precisely what *it* was, she knew that she longed for *it* in a way that she longed for water after a hot and dusty ride. And *it* was not his admiration of her artistic skills or his approval of or participation in her dreams of becoming a professional artist that she longed for. No, it was purely and simply that she longed for him as a man, longed to trace the square jaw with her fingers, to run her hands through the thick dark hair, to be pressed against the broad chest, and to feel his lips on hers.

Sophia shook her head in frustration. She had thought she was immune to such things. She had lived her life among so many men that she saw them all as brothers. None of them had ever made a deeper impression on her than that, until now. Though female companionship had been rare in their circumscribed existence, Sophia had heard enough gossip among maids and the occasional conversation among the wives of people they knew in Lisbon to know how most women thought of men. In fact, most of them seemed to dedicate a good deal, if not all, of their time and energy trying to attract the attention of one man or another.

Such machinations had always seemed ludicrous and trivial to Sophia and she never could understand all the fuss over winning a man's admiration when it was so much more pleasant and so much easier just to be friends with one. She had felt rather superior to all these female conspiracies. So much for superiority, she thought grimly. It was turning out that she was no different from the rest of them after all; it had just taken her longer.

Sophia had almost reached their hut by now, but she was loath to enter until she had resolved this thing in her mind. Her mother was far too acute, and she would recognize in a moment that something was wrong.

No, she would take her sketchbook a little way on the other side of their quarters and sketch the scene beyond. The Pyrenees rising ever higher in the distance made a magnificent picture and she had been wanting to capture it. Sketching would take her mind away from the dangerous channels into which it seemed to be drifting. The mere act of committing the scene to paper, the feel of the pencil in her hand and the paper beneath it, would have a calming effect on her; it always had in the past.

Seeking out a comfortable boulder, she seated herself and pulled out her sketchbook and pencils. Her hand hovered over the paper for some minutes while she decided just where to begin. Then swiftly and surely she began to make the first broad strokes, but the outline that emerged was not that of the towering mountain peaks, instead it was the angular planes and the strong features of the face of Major Lord Mark Adair.

Sighing at her own weakness, Sophia gave in to her artistic imperative and continued to sketch, slowly at first, and then more feverishly as the image took hold.

How long she sketched, she could not have said, but the sky over the mountains had turned from blue to pink and now the deep sapphire of twilight. Her fingers ached and her knees, as she rose to gather her things, were so stiff they could barely support her, but her soul felt more at peace than it had since she and the major had parted that afternoon.

She picked up her things and turned back to the hut with a sense of relief. Perhaps she was not attracted to him after all. Perhaps the urge she had felt was only the urge to capture his image on paper.

Sophia studied the portrait again before putting her sketchbook in her satchel and smiled to herself. Yes, she had done him justice. She had captured the bold features, the energy that always seemed to emanate from him, the sparkle of adventure in his eyes, and the touch of deviltry in his smile. Satisfied, she closed the sketchbook and went to help her mother with dinner.

The weather grew appreciably cooler over the next few days. Several mornings they awoke to a ground glistening with a heavy frost. "They say that over at Roncesvalles it has snowed so hard that many a morning the Pioneers have had to dig the Thirty-fourth out of their tents," Speen remarked to Sophia one afternoon as she was darning her stockings and he was brushing off the general's uniform.

"I do hope we march soon, for the last rain we had was so torrential that it was all over mud and we shall never be able to move if we have many more storms like that." Sophia snipped the thread and laid another completed

stocking on her pile. "I expect it will not be too long now.
I heard the general telling Mama that the French were
soundly beaten at Leipzig and a great deal of Napoleon's
army destroyed."

"It is true. And what with Pamplona surrendering, Old
Douro has only Soult and Clausel to contend with, and no
Grand Aremée to come to their rescue. Mark my words,
we shall be moving on soon."

Not very many days later, General Curtis announced to
the women at breakfast, "We shall be moving out today.
We mean to drive down the valley of the Nivelle, storm
the French fortifications on top of the Petit Larroun and
the Harismendia Ridge, and take Saint Jean de Luz. You
two"—he frowned heavily at them—"are not to follow, but
to wait until I send word that Saint Jean has surrendered.
Then you may join me."

Recognizing that there was to be no argument this time,
Lady Curtis agreed. "Very well, my dear. We shall stay
here until everything is quiet and our army well established
in Saint Jean. I only hope it does not take very long, for
the rains we have had of late have swollen the rivers a
good deal and the roads will be impossible."

"I believe that it will not be long. Wellington has said
more than once, *Those fellows think themselves invulnera-*
ble, but I shall beat them out, and with ease. They have not
men to man the works and lines they occupy. I can pour a
greater force on certain points than they can concentrate to
resist me.

They bid good-bye to the general and Speen and prepared themselves to wait for news of the capture of Saint
Jean de Luz with as much patience as they could muster.

Sophia kept an eye out for the major, hoping to have
the opportunity to wish him luck on the campaign, but she
only caught sight of him once, and then it was the briefest
of encounters. He was mounted on Caesar and was covered
with dust. "Wellington has me hopping, carrying dispatches
to Hope advancing against Urrugne, to Napier attacking
the Petit Larroun, to Beresford who is to attack Clausel at
Sare, and then to Hill over by the Harismendia Ridge and
the country is rough, to say the least." In spite of the dust
and his travel-stained appearance, he looked more exhilarated than exhausted by his exertions and Sophia could not

suppress a twinge of envy at the active role he was playing while she and her mother were forced to sit quietly by as the British gained a stronger foothold for themselves in France.

They did not have to wait long, however. The very next day Speen returned with the news that the French had abandoned Saint Jean and were retreating toward Bayonne. "The general says that I am to help you move and that he will have found quarters for you by the time we arrive."

"So soon?" Lady Curtis exclaimed. "Is it safe to travel?"

"Yes, my lady. We have those Frenchies on the run. Believe me, if there are any around, they are deserters and won't trouble us. Now that we are in their own country they have lost their nerve. Why they hardly put up a fight even behind the redoubts at the Petit Larroun."

"Good. I shall be glad to get out of the mountains, not that it is not lovely here, but the weather is growing colder and there is no telling when the rain that has fallen will turn to snow." Lady Curtis began bustling about immediately.

Since they had not settled so fully into these quarters as the ones in Lesaca, the carriages were packed in very little time and were soon lumbering slowly down the rough mountain road to Saint Jean de Luz.

As she rode alongside the first carriage, her eyes sweeping appreciatively across the magnificent view of the plains before her, Sophia could not help comparing it with their last journey, reluctantly admitting to herself that she missed the major's companionship. The sight of that powerful figure riding ahead of them had made her feel as though nothing could go wrong.

Chapter 20

They reached Saint Jean just as night was falling. Speen led them to headquarters, where General Curtis greeted the ladies enthusiastically. "It was a magnificent operation, Wellington's finest so far. Our lads were absolutely unstoppable and the French lost heart completely. But come, I have found us a snug little house near the Église Saint Jean Baptiste. It is owned by a banker who was only too happy to retire to his country estate once the British arrived, but he has left some of his staff."

He led them to a spacious house whose balconies afforded a view of the ocean and whose reception rooms were spacious enough to please his wife. "Excellent, my dear." Lady Curtis surveyed the dining salon with satisfaction. "Now we can entertain the duke himself without apologizing for our surroundings."

"Nonsense, my dear. Everyone enjoys your good company and Jorge's excellent cooking so much that they have not the least notion of their surroundings. However, I think you will find that there are considerably fewer fleas and flies here than in Lesaca."

They fell gratefully into their beds and awoke the next morning to the bells of Saint Jean Baptiste, refreshed and ready to establish the household to their liking. Lady Curtis was pleased with the two spritely serving girls who, once they had seen how ladylike and civilized the general's wife and daughter were, fell to their tasks happily enough and were delighted to recommend the local dressmaker to the two ladies.

"I feel certain that with winter setting in we shall be here for some time and if I know the duke, he will soon be entertaining. We would not wish our wardrobes to look as though we had spent the last few months in a small Spanish village," Lady Curtis confided happily to her daughter.

"Even though we have." Sophia turned to smile at her mother as she straightened the looking glass Luis had just hung in Lady Curtis's bedchamber.

"Jeanne assures me that this dressmaker is seamstress to the Condesa de Gonsalvo y Coruna, who is extremely à la mode."

"A condesa, here in France?"

"She is the daughter of the Comte de Brissac. According to Jeanne, the de Brissacs are a noble Gascon family of ancient and illustrious lineage. During the revolution they fled across the border into Spain where the daughter, Diane, grew up and married the Conde de Gonsalvo y Coruna. When Napoleon allowed the emigrés to return to France, her father, then a widower, returned to claim their estates while his daughter remained in Spain with her husband. However, the conde was a good deal older than his wife and when he died several years ago, the condesa returned to France. I believe that the de Brissac chateau was destroyed during the revolution, but their hôtel in Saint Jean was not, and it is here where the condesa acts as hostess for her father."

"And has her dresses made up by the seamstress you hope to patronize. You certainly learned a good deal of information in your quest for improvements in your wardrobe, Mama."

Lady Curtis smiled apologetically. "Well, it will be rather nice to be back in civilization again. The duke and his lads were fine fellows, and excellent company, but it would be nice if we were to enjoy some female society as well for a change."

Lady Curtis was not the only one among the British occupiers of Saint Jean to learn about the Condesa de Gonsalvo y Coruna. The duke himself had met and been favorably impressed by the lady. True to form, the moment he had settled himself into headquarters, he set about extending dinner invitations to the most influential members of what constituted society in Saint Jean de Luz, explaining to Fitzroy Somerset, "If I am able to win the good will of the population, I shall need less of the army to hold the territory we have already gained and can put them to use gaining us more." And among the first to be included in one of these invitations was the Comte de Brissac and his daughter.

Seated near the foot of the table headed by Wellington with the condesa on his right, the comte on his left, and numerous other aides de camp and staff in between, Mark had ample opportunity to observe the vivacious condesa. He was only one among many whose eyes strayed hungrily to the guest of honor.

Diane de Gonsalvo y Coruna was at the height of her charms. Married very young, she had been widowed at an age not much more advanced than that of many young misses in their first Season. Deprived of the delights of any sort of society, first by her widowhood and then by the war, Diane had languished in Saint Jean, desperately hoping for some opportunity that would take her to the gaiety of the French capital or, failing that, even to Bayonne.

Starved for society, it was she who had urged her father to accept the duke's invitation. "Papa, you can not refuse him. He is not one of these jumped-up bourgeois dukes that we have in our army like the Duke of Dalmatia." Diane had not been impressed by Marshal Soult when he called on them. "He is a true member of the British aristocracy, and it is said that his staff is made up solely of men from the finest families."

"Very well, but we accept this invitation only to demonstrate to these English barbarians true politesse." The Comte de Brissac grumbled, but he, too, was secretly pleased by the opportunity to dine with peers. Though proud of the French victories throughout Europe, the comte had refused to have anything to do with the *Corsican upstart* or his cohorts, with the consequence that he was nearly as starved for society as his daughter.

The young widow was as vivacious as she was beautiful and a table full of dashing well-bred young men offered the perfect opportunity for her to display her charms to their fullest extent. The comte enjoyed the company as well and on the drive home was forced to admit grudgingly to his daughter, the duke at least, appeared to have excellent manners, for an Englishman.

"Then, Papa, we must and show him the graciousness for which the French are so famous." Though flattered by the

duke's obvious admiration, Diane had been far more intrigued by the appreciative glances of some of the younger
members of Wellington's staff and was already scheming to
become better acquainted.

It was at the ball held by the mayor at the Hôtel de Ville
that Mark had the honor of being introduced to the lady.
Still unsure of the English barbarians, very few of the wives
and daughters of the town's leading citizens made their
appearance so it fell to Diane, Lady Curtis, Sophia, and
Lady Waldegrave, who was living with her husband at
headquarters, to serve as partners for all the young men.

Diane was in her element, dancing and flirting with the
officers crowding around her, but Mark, waiting for an opportunity to approach her when there was not such a crowd
around her had caught her gaze straying in his direction
more than once. He stifled a grin as, catching her eye, he
sketched a bow. It appeared that the lady was piqued that
one officer at least had not fallen under her spell. He had
rather thought that might be the case and used his aloof-
ness to attract her attention.

Caught in the act of looking at him, the condesa haughtily turned her attention elsewhere, but not before she had
surveyed him appraisingly. Mark knew that look. He had
seen it in the eyes of several ladies of his acquaintance who
had been starved for attention until he had come into their
lives, and he had little doubt that sooner or later, the Condesa de Gonsalvo y Coruna would find the opportunity to
speak to him.

His predictions were entirely correct. Somehow, and
Mark was not certain how she managed it, Diane materialized at his side as he gazed out the window at the moonlit
town and the sea beyond.

"You find our provincial company so very dull that the
empty streets outside are more to your taste than the people inside? We must do what we can to change that, Milord Adair."

Mark cocked an inquisitive eyebrow.

"It is the duty of every hostess, and as one of the few
Frenchwomen present, I count myself a hostess, to make
sure that our guests are well taken care of. Naturally, one
of the first things one does as a hostess is to discover the
identity of the guests." The condesa's sly smile revealed

pearly white teeth and an enchanting dimple at the corner
of her full red lips.

"You mistake my actions, madame. It has been so long
that I have been part of such a gay gathering and such
delightful company that I find myself rather overwhelmed."
Mark's gaze drifted appreciatively from the tempting mouth
to the expanse of soft, white skin revealed by her daring
décolletage. She was delectable enough to turn any man's
head, from the dark curls arranged in provocative disarray
and threaded with pearls to the brown eyes fringed with
long, dark lashes and set under delicately arched brows.
Her mouth, with its full lower lip, invited passionate kisses,
an invitation that was also reflected in her eyes.

As he drank in the condesa's magnificence, Mark welcomed the wave of desire that washed over him. Lately, he
had begun to wonder about himself. His growing preoccupation with Sophia Featherstonaugh had shaken him severely and he had found himself thinking the most unlikely
thoughts about her, thoughts such as wanting to help her
fulfill her dreams, wanting to prove that not all men were
as selfish and unreliable as her father, wanting to protect
her from the discomfort and danger of campaigning, wanting to be with her, talk with her, share things with her.

Mark had never been so obsessed with a woman in his
entire life and he found it to be disconcerting in the extreme. Much as he scorned his brother's and his father's
passionless, rule-bound approach to life, Mark himself enjoyed a good deal of control over his emotions, especially
with women, but his acquaintance with Sophia had more
than once threatened that control and he had begun to
wonder if he had become as weak-willed as his fellow officers, who fancied themselves in love with every pretty face.

He had always prided himself on never having been in
love before, never having done things for a woman (that
were contrary to his character) just to win admiration, and
at this stage of maturity and with his vast experience, he
had thought himself immune to such weakness until he had
met Sophia. For some unfathomable reason, the self-sufficient Sophia had aroused feelings of protectiveness, tenderness, and concern in him that he had not felt since the
disastrous day he had spoken in his mother's defense.

Running his eyes over Diane de Gonsalvo y Coruna's

enticing figure, Mark was relieved to feel only one emotion, desire—a desire that was purely and delightfully physical and not complicated by any concerns for her welfare or happiness. It was unencumbered by a wish to protect her from anyone or anything. He sighed with relief. He was himself again. As he had suspected, his feelings for Sophia had been just a momentary lapse after all.

"Would you care to dance?" Mark held out his hand.

"You English are so arrogant." The lady teased him, fluttering her dark lashes. "You are always so sure the French will capitulate immediately." But she clasped his hand with a warmth that made Mark wonder who was doing the capitulating.

Chapter 21

Major Lord Mark Adair was not the only one to be affected by the bewitching condesa. Across the room, Sophia, discussing with Fitzroy Somerset the merits of the duke's pack of hounds and the hunting to be had in the area, was assailed by the most unpleasant sensation in the pit of her stomach as she caught sight of the major and his lovely partner whirling around the floor. Resolutely ignoring it, she tried to focus on the conversation instead.

"So you too agree that Lascelles's is the best going across country."

"What?" She looked up in dismay to see that Wellington's secretary was waiting for her answer. "Oh, er, ah Lascelles's, you say." She groped wildly for an answer. "Perhaps, but his horse invariably runs away with him."

"Yes, of course you are right. I do recall now that he has more than once nearly caused the duke to come to grief," Fitzroy Somerset agreed almost too heartily. What was wrong with Miss Featherstonaugh? Usually as knowledgeable in conversation as any man, she had suddenly seemed to lose her bearings, but to his infinite relief, she appeared to recover from her momentary lapse.

But she had not. Sophia had recovered herself in conversation, but found herself completely at sea where her emotions were concerned. The sight of the major smiling down at the condesa and leaning over to catch every word in the same intimate manner he had shared with her struck her with all the force she had once suffered when a low branch had knocked her off Atalanta's back. She was experiencing the same difficulty catching her breath now as she had then when a momentary loss of attention had caused her to be thrown to the ground with the wind knocked out of her before she even knew what had happened.

Drawing a deep breath, she steadied herself and, on the pretext that she needed to speak with her mother, excused herself to escape to the same deserted corner of the room that the major had just left and gaze out over the scene that had captured his attention.

You are a fool, Sophia Featherstonaugh, she scolded herself, *to think that you meant something special to him. The only thing special about it was that you were the only available female at the time. Now that another one has appeared, you can see that how he treated you is how he treats them all. You were not special, you were simply a woman.*

Actually, she reflected, she was glad to learn this, for the major had begun to distract her in a most upsetting way. She was relieved to see that she was not special to him because now she could once again focus on her life, her work, and making her dreams come true. Taking a last glance at the scene below lit by a moonlight as bright as day, Sophia squared her shoulders and returned to the crowd surrounding her mother and General Curtis.

Unaware of the effect he was having on one woman, Mark was concentrating all his attention on another as she alluded, ever so delicately, to the loneliness of her existence.

"Mama died not long after we fled to Spain so I have not really had anyone to guide me except Papa, who, try as he did to be everything to me, could not teach me all those things that a daughter learns from a mother. My life lacked the feminine guidance that every young woman needs. You can have no notion how isolated a life I have been forced to lead."

"It appears to me that you have succeeded admirably on your own. I fail to see how a mother could have helped you become any more of a woman than you are now." The look in Mark's eyes as they swept appreciatively from the provocative lips to the smooth white shoulders and the long line of hips and thigh revealed by the clinging white satin slip gleaming through the Venetian crape draped over it, left no doubt that he considered her to be more than adequately endowed with feminine qualities.

"Ah, but you are a man, you can not know what a young girl misses in a mother's affection." The condesa licked her lower lip in a way that suggested that the concentrated attentions of a dashing cavalry officer might possibly make up for some of that lost attention.

"That is true, of course, but none of us, man or woman, can truly understand someone else's needs and wants." The condesa's conversation was moving a little too fast for Mark, who was beginning to feel more and more that he was the pursued instead of the pursuer, a feeling he tried to avoid at all costs. "But now that we are here in winter quarters perhaps some of that loneliness you allude to can be dispelled. For . . ."

"I certainly hope so." There was no mistaking the invitation in the condesa's dark eyes.

"For there are several English ladies attached to headquarters who would be only too happy to make your acquaintance." Mark tried desperately to regain control of a situation that was slipping rapidly away from him. "Allow me to introduce you to two of them, Lady Curtis and her daughter, Miss Featherstonaugh. Miss Featherstonaugh, who has also spent much of her life as the only young woman among many men, will be most sympathetic to your situation."

And taking her by the arm, Mark hurried the condesa over to meet Sophia and her mother.

There was little Diane could do to protest as her partner grabbed her almost rudely and forced her over to meet a slender, quiet-looking young lady and another older woman, who was obviously her mother. Approaching the two of them, Diane realized that it was the demureness of the young lady's costume rather than her face that made her appear somewhat mousy. The blond lace frock over a slip of white satin was almost devoid of ornamentation with the exception of a quilling of blond lace at the hem and the bodice, which was cut higher than any Diane had seen in some time. The dark hair, too, was simply dressed, pulled smoothly into a knot at the back of her head. However, there was nothing mousy or demure about the large hazel eyes that examined her with lively interest. It was not quite true that Diane had been entirely deprived of feminine companionship. Though she certainly did not consider the wives of Saint Jean's mayor and its bankers to be on a level high enough to offer companionship or competition, she had had enough contact with females to recognize that

Miss Featherstonaugh was an unusual young woman. She
made no attempt to hide her obvious intelligence with fluttering eyelashes or a self-deprecating smile, and her bearing, though self-possessed, exuded an energy that most of
the ladies of Saint Jean would have concealed with a graceful languor. It was abundantly clear that it would take more
than beauty and social position to impress this young lady.
And it was also clear that Major Lord Mark Adair expected
the two of them to become instant friends.

"Miss Featherstonaugh, I would like to introduce you to
the Condesa de Gonsalvo y Coruna, who is eager to become acquainted with the English ladies just arrived in
town."

Before Sophia could do more than acknowledge the in-
troduction, Diane, flashing a bewitching array of dimples
and beaming dazzlingly at her escort, launched into a dis-
quisition on the excellence of the British officers attached
to headquarters. "They are all so dashing that I am quite
bouleversée. I hate to admit it to you, mademoiselle, but
we had been led to expect barbarians so it is altogether
delightful to discover that they are so charming." Casting
a seductive sideways glance at Mark, she clung to his arm
even more possessively than before.

"Naturally we British do not possess the *politesse* for
which your countrymen are so renowned, but we do try to
behave with a modicum of civility."

Mark's lips twitched at Sophia's acid response, but the
ironic note was lost on the condesa, who continued as
though Sophia had not even spoken. "I have never seen
such handsome men. But are they all so large?" Again a
provocative glance was directed at Mark. "And the way
they ride, *mon Dieu,* on such magnificent horses. We in
France have nothing to compare with your English horses.
Surrounded by such officers, you must have lost your heart
to more than one of them. What?" She exclaimed in horror
as Sophia, bemused by the spritely banter, shook her head
slowly. "Not even one handsome cavalry officer who makes
your heart beat faster?" Again Sophia shook her head,
though much to her horror, she felt her cheeks growing
hot, but the condesa was concentrating too much on the
major to notice. "You must be made of ice, mademoiselle.

One hears of the coldness of these English young ladies, but *c'est incroyable,* such lack of interest is unnatural."

"Madame does not realize that I look upon them as brothers." Gathering her wits at last, Sophia defended herself.

"Brothers? What young lady could possibly consider the major here as a brother. He looks to be the *beau ideal* of any young woman's romantic dreams." Though she addressed Sophia, Diane's words and expression were all for the benefit of Mark.

Acutely uncomfortable, Sophia struggled to find something clever to say that would dampen both the condesa's monopolization of the major and her condescending attitude toward Sophia. While it was true that the condesa was stunningly beautiful and seductive, and sumptuously and provocatively dressed, Sophia knew, that despite her sophisticated air, Diane de Gonsalvo y Coruna was in fact not much more sophisticated than Sophia, and that, as far as worldly experience was concerned, she actually had less than Sophia, never having traveled more than a hundred miles on either side of the rugged mountains that divided France from Spain. All this led Sophia to ask herself why she should feel at such a disadvantage in the presence of this woman. "Romantic dreams are usually the longings of one's imagination for the unfamiliar, for something that one does not have, but I grew up among military men, such as Major Adair, so, you see, they are hardly the stuff of dreams." There, she had at last come up with a reply that wiped the fatuous smile from the major's lips and the self-satisfied expression from the condesa's lovely face.

"Ah, yes, I do see your point, Miss Featherstonaugh. What a shame you can not enjoy it, for I find their company quite exciting. But I see my father looking for me, Major. Perhaps you will be so good as to restore me to him. It is a pleasure to welcome you to Saint Jean, Miss Featherstonaugh," Diane remarked over her shoulder as she swept Mark off to a knot of officers clustered around a courtier dressed for an evening at Versailles.

Trying not to grind her teeth too audibly, Sophia turned her attention back to the group that included her mother and General Curtis. She could not say precisely what it was about the condesa that made her feel so ill at ease, but she sensed that the condesa felt no more comfortable with her. In order to reassure herself of her own value, she suddenly found herself listing all the characteristics she possessed that the condesa undoubtedly did not, horsemanship, for example. Surely a lady so exquisitely turned out would not want to mar her seductive image with anything so rough and dirty as riding.

Chapter 22

Sophia was wrong in her assumption. Though Diane's isolated existence had robbed her of the opportunity to grace a society worthy of her charm and beauty, she possessed an innate sense of what was pleasing to the male sex, and horses were an integral part of the masculine world. Therefore, though she did not care for the exertion or the inevitable dirt and discomfort associated with horses and riding, she had forced herself to acquire enough equestrian skill to show herself creditably in most circumstances. And she definitely enjoyed selecting riding costumes designed to show her superb figure to the utmost advantage.

The condesa de Gonsalvo y Coruna also knew that the best way to arrange a seemingly accidental encounter with one of Wellington's aides was to take up a regular routine of riding, preferably early in the morning. Diane's distaste for early rising was even stronger than her distaste for exercise and dirt, but the handsome major was worth the effort in both cases.

For a number of days her plans were thwarted by the weather, which remained cold, gray, and rainy, but at last, several crisp sunny days dried out the soft ground and beckoned to all sorts of people who had been forced into confinement by the bad weather.

Diane, mounted on a stylish-looking though utterly docile bay mare, was trotting sedately along the promenade that ran the length of the beach when she spied a lone horseman galloping along the hard sand left by the retreating tide. It took no time at all for her to recognize the major and turn her horse toward him so that as he slowed at the northern end of the beach she was directly in front of him, a picture of desirability in a clinging riding habit of deep crimson with a military cut that showed off her figure to perfection. The daring color called attention to the beauty of her complexion, sparkling dark eyes, and full red lips. A dashing shako bonnet perched jauntily on her brown curls completed the ensemble and was quite enough to take Mark's breath away.

"Good morning, Condesa. How fortunate I am to have this beautiful landscape made even more lovely by your presence." As he uttered these words, Mark could not help thinking of the derisive expression such a speech would elicit from Sophia. The condesa, however, appeared to find nothing amiss with such a fulsome compliment, and smiling graciously, accepted it as her due.

"I, too, am surprised to see you, Major. I thought that all those on Lord Wellington's staff were too busy planning the next campaign to have a moment to spare."

"Oh no. Old Douro would never have us miss our daily gallop. We must spend too much time in the saddle during campaigns to allow ourselves to go soft in between them."

"Then you are between campaigns. I am delighted, for it must mean you intend to remain in Saint Jean for some time. If the reports one hears are true, you will be settling in for a month or so at least, which means that we must keep you amused so that you do not return to England complaining of French hospitality."

"Certainly I would welcome a chance to remain long enough to experience a great deal of French hospitality." Mark smiled appreciatively at the face turned up to his. Yes, he would enjoy forgetting the cold of winter wrapped in the condesa's soft white arms, for he had no doubt he would be enjoying the warmth of her embraces fairly soon. He had seen that inviting look in women's eyes too often not to know what was coming next, and he smiled in anticipation. Campaigning of one sort might have ceased for the winter, but campaigning of another was just beginning.

"But tell me, Major, after all the activity of the past year, how do you plan to spend your time if you remain quietly quartered in this fishing village?" Diane dismissed the cluster of whitewashed houses dominated by the tower of the Église Saint Jean Baptiste with a scornful wave of her riding crop.

"Delightfully, I assure you." The expression in the eyes fixed so intently on her left Diane in no doubt as to how the handsome major intended to amuse himself. A shiver of delicious anticipation ran down her spine. La, the gentleman was bold. If his lovemaking was as bold as his conversation, she was going to find the British occupation even more enlivening than she had hoped. "I, for one, shall do my best to see to it that you do." She ran her tongue slowly, provocatively over her lower lip. "But come, Major, I must show you the few picturesque sights we have to offer in Saint Jean." With a flick of her crop, she was trotting toward the rocky headland at the end of the beach.

Grinning, Mark urged Caesar after the condesa's mare. Catching up to her easily, he reined in as she pointed out the jagged promontory that thrust itself into the sea. "After the sublime heights of the mountains you undoubtedly find our gentle beach quite tame, but we do have our Pointe Sainte Barbe to add a little drama to our landscape."

"I see. And I also see that a far more artistic eye than ours is appreciating it at this very moment." Mark nodded toward a solitary figure seated on one of the rocks, head bent over a sketchbook in her lap, and he turned Caesar's head in Sophia's direction.

Diane had no notion of the artist's identity, but the fact that she was a female dampened any curiosity she might otherwise have entertained. It seemed, however, that the major was intent on speaking to this person, so there was little she could do but follow him with what little appearance of interest she could muster.

"Good morning, Miss Featherstonaugh. I should have known that you would be part of the most picturesque scene Saint Jean has to offer."

"Good morning, Major." Having recognized the major from a greater distance than she was willing to admit even to herself, and having guessed the identity of his fair companion, Sophia was prepared for the meeting though she had not been prepared for the stab of disappointment she had felt when she had witnessed the encounter between the two riders. The fact that the female had obviously sought out the male did very little to diminish this unwelcome feeling. If she had stopped to consider it, Sophia would have agreed that it would have been more disappointing to have the major seek out the condesa rather than the other way around, but at any rate they were together and it was quite clear to Sophia, at least, that the condesa was intent on exercising all her charms on the major.

Once again, Sophia felt at a dreadful disadvantage. She had not given a second thought to the plain white cambric dress she had put on that morning or the deep yellow three-quarter pelisse except to make sure that she looked neat and that her bonnet of yellow satin was securely tied. But now, surveying the condesa's dashing ensemble, she felt positively dowdy. And once again, Sophia felt an irrational defensiveness rising up within her in the face of the condesa's clear assumption of her power to attract.

"I see that you are sketching. What a talented thing you are, Miss Featherstonaugh, to be able to cultivate such refinements in the midst of such barbaric company." The condesa darted a playful glance at her companion.

"Miss Featherstonaug's sketches are no mere feminine accomplishment. You must see for yourself how talented she is. With your permission, Miss Featherstonaugh, I would love for the condesa to see them." Mark dismounted and strolled over to help the condesa down so she might get a closer look at Sophia's work.

Torn between gratitude at his defense of her art and annoyance at his calm assumption that she wished to share her work with just anybody, especially the condesa, Sophia protested. "The major is too kind. One must have something to occupy one's time while everyone is off fighting. Music does not lend itself to military life. Campaigning with a harp or a pianoforte is next to impossible."

The condesa glanced briefly at the sketchbook. "Very pretty. You certainly have done justice to our landscape, though I confess to a weakness for portraits myself. I find people so much more interesting than trees or rocks." The dark eyes barely took in the picture before focusing suggestively on the major.

Feeling utterly excluded by this intimate byplay, Sophia remained seated, clutching her pencil and wishing desperately that they would continue their ride, take their flirtation elsewhere, and leave her alone.

"Oh Miss Featherstonaugh is even more skilled at capturing people than she is at portraying landscapes. May I?" Mark held out his hand. Short of refusing him outright, Sophia had no choice but to give him the sketchbook. She certainly did not wish to appear churlish in front of the condesa, but she did not relish sharing her own private view of the world with someone who was so clearly interested in other things.

Diane was no more pleased with the way the conversation was going than Sophia was. It was bad enough to have her tête-à-tête with the dashing major interrupted, but to have it interrupted by another young woman, even a *petite Anglaise* who had no idea how to dress for a man, was annoying in the extreme. Reluctantly she took the proffered sketchbook and glanced at the half-finished landscape. "Yes, it is really quite well done."

The tiniest of smiles tugged at one corner of Sophia's mouth. She had regained her equanimity and her sense of humor enough to be amused by the Frenchwoman's utter lack enthusiasm for her, her pictures, the scenery, everything, but Major Lord Mark Adair.

A gentle puff of wind ruffled the pages of the book and the condesa's expression of polite boredom suddenly vanished. "Why here is a picture of you, Major." She darted a quick, speculative glance at Sophia, who was struggling to maintain her own expression of polite boredom. "Why it is very like you indeed—that firm jaw, the noble forehead. Miss Featherstonaugh has captured your very essence—that aristocratic bearing, the forceful character. Of course no one could quite do justice to the man, but I can see you agree with me, Miss Featherstonaugh, that the major is a fine-looking man and a most fitting subject for a portrait."

Sophia gave up hoping that the earth would open up and swallow her or that a sudden tidal wave would sweep her out to sea. She would rather have died than agree to sharing anything with the Condesa de Gonsalvo y Coruna, but to disagree with her opinion at this point would appear pettishly contrary. "I, er, have been doing portraits of nearly everyone at headquarters. As you see I have completed a number of them already—Fitzroy Somerset, Francis Larpent, Major General Morillo, Andrew Leith Hay." Sophia opened to the other portraits in the book, but even to her ears, her explanation sounded halfhearted and Mark, observing her closely, did not miss the self-conscious flush that rose to her cheeks.

During the entire exchange Sophia had resolutely avoided looking at the major. Intrigued by this uncharacteristic evasiveness, he leaned to look over the condesa's shoulder at the picture. Even he, accustomed as he was to confronting himself in the looking glass every morning, was caught off guard by the closeness of the resemblance and the intensity of the portrait.

There was a fire in the eyes looking back at him that was surprising even to him, a passion expressed in the tight line of the lips and firmness of the jaw that made it appear that the subject had been captured in the midst of some desperate and heroic act—leading a cavalry charge or scaling a heavily defended fortress—by someone who was fighting right at his side. It was the work of an artist who understood completely what it was to brave enemy fire, and plunge into battle with no expectation of emerging alive. Familiar as he was with Sophia's skill, Mark found his breath quite taken away.

"But none of the others is nearly so dashing as this." The condesa's remark fell on deaf ears. Neither Mark, his attention riveted to the reproduction of himself, nor Sophia, warily observing his reaction, was even aware of Diane's existence, much less paying attention to her.

Mark turned back to Sophia. "It is incredible! Do I really look like that?"

"To me you do."

It was a simple answer, simply stated, but Mark, overwhelmed by the heroic persona of the man on the page in front of him, was humbled by it. Was it true, then? Was he really this way? He had always striven to be the man in the picture, idealistic in the causes he fought for, courageous in the heat of battle, steadfast in the face of danger, but he had never been sure whether or not he had succeeded. Apparently he had. "Thank you."

It was barely a whisper and Sophia was not even sure whether she had heard it or whether she had read it in his eyes, but the message was abundantly clear. "You are welcome."

If the condesa's plan had not included meeting up with the young Englishwoman who boasted a prior acquaintance with the major, it definitely did not call for the long, deep, significant look that passed between them, and the condesa was not about to stand for it, no matter how plain or how unfashionable the young woman. "Goodness, how the time has flown! You are such a distraction, Major. I had no idea it was so late. Papa will be frantic with worry. You must accompany me to vouch for me when I assure him that I was not abducted by soldiers from either army."

Mark saw the scornful little smile that curled Sophia's lip ever so slightly at this obvious ploy, but short of being barbarically rude, he was helpless to refuse the condesa's obvious command. "But of course, Condesa." He sauntered over to help her back on her horse, hoping against hope that Sophia had heard and understood the ironic note in his voice.

He could not have said why it was so important that Sophia Featherstonaugh understood that he was not a slave to the woman that only days ago he had welcomed as an antidote to his preoccupation with Sophia, but it was. He glanced at her quickly as he mounted his own horse and was relieved to glimpse one delicate eyebrow raised in an expression that was both amused and conspiratorial. He grinned in return and then wheeled Caesar around to join the condesa.

Chapter 23

Mark was not the only one who was relieved. The grin told Sophia all that she wanted to know. Attracted though he might be by the condesa's obvious beauty, Major Lord Mark Adair was not about to be taken in by her feminine ploys.

Gathering up her things as she watched the tide roll in, eating up the wide, flat beach that was her path back to town, Sophia puzzled, not for the first time, how a clever man could be led by a beautiful woman even though he was fully aware of the machinations being practiced upon him. Sophia was now reasonably certain that the major was as alive to the fact that the condesa had lain in wait for him as Sophia was, but that knowledge had not stopped him from falling in with her plan. If she had been in the major's place, Sophia thought angrily as she strode along the hard-packed sand toward town, she would have refused to accompany the condesa purely on principle, and the more the condesa tried to coerce, the more she would have resisted.

But men apparently did not see things this way. Sophia had witnessed time and again in army camps from Lisbon to Saint Jean how easily men were swayed by a pretty face and a coy manner, no matter how obvious or how false, to make perfect fools of themselves. At least she could say of the major that he knew he was being led a merry dance by the Condesa de Gonsalvo y Coruna.

Struggling to put the entire episode out of her mind, Sophia trudged homeward, hoping desperately that the major had forgotten about the appearance of his face among the other portraits in her sketchbook. The condesa had been entirely correct in thinking that he was more carefully drawn than the other subjects, and Sophia did not want the major to arrive at the same conclusion. In fact, the less he thought about the portrait, the better.

Fortunately for Sophia's peace of mind, Mark's attention was taken up with other things. With winter setting in in earnest, Wellington and his staff settled into the task of making their winter quarters as gay as possible. Headquarters was filled with the sounds of dinner parties, regimental bands, and animated conversations, and the smells of good food and wine.

While many of the Frenchwomen were still leery of the occupiers of Saint Jean, Diane de Gonsalvo y Coruna, daughter of the *ancien régime* and widow of a Spanish grandee, was not. She and her father were frequent guests at the duke's table, which gave Sophia ample opportunity to observe the beauty's wiles.

Though she laughed and flirted with any and every officer, Diane appeared, to Sophia at least, to demonstrate a distinct partiality for Major Lord Mark Adair. Though she hated to admit it, and though she loathed the thought of having anything in common with the condesa, Sophia could not help agreeing that the Frenchwoman's partiality was natural enough, for she, too, preferred Mark's company over all the others. His conversation, though witty, was more serious, and his genuine interest could not help but make Sophia feel understood and appreciated in a way that she never had been before. Only one thing troubled her, and that was his assumption that simply because both she and the condesa were young females without husbands they were bound to become friends.

"I do think that the condesa would appreciate it if you called on her," Mark volunteered one morning as, encountering Sophia on her way home from the inn that served as a hospital, he fell in step with her.

"Might she not think that rather presumptuous of me?" Sophia had seen enough of the flirtatious Diane to know that they had little in common except their gender and their unmarried state.

"Oh no. The condesa is always telling me how she longs for company. She has led a most solitary life, you know."

"Ah."

"I can see that you are skeptical. But remember, her

family has been opposed to Bonaparte longer than we have."

"Oh, I realize that."

"Yet you seem hesitant."

"From what I have observed of the condesa, I am not sure that we would have very much to talk about." Seeing the puzzlement in his eyes, Sophia tried to explain. "She is so fashionable and a very . . . ah . . . sociable person."

"No, that is where you are wrong. She may seem to be more flir . . . er . . . gay, but that is because it has been so long since she has had any society to speak of. Her husband died not long after they were married so she was in mourning for some time. Then she returned to France to be with her father and, as royalists, they felt it best to remain very quiet. It has been such a relief to her now to have people to talk to that she may appear gayer than is usual, but she has a serious side to herself. Why, she is almost as knowledgeable about the troops as you are, and she certainly is as interested as you are in all that we are doing."

"Is she?"

"She is forever asking me about the regiments stationed here and never tires of hearing about all the details." Mark was so intent on convincing Sophia of the mutual interests she shared with the condesa that he missed entirely the sarcastic note in her voice and the ironic gleam in her eyes.

"In that case, she is far more likely to enjoy your company than mine."

Mark *did* hear the edge in her voice that time and he quickly turned his head to hide a grin. So the serious artist was jealous of the beautiful condesa, was she? It rather pleased him to think that Sophia Featherstonaugh could fall prey to such a lowering emotion.

"But she, like you, has had nothing but male company for years. It is a new thing for her to have a woman of her own social level for companionship."

"I suppose it is." Sophia refrained from remarking that just because something was new and different did not mean it was welcome. She had had the distinct feeling every time that she and the condesa were in one another's vicinity that the captivating Diane avoided her more assiduously than she sought her out.

They had reached her quarters by now and Sophia,

thanking the major for his escort, bid him good day. She continued to ponder the conversation as she went to her bedchamber to freshen up and wash off the scent of sickness and death that always seemed to cling to her after her visits to the hospital.

But it was not visions of the wounded and the dying that occupied Sophia's mind as she sat looking out her window at the sea of red tiled rooftops and the bell towers of the Église Saint Jean Baptiste, it was the condesa's singular interest in the British forces. Naturally, the condesa, who obviously reveled in masculine attention, would discuss topics that were important to the men with whom she was flirting, but Sophia had seen enough of the condesa to know that a woman such as Diane de Gonsalvo y Coruna was far more likely to wish to talk about herself than anything else. Such a woman craved flattery and demanded a steady supply of it from any and all men in her vicinity. So, why were there the questions about troop strengths? Even to Sophia's critical eye it seemed that the condesa had very little need to suit her conversation to the major's tastes in order to captivate his attention. It was abundantly clear that he was supremely attracted to her person as it was, without needing a feigned interest in his affairs to keep him at her side. Her curiosity roused, Sophia vowed to keep an eye on the Frenchwoman, for even the briefest of interactions with her had been enough to convince Sophia that nothing about that particular lady was without purpose. Every gesture, every glance, every smile, was calculated to create a certain effect. If she discussed troop movements with Wellington's aides-de-camp, it was not idle chatter.

Chapter 24

Idle chatter was certainly not part of the condesa's plan for her next encounter with the major. Knowing full well that her father was off overseeing repairs to the roof of their now uninhabitable chateau, Diane gave her maid the afternoon off and, attiring herself in a promenade costume more suited to the hot, sunny days of midsummer than he cold and damp of winter, she glanced out the window to reassure herself of the likelihood of a downpour at any minute, threw on a Cossack mantle of heavy silk, and tripped off in the direction of headquarters at the moment she knew Mark would be heading to the stables for a stable call.

Sure enough, precisely according to her calculations, the wind came in off the ocean, bringing with it a driving rain. Hurrying down the steps, Mark was just in time to see Diane pull her mantle around her and hasten to the inadequate shelter of a doorway. She was not quick enough to keep the mantle from becoming thoroughly soaked and it clung to her like the revealing draperies of a Greek statue, outlining her magnificent figure to its fullest advantage.

Mark ran across the street. "You must be wet through, let me take you into headquarters." He quickly stripped off his own coat and wrapped it around the condesa's shoulders.

Leaning back so that his arms practically encircled her as he draped the coat around her, Diana replied through chattering teeth. "No. I should be much too self-conscious. Look at me, my gown is so wet I feel practically naked." She gestured in such a way as to open the coat and mantle, giving him an enticing view of her white muslin dress now plastered to her thighs and bosom. "Please"—she looked at him with pleading eyes—"take me home."

"But you will be thoroughly drenched."

"I am wet through already. I can hardly get any wetter, and besides, I must get out of these damp things."

Mark had a sudden intoxicating vision of the condesa stripping off the flimsy muslin gown, and his throat tightened. "Very well, if that is what you wish."

"That is what I wish."

He held out his arm and they hastened through the downpour, hugging the buildings for what little shelter they afforded.

When they entered the Hôtel de Brissac, Mark was too intent on getting the condesa in out of the rain to notice the singular silence that reigned in the household. Not a servant was in sight. No one came hurrying up to relieve the mistress of her mantle or to rush her off to her bedchamber to take off her wet things.

Diane led him into a graceful salon hung with pale green damask and crammed to the fullest with the boulle chests, marquetry tables, and gilt chairs of a previous generation. Pulling off the major's coat and her own wrap, she tossed them across the back of one of a pair of bergère chairs next to the fireplace. "I gave the servants the afternoon off, as I expected to be out making calls the entire time so there is hardly any fire left, but . . ."

"Allow me to see what I can do." Taking his cue, Mark crossed over to the fireplace, poked at the embers, and managed to rekindle the few half-burned logs at the back of the fireplace. If he thought it odd that the condesa, born into a world notorious for ignoring its servants, seemed to have succumbed to a sudden burst of generosity, he made no comment except to remark that perhaps he should leave so that she could change into dry clothes.

"I would not think of sending you out into this weather until you had a chance to warm yourself, and you are even more wet than I." Diane allowed her eyes to wander over the broad chest and muscular shoulders so clearly revealed by the damp cambric shirt that clung to him. La, but the man was handsome! She drew a deep, shuddering breath and rose from her chair to join him in front of the warming blaze.

"I can feel how drenched you are." Diane reached out and stroked his chest with one small white hand. "You must be chilled to the bone, for you gave me your coat. I had no idea the British were so chivalrous."

Mark looked down at the condesa, who was so close to him that he could feel the warmth rising from her body and smell the rosewater on her skin. The dark eyes looking up at him were full of promises, and the full red lips parted invitingly as the hand on his chest slid slowly, tantalizingly, up his shoulder, and then to his neck.

He could not tell whether she pulled his mouth down to meet hers or whether, drawn by an urge too strong to resist, an urge he had no desire to resist, he bent to crush her lips beneath his. His arms went around her waist, pulling her to him. The soft fullness of her breasts pressed against his chest, and the gentle pressure of her hips as she arched against him, drove all thoughts but one from his mind.

In a daze, Mark felt her loosening his neckcloth and sliding one hand under his shirt, where it seemed to burn against his bare skin. Desperately he reached around her and undid her gown.

Gazing up at him under half-closed lids, Diane smiled a slow, sultry smile. Yes, she had known the major would be an experienced lover—why he was undoing her gown far more expertly and efficiently than her maid Marie ever did. She sighed with pleasure as he pulled it off her shoulders and trailed passionate kisses down her neck. With a moan of satisfaction and anticipation, she fell back onto the sofa, pulling him down on top of her.

The next moments were a confusion of flesh against flesh, hands buried into dark curls, lips seeking lips, as they both gave themselves up with abandon to sheer sensuality.

After what seemed hours later, Diane lifted her head to gaze down at the man beneath her, his chest still glistening with sweat. *"Merci, mon chère,"* she whispered, slowly licking her lips, "you were *magnifique."*

One cynically raised dark brow told her that this was a little excessive, even taking into account the intensity of their lovemaking. She hastened to retrieve her credibility. "I know, I know, it does sound extravagant, but you must make allowances for a woman who has known nothing but loneliness her entire life." Diane looked deep into his eyes, her fingers playing with the thick hair on his chest. "You do not know what my life has been. Now, yes, I look happy, gay. You see me laughing and making conversation with your officers, but until now, my life has been most dreary and empty. I was just a little girl when the Revolution came and we fled to Spain. Only a few months after my marriage Napoleon gave amnesty to all exiles. Papa went back to France and I was left behind. I had no one to turn to except my husband, who was more a father to me than a husband. Then Napoleon made his brother King of Spain and my husband left to join the others who declared war against the French. He died of a fever soon after and I came home to Papa. I have always been an exile and Bonaparte has made it impossible for me to enjoy any sort of society until now." This was not entirely true as the de Brissacs had established themselves in Madrid to the extent that they attracted the attention of the Conde de Gonsalvo y Coruna, but Diane saw no reason to mention anything that might dispel the expression of deep sympathy she saw on her lover's face.

If Mark wondered how the condesa, living a life that she claimed to be so sheltered, had become so skilled at making love, he dismissed it with the excuse that desperation was taking the place of experience and was pushing her into an affair that more sophisticated and cynical women would have drawn out into a prolonged seduction, building up anticipation and extracting expensive presents before finally giving in. He told himself that her impulsiveness was naive and charming, that it was as attractive as it was novel to find a woman who did not continually temporize with the excuse that she was concerned with her reputation. Her lips came down on his and, pushing all rational thoughts aside, Mark gave himself up to all the sensual delights that the lady's passionate nature inspired.

At last, completely exhausted by the condesa's appetite, Mark glanced at the clock on the mantel and, astounded by the time that had passed so quickly, turned to his companion. "Surprising and delightful as this time has been, my lady, I must return to my duties."

"I know." She sighed gently. "It has been all too brief, but you officers have so many things to do. You must be planning to move against Bayonne as soon as the roads are passable again."

"Of course, I would rather remain here." Mark was

touched by her understanding. No other woman he could think of, except one, would have realized that despite the army's temporary inactivity, there was much to be done, but that woman would never have been so rash and reckless to do what the condesa had just done.

He pulled on his clothes and, planting a final kiss on the lady's lips, took his leave. "This has been a most charming and delicious interlude. I hope you know that you are no longer without friends or society. You must always count me as a friend and not hesitate to ask for anything you need or desire."

Diane flashed a bewitching smile. "You English are so chivalrous and you are the most chivalrous of them all, but what if I find that your services become indispensable to me?"

"I would count myself most fortunate to be your servant." He raised her hand to his lips, pressed a kiss in the soft palm and, opening the door, glanced quickly up and down the street to make sure no one witnessed his exit. When he had assured himself that the coast was clear, he hurried back toward headquarters.

Back in her boudoir, Diane sat down at her dressing table and regarded her reflection in the looking glass with a good deal of satisfaction. Lovemaking always brought out the best in her looks. There was a sparkle in her eyes that seemed to illuminate her whole being. Yes, the major had been all that she had hoped for, except—Diane frowned at her reflection, but seeing the wrinkles it put in her forehead, quickly banished it—except that he was not so blindly adoring as she liked her men to be.

While it was true that he sympathized with her pathetic tale, there had been a suavity in his voice that made it appear more like a practiced response than a genuine commitment to run to her side at her least command. He had also not believed her flattery of his lovemaking. She leaned forward to inspect her perfect complexion for any possible hint of a blemish and, satisfied that nothing had changed since the morning, remained staring speculatively into the glass.

Ordinarily she liked a clever man, but at this particular moment, Diane de Gonsalvo y Coruna was not looking for a challenge; she was looking for a dupe. Perhaps it did not have to be the major, perhaps there was someone else at Wellington's headquarters who would be more susceptible, but no one made her pulses race the way Major Lord Mark Adair did.

Chapter 25

Though Sophia felt certain the condesa had little need and even less inclination for the company of other women, she did make several attempts to seek out her company at a few of the gay evenings at headquarters. Each attempt served to convince Sophia more strongly that not only was the condesa doing her best to ignore her, but she appeared to spend a great deal of time discussing with various officers the strength and disposition of the troops stationed in the area.

That the officers' replies were generally rather vague did little to reassure Sophia, who by now was beginning to suspect the beautiful condesa of more than casual flirtation. But before she spent too long wondering what to do, the major provided her with an opportunity.

The ardent episode after the condesa's soaking was repeated regularly whenever the Comte de Brissac rode out to his estate, and the rapport that had been established between Diane and the major deepened.

Ordinarily Mark, accustomed to being sought out by the female sex, would have been on his guard and careful not to give anyone the wrong impression, but unlike other women, the condesa did not seem to expect anything from him except ardent lovemaking and he dismissed any uneasiness he might have felt along those lines by reassuring himself that she was, after all, a Frenchwoman, and Frenchwomen had a much more pragmatic approach to such affairs than their English counterparts.

One afternoon, feeling agreeably tired after an especially passionate encounter, Mark allowed his eyes to drift around the salon. It was obvious from the quantity of furniture that all the de Brissacs had been able to retrieve from the ruined chateau had been brought to their hôtel in Saint Jean.

Portraits of de Brissacs going back two centuries covered the walls and Mark, examining them for a likeness to one of the present members of the family, made a discovery. "I see that there is a fine portrait of your father and that"—he motioned to a lovely lady who appeared to possess Diane's coloring without her dark eyes—"must be your mother. Does one of the current condesa hang in some castle belonging to the Gonsalvo y Coruna?"

"No. There has been no time in my life to sit for portraits. Revolutions and wars are not conducive to such things."

"That is a great pity. We must see what we can do to remedy the situation."

Dismissing this as idle flattery, Diane forgot entirely about the discussion and was a good deal surprised when several days later Mark informed her that as a present to her and her father he had arranged for her portrait to be painted. All she needed to do was to agree to the sittings.

"But that is too kind of you, Major." For her part, Diane preferred to receive more personal remembrances from her admirers—jewels, for example, that were so much more useful to a lady than a picture—but she did her best to muster up enough enthusiasm to thank the major very prettily for his thoughtfulness.

She was less enthusiastic, however, when she learned the identity of the artist. "Mademoiselle Featherstonaugh? But she is not a true artist, she is a woman."

"I have seen portraits done by Miss Featherstonaugh that compare favorably with those done by Lawrence, Hoppner, and Reynolds, and after all, Angelica Kauffmann is a woman.

Mark did not acknowledge to the condesa that when asked, Sophia herself had been less than enthusiastic over the project. "And does the condesa agree to this?"

Mark had been somewhat taken aback by the skeptical note in her voice. "Naturally she does."

"Very well. Then I shall be happy to do so. All that remains to be done is to arrange a time when I may call on her for the first sitting. You may inform her that it would only require one or two sittings at the most."

"Thank you. I shall tell her that." It had been clear from Sophia's expression that the discussion was at an end.

As she went about her tasks that day, Sophia could not
help wondering if the major's scheme had been concocted out
of a desire to please the condesa or out of his misguided
conviction that the condesa and Sophia ought to be friends.

The condesa welcomed her graciously enough when Sophia
called on her at the Hôtel de Brissac several days later, but
the faint air of condescension left no question in Sophia's
mind that the Frenchwoman considered her to be nothing
more than the little English artist who had been commissioned to paint her portrait.

As Sophia selected a corner of the salon where the light
was best, the condesa made it absolutely clear that this
arrangement had been none of her doing "There was no
need to have a portrait done of me, but the major is such
a dear man and so devoted."

Sophia glanced at the condesa in some surprise. There
were many words one could use to describe Major Lord
Mark Adair, but in her estimation *dear* was certainly not
one of them.

"Well"—the condesa sniffed, not a little put out by Sophia's obvious incredulity—"he is certainly quite dear to
me. He simply will not take no for an answer where my
happiness is concerned."

"Oh."

"Yes. The man is forever trying to think of things he can
do for me. In fact, I am quite *bouleversée* with his attention." Diane tossed her head, a defiant sparkle in her eyes.
There, let the *petite Anglaise* reflect on that. No true man
would waste his time trying to please as cold and reserved
a young woman as Miss Featherstonaugh; there would simply be no point in it, especially when the Condesa de Gonsalvo y Coruna was around to command attention. Men
such as the major liked their women to be passionate as
well as stunningly beautiful. Diane smiled smugly as Sophia,
obviously abashed, indicated the chair where her subject
was to sit.

For her part, Sophia was struggling to maintain her air
of cool detachment, difficult though it was under such prov-
ocation, but the condesa's insistence on the major's devotion
to her told Sophia a good deal more than the condesa
intended.

Sophia quickly bent over her box of supplies to hide the tiny smile of triumph she could not entirely suppress. Until this moment she had not realized how concerned she had been over the major's relationship with the condesa. She could not say precisely what it was that had bothered her every time she had seen his tall form next to the condesa's as they took advantage of the rare mild day to walk on the promenade or when, seated next to her at one of the duke's dinners, he served her with the choicest morsels from every platter that was presented, but Sophia had been uncomfortably aware of all these intimacies between the two of them, and now one of the two was going out of her way to claim a relationship with the other. To Sophia, this meant that the condesa was not so sure herself how much power she had over the major.

There was no further discussion between the two ladies. Sophia sketched rapidly while the condesa did her best to look beautiful but bored as though men clamored every day for pictures of her. By the time the light had begun to fade, Sophia had captured enough of the subject that much to her relief she decided to dispense with future sittings.

Sophia glanced again at the sketch in front of her. "I believe, madame, that I shall have no further need to trouble you for future sittings so that you will be spared more hours of maintaining one position like a statue."

"What? Are you done? Good heavens I have been sitting like a block when I should have been asking you to tell me all of your adventures with this army of madmen."

"Madmen? I do not understand."

"Oh the English are definitely mad. To risk their lives to save Portugal and Spain, to beat the Corsican Monster when they might remain in comfort and safety on their own little island. Do you not find there is something definitely mad, but absurdly gallant about it all? The officers I talk to say it is nothing, all this marching and fighting and marching and fighting so far from home. But you are a woman, you see the conditions they live in. How ever do they find enough to eat? Surely one can not count on ships to bring supplies in this weather? Soon they will have to move on or they will have eaten all the provisions from the surrounding countryside."

Such sudden loquacity, just when she was about to depart

would have struck Sophia as odd under any circumstances, but Sophia had already formed certain suspicions where the condesa's interest in the troops was concerned. "Ah, the duke is forever saying that an army travels not on its feet, but on its stomach, and he would never allow himself to live off the countryside." Sophia did her best to sound as noncommittal as possible. "Now as to the costume you wished . . ."

"I shall instruct my maid, Marie, to deliver to you the gown I wish to appear in so you may study it. Now if you will excuse me, Antoine will show you out. I find that I have developed such a *migraine* from all this posing." The condesa rang the bell and rose to leave just as the ancient retainer who had admitted Sophia appeared in the doorway. "Antoine, Mademoiselle Featherstonaugh is leaving. You will inform any further visitors that I am indisposed."

The condesa swept from the room before Antoine could even respond, *"Très bien, madame."*

As the door of the Hôtel de Brissac closed behind her, Sophia could not help congratulating herself on the brevity of her response to the condesa's questions concerning the army, and it was obvious that this brevity had been the cause for her speedy dismissal.

Sophia knew she ought to tell someone that the condesa de Gonsalvo y Coruna was more than casually concerned with the welfare of the British forces, but what person in a position important enough to do something about it would listen?

Major Lord Mark Adair could have been a possible confidant were it not for his obvious partiality for the condesa. If he believed Sophia's suspicions at all, which was highly unlikely, he would simply ascribe them to the fact that Sophia had never been particularly enthusiastic about the condesa, or, worse yet, that she was jealous of her.

It was clear to Sophia that for the moment, at least, there was nothing she could do except keep an eye herself on the condesa, or perhaps ask Luis to while she tried, as she had so many times before, to forget her problems by throwing herself into her work.

Chapter 26

Devoting herself to her painting brought positive results in two ways: Sophia was able to set aside upsetting thoughts about the relationship between the condesa and the major; and she was able to finish the portrait in record time.

Sophia's work space had been set up at the far end of the salon where the large windows faced north, affording her the best light and, when the rains let up enough to allow visitors, gave them easy access to the work in progress.

"Damn fine likeness of the condesa, damn fine," General Sir Thomas Picton declared one morning when he dropped in to discuss supplies with General Curtis. Sophia thanked the bluff general, but it was the praise of the others, Fitzroy Somerset and Andrew Leith Hay, that told her she had succeeded in capturing the condesa's likeness to perfection.

There was one person, however, who did not share in the general enthusiasm for Sophia's creation. One morning before going to exercise Caesar, the major called at General Curtis's quarters expressly to see the portrait which now, lacking only a frame, was completed.

"I heard from Fitzroy Somerset that the portrait is nearly finished," Mark greeted Sophia as he handed his cloak to Jeanne, who had opened the door, "and Andrew said it was superbly executed so I have come to see for myself."

Sophia led him up the stairs and, opening the drapes further for better light, indicated the portrait sitting on the easel near the windows.

"Ah." The major stood in front of it for some time, not saying a thing. Nor did his expression afford the least indication of his reaction to the work he had commissioned.

Sophia waited as patiently as she could, but when no

remark was forthcoming, she at last ventured to point out that Andrew Leith Hay, who was an artist himself and familiar with much of her work, had labeled it her best picture yet.

"Did he. Hmmmm."

"It does not meet with your approval, Major?" Try as she would, Sophie could not hide the anxiety in her voice.

"Yes. Er, well. It is very like." The major fell silent again. "But do you really think the condesa is as sly as you portray her?"

"Sly, my lord? She is gay and flirtatious, but . . ."

"Yes. Sly. Now, Miss Featherstonaugh, I am familiar enough with you and your talent to know that you can produce whatever effect you care to. Certainly there is a coquettish smile there, but the eyes are full of secrets. Do not tell me you did not intend it for I know you better than that."

"You are the only one who has interpreted it that way, Major. No one else has even hinted at such a thing."

"Which does not mean that I am not correct. I am more than seven, you know."

There was no avoiding it. The dark eyes fixed so intently on her seemed to see right through her. "I am aware of that, Major. But I did not *make* her anything. I merely painted what I saw."

"What you saw this time was wrong. The condesa may be flirtatious, perhaps, but she is not deceitful. I can not understand why you would paint her that way."

Sophia twisted her hands together uncomfortably. She had hoped against hope that the major would come to suspect the Frenchwoman of duplicity, but all on his own and not this way, not in a way that would make him doubt Sophia rather than the condesa. "As I said, Major, no one else who has seen the portrait has interpreted it that way. Even the lady herself was pleased by it when she called the other day."

While this was not entirely true, it was close enough. The condesa, invited by Sophia to pass judgment on the portrait before the finishing touches were completed, would rather have died than offer a comment that implied that the *petite artiste Anglaise* possessed anything akin to talent. She had stood for quite some time gazing at the picture, a self-satisfied smile on her face. It was only when she was leaving that she acknowledged Sophia's skill. "Yes, it will do—very pretty," she pronounced before sweeping out the door.

Sophia, well aware what even that small concession had cost the condesa, had been pleased. If the condesa, who was looking for faults, had not voiced the objections that the major now voiced, then surely it was his own doubts about the lady that were affecting his reaction to her portrait. Naturally, Sophia was not about to point this out to him, but it did give her some small sense of satisfaction.

"I am sure the condesa is too well mannered to say anything that was not highly complimentary. Besides, she does not know you as well as I do. It would also never occur to her that someone might be jealous of her."

"Jealous! Is that what you think?" For a moment Sophia was too furious even to speak. That the major could think such a thing of her was infuriating enough as it was, but that he believed she would allow such a petty emotion to compromise her art was beyond bearing. White with anger, she clenched her hands at her sides in an effort to contain her fury. To respond in anger would only make him think that his absurd accusation was true, and Sophia would rather have died than allow anyone to be of the opinion that she had wasted a moment's thought on someone who was as obviously shallow and self-centered as the Condesa de Gonsalvo y Coruna.

Drawing a deep, steadying breath, Sophia at last gained enough control over herself to speak. However she was not able to control the blood that rushed to her cheeks or the painful throbbing in her temples. "Jealous? Why would I be jealous?" She felt quite proud of herself for getting the words out without the slightest quaver. Even to her own critical ears, her voice sounded coolly conversational.

"Well, because I have . . . I mean the condesa and I . . ." Mark felt his own face growing hot as he recognized the pit he was digging for himself. It didn't help that Sophia with her damn-your-eyes expression and her eyes flashing scornfully looked more beautiful than he ever recalled seeing her. She was magnificent in her indignation and he felt like the veriest fool, and a cad to boot. "It is just that, well, the condesa has attracted, er, so much attention, and the men are always flocking around her that I thought you,

I mean it is only natural, well, any woman might find that difficult to take.''

"What I find difficult to take is that she is asking all those men such pointed questions about troop strengths and troop movements. And what I find even more difficult to take is that many of them may be giving her answers without the least thought as to why she might be asking them."

"She is interested. The Condesa de Gonsalvo y Coruna is a lovely woman who knows that the quickest way to charm a man is to ask him about himself." Even as he uttered these words, Mark could not help thinking how different the condesa was from Sophia who could actually speak knowledgeably about such things, actually carry on a conversation while the condesa bombarded one with questions, fluttered her eyelashes, and smiled seductively.

"Perhaps you are right." Sophia had suddenly grown very tired of the entire discussion. She turned to gaze out the window—a clear indication of her desire to let the entire conversation drop.

Tilting his head to one side, Mark scrutinized her averted profile. He was not sure what to think. One moment she had been blazingly angry and now, the carefully neutral tone and wandering eyes suggested that she had lost all interest in the conversation. With any other woman, he would have been extremely suspicious, but Sophia was not any other woman. She was not coy or flirtatious. She did not leave a man guessing what she meant or what she wanted, but was as forthright as any man in her actions and her speech. Clearly he had offended her, and just as clearly she had no intention of being drawn further into any explanation. There was nothing to do in the face of such a position but retreat, even though he was far from satisfied as to why she had painted the condesa the way she had or her refusal to discuss it.

"Well, er, thank you. If the condesa and her father are pleased with the portrait, that is all that matters. I shall send my batman to collect it and deliver it to the condesa. And now you must tell me what I owe you."

"Owe me? You owe me nothing."

"On the contrary, I owe you a great deal. I commissioned

you to do a portrait which you have done extremely expeditiously, and the subject is well pleased."

"I can not take anything from you for this."

"I do not see why you can not. I am like any other patron. If you are hoping to become another Angelica Kauffmann then you must learn to accept commissions which are an indication that your talent is recognized and appreciated by the world at large."

"Oh." This time Sophia truly was at a loss for words. She had been striving over the years to perfect her skills, dreaming of being sought out for them, but now, when someone was doing just that, she felt extremely uncomfortable with the entire notion.

A tiny smile tugged at one corner of the major's mouth. She had no difficulty defending the rightness of her vision or her skill, but when it came to accepting reward for it, the part that most women accepted as their due, she was obviously uneasy with it. Mark laid a hand on Sophia's shoulder. "You must accept payment, Miss Featherstonaugh. Not accepting it is tantamount to saying that you do not believe in yourself or your talent." He looked deep into her eyes and smiled. "I will send your commission with my batman, and that is that."

He turned and was gone before Sophia could respond in any way. She stood staring blankly at the door for a few minutes before sinking into a chair by the window and gazing out over the red tile rooftops toward the sea as she tried to collect her thoughts, which were in a perfect jumble.

How could Major Lord Mark Adair understand so completely what she was thinking and feeling and yet be so blind to the possibility of the Condesa de Gonsalvo y Coruna's schemes? How could he be sensitive enough to mistrust the portrait, but not mistrust the woman? It was an absolute enigma. On the one hand Sophia was furious with him for daring to think, much less suggest, that she was jealous of such a woman, but on the other, she was touched by his interest and concern for her dream of becoming a professional artist, and she was grateful to him for trying to help her make something of it.

Chapter 27

Mark, too, felt a need to sort out his thoughts, and saddling Caesar, headed straight for the rocky headland at the end of the bay. The stiff breeze from the ocean and the clouds scudding across the gray sky were likely to keep most people indoors and certainly away from the windswept beach. He needed to be alone with his reflections, some of which were most uncomfortable. But as he rode, he caught sight of a lone rider trotting across the fields and away from town. It was later than the customary hour for cavalry officers to exercise their mounts and since few of the inhabitants of Saint Jean de Luz engaged in equestrian pursuits, his curiosity was piqued. He squinted into the distance, trying to make out the identify of the dark figure on horseback, which on clearer inspection appeared to be a woman. The only woman he knew who could possibly be out taking the air in such a manner was Sophia, but he had just left her. That left the only woman besides Sophia whom he had seen riding since he had been in Saint Jean, the Condesa de Gonsalvo y Coruna.

Mark strained to get a better look. The habit was dark, not the eye-catching crimson that the condesa had been wearing the day of their encounter on the beach. However, there was no mistaking the bay mare with the white stocking on the right foreleg.

It must be the condesa, but why? Alone, and heading away from the town, so somberly dressed, it appeared that she was not hoping to encounter Mark or any other cavalry officer whose attention she wished to attract. Mark frowned in puzzlement. It did not add up. The condesa was a woman who thrived on company, especially company of the admiring, masculine kind. So why would she be riding alone, away from the possibility of such company unless she were riding toward something else, but what? Bayonne? The French? *What I find difficult to take is that she is asking all those men such pointed questions about troop positions and troop strengths, and what I find even more difficult to take is that many of them may be giving answers without the least conception as to why she might be asking them,* a nagging voice repeated over and over in his head.

Had Sophia been right in being suspicious of the condesa? Mark could think of nothing but the French forces that could make the condesa head toward Bayone rather than Saint Jean. She was not the sort of person to indulge in a long ride for the sheer pleasure of exercise and fresh air.

He turned Caesar around to ride slowly, thoughtfully, back toward town. There was nothing more he could do at the moment. He was expected back at headquarters and it would be difficult to get close enough now to the condesa without being seen. He would have to come up with some way to discover what she was up to. His days as an exploring officer were not over after all, it appeared.

Sophia might have felt a good deal better if she had known the direction the major's thoughts were taking. As she sat looking out the window she realized that it was not so much anger at the major's accusation of jealously as it was distress that a man who had seemed so close to her in so many ways could take so diametrically opposite a point of view on something as important as the trustworthiness of the Condesa de Gonsalvo y Coruna. Knowing that he disagreed with her so completely was bad enough, but knowing that he ascribed her opinion to some petty female rivalry was almost more than Sophia could bear, and the rest of the day she went about her customary chores, weighed down by a corrosive sense of loss. If she had been able to observe the major's straight dark brows frowning suspiciously at the back of a retreating female rider it would have gone a long way to easing Sophia's unhappy state of mind.

As it was, her mind was soon occupied with other, more serious concerns that evening as Lady Curtis, back from another afternoon comforting the sick at the hospital, complained of a slight fever. "If you do not mind, I shall just

have a bowl of soup in my chamber." She excused herself
after greeting her husband and daughter.

"I hope that you are not ill, Mama." Sophia rose from
the chair by the fire where she had been reading a six-
week-old copy of *The Times,* delivered the day before.

"So do I, but I fear that I may have contracted something, what with the weather being so cold and damp and
there being so much illness at the moment. While the bad
weather is a blessing in that it has kept us from fighting
the French such a long time that there are hardly any casu-
alties, it has filled the beds with men suffering from catarrh,
inflammation of the lungs, and fevers of every sort."

Checking on her mother after supper, Sophia was most
alarmed by the unnatural brightness of her eyes, her shallow breathing, and the heat of her forehead. "Do let me
call one of the surgeons, Mama. You do not look at all
well."

"Nonsense, my dear. They have enough to do looking
after all those men. I need nothing more than some rest.
A good night's sleep and I shall be right as a trivet in
the morning."

But she was not, and Sophia and General Curtis, waiting
anxiously for the report of the surgeon they had called in
the next morning, had no appetite for the breakfast Jorge
had prepared for them.

The surgeon, more accustomed to patching up wounded
men than ailing women, was not encouraging. "There is
little that anyone can do, except keep her warm and try to
get her to drink some beef tea, but I fear it will not be
long now. I am sorry." He spoke bluntly, but not unkindly
as a man who had seen too much suffering and disease to
waste his and everyone else's time by offering false hope.
Before taking his leave, he laid a fatherly hand on Sophia's
shoulder. "I would spend as much time with her as I could,
if I were you."

"Thank you." Sophia would barely make out his craggy
features through her tears. "If you will excuse me." She
looked at the general, who, his own eyes far from dry,
nodded sadly.

The next few days were one long indistinguishable blur
of watching and waiting by her mother's bedside, watching
the shallow rise and fall of the coverlet or the feverish

tossing and turning, waiting for the intermittent moments
when Lady Curtis would open her eyes and recognize her
daughter or the general, who was a regular visitor, sitting
at the head of his wife's bed, holding her hand and staring
fixedly at her face.

The surgeon's grim prediction, however, proved all too
true, Only a few days after she had come home feeling
feverish, Lady Curtis struggled to raise herself from her
pillows and turning to her husband and her daughter, whispered, "Take care of one another." The effort was too
much and she fell back gasping for breath. Then, closing
her eyes, se fell into a trance, lying so still that Sophia
could not be sure she still breathed. A few minutes later,
there was no doubt that Lady Curtis was gone.

Too overwhelmed by the suddenness and unexpectedness
of it all, Sophia just sat motionless, dry-eyed, not uttering
a sound until the general, wiping a hand across his own
eyes, rose and, laying a comforting hand on her shoulder,
urged her to leave the room. "Come, my dear. We can do
nothing further here, and you must have something to eat
and get some rest yourself."

Reluctantly Sophia allowed him to lead her away. She
could not have felt less like eating or sleeping, but she
knew the general was right; she could do nothing more,
and she would need all her strength to face the ensuing
days without her mother's comforting presence.

All of her life, the one thing she had been sure of, the
one thing she knew would remain constant in their ever-
changing circumstances, was her mother's affection, and
now, abruptly and without warning, it had been taken
away forever.

Following the general's instructions, Sophia picked at the
chicken that Jorge, sighing gustily and muttering *povere senhora* over and over, had prepared for her. Then she lay
down on her bed fully clothed. It was impossible to sleep,
but she lay staring at the ceiling until the cold, pale light
of dawn told her that her first day alone in the world without her mother had arrived.

Wearily she rose and went to dress her mother's body
for a simple funeral conducted by Wellington's own chaplain. The duke, upon hearing the news of Lady Curtis's
death, had kindly offered the chaplain's services. "I could

do no less for a lady who has remained steadfast and comforting to so many of our lads for so many years," he had responded to the general's thanks.

The general, who had hurried home to tell Sophia of the duke's kindness, left again immediately for headquarters, where he buried himself in his work for the rest of the day, coming home to share a lonely supper with Sophia before retiring.

Sophia envied him his business. There was no doubt that he grieved deeply, but he was able to distract himself with requisitions and supplies, and conversations with fellow officers, while she had no one. Every room in their little house reminded her of her mother—a basket of mending here, an arrangement of dried flowers brightening a bare corner there, the needlework on the fire screen that she had done one winter in Lisbon.

Unable to stop herself, Sophia wandered from room to room, touching the things her mother had touched last, desperately trying to recapture some tangible connection with the woman who had been everything to her for as long as she could remember.

Chapter 28

One gray, meaningless day followed the next as Sophia took over the running of the household, glad to have the extra burden of her mother's duties so that she had less time to reflect on her loss. Dry-eyed, she went through the motions of ordering the meals, overseeing the airing of the linens, the dusting, and the shopping, but inside she felt empty, numb, lifeless.

Encountering her in the street some days after Lady Curtis's funeral, Mark was at pains to identify the vital, energetic Sophia Featherstonaugh in the gaunt, worn-looking woman who passed by him, not even recognizing her until she had passed him.

"Miss Featherstonaugh."

The slender figure, eyes fixed on the ground, trudged on.

"Sophia." Mark had to catch her arm to get her attention.

"Oh. Good day, Major."

"I wanted to ask you, did you receive . . ." Mark paused, his heart turning over at the sorrow he read in the large hazel eyes.

"Come." Without further conversation, he guided her unresisting toward the promenade. It spoke volumes for Sophia's misery that, utterly passive, she let him lead her to the beach, and the lonely grandeur of the Pointe Sainte Barbe.

Neither one spoke until they reached the rocky promontory. At last Mark halted and turned her to face him. "I heard about your mother. I am sorry, so very sorry."

"Thank you." It was a whisper, so low that he saw her response rather than heard it.

"I know she was everything to you. If I can do anything . . ."

"No. Thank you. There is nothing anyone can do."

"Sophia." He felt utterly helpless in the face of her sorrow, more helpless than he could ever remember feeling except for those miserable months when he had watched his own mother fade away before his eyes. There was nothing he or anyone could do for Sophia to help ease the pain of her loss. As a soldier he had dealt with death on a regular basis, and though he never grew accustomed to it, he had learned how to cope with it and to help others cope with it, but only on a military basis. The way he and others handled it was to throw themselves into their jobs, to continue to fight the fight that had cost others their lives. But he could not even offer Sophia this consolation, meager as it was.

He looked into her eyes, dark with hopelessness, but without a trace of tears in them. Mark was willing to bet that she had not even cried—the loss had been too devastating for her to allow herself to acknowledge it or to give way to an emotion so strong that it might completely overwhelm her. "My poor girl," he whispered, pulling her close to him.

At first her body remained rigid in his arms as she struggled to maintain control. Carefully, he stroked her back until he felt some of the stiffness go out of her. Pulling her closer, Mark slid one hand up her neck, undid the ribbons of her bonnet and deftly slid it off so it hung down her back, then slowly, gently pulled her head down on his shoulder.

For a moment she resisted and then, with a sigh, she gave up. The tension slowly drained from her and she allowed herself to lean against him for support.

"There, there. That is better. You must give in to your sorrow or it will never leave you," he murmured into the dark curls that brushed against his cheek.

There was no response. He continued stroking her hair for some time, letting her relax against him, absorbing some of his strength, but at last, gently but firmly clasping her arms, he set her away from him. Then, cupping her chin in one hand, he looked deep into the eyes that were still so full of pain and as dry as they had been when he had first encountered her.

"Sophia, my dear girl, it is not natural to resist giving in to grief. Sometimes silent bravery and self-control are not good things, especially if they keep you from living. If you do not acknowledge your sorrow or give in to it now, you will never get beyond it. Believe me, I know."

"You know?" The look of patent skepticism, which almost verged on scorn, was not promising, but at least it was a reaction, and any reaction was better than the lifeless tone and blank expression she had maintained up until that moment.

"Yes, I do. I lost my mother, too, in far worse circumstances than yours, and I was younger than you at the time."

"But that was different. You were young, you had your father and your brother, you had family."

"No, it was worse because I killed her."

That got her attention. "You what?" If there had been skepticism before, there was patent disbelief now. "I can not believe it, how could a young boy . . ."

"I did not actually, physically kill her, but I was as responsible for her death as if I had. She was so lonely. My father, who should have known how much she thrived in company, kept her immured in the country at Cranleigh, miles away from the gaiety and society she craved and far away from any of her countrymen. When we did go to town she was a changed creature. She entertained a great deal, especially those attached to the Spanish embassy, for she was eager for news of her family and the friends she left behind in Spain. There was one young man in particular who, homesick himself, delighted in talking with her for hours, not only of common friends and family, but Spanish literature, painting, and music. Now that I look back on it, I realize he was very young and to him, my mother was not only someone who spoke his language, she was the mother and the family he missed back home. My father, however"—Mark broke off as he recalled the icy tones his father's already cold and distant voice took on whenever he spoke of the young Spaniard. How could his father have been so lacking in sympathy or understanding not to have seen a that the boy was simply lonely? How could he have known so little of his own wife that he so badly misjudged her affectionate nature? Mark swallowed hard, and with an effort, continued. "My father, however, only saw one thing—a man who spent a great deal of time with his wife, the Duchess of Cranleigh. Oddly enough, now that I think back on it, he was less concerned with what actually was occurring than with what *appeared*—to be occurring, or, to be more exact"—Mark laughed mirthlessly—"with what he thought the world believed to be occurring.

"But surely you had nothing to do with that."

"No. But I was the one responsible for the final act of the sad little drama. Signor Alvarez also missed his younger brothers and he always asked Mother to let me stay if he happened to call when I was with her. He brought me a toy sword of which I was inordinately proud and naturally, because I was always eager to prove my maturity and my worth to my father, I showed it to him.

"I was bitterly disappointed by his cold dismissal of my new toy, but what followed was even worse. I happened to walk by the library when I heard my father berating my mother for seeing Signor Alvarez. Hoping to defend her, I ran in to tell him that the Spaniard was not the blackguard and traitor my father said he was, but a very nice man who often called on us.

"I will never forget what ensued. My father's face already looked like a thundercloud and it took all my courage to enter the room, but as I said my piece, his expression grew positively murderous. I was almost relieved when he ordered me from the room, but I worried about my mother. She looked so unhappy."

Unable to go on, Mark stopped, and blinking rapidly, gazed out to sea for several minutes. At last, clearing his throat, he continued. "That was almost the last I saw of my mother. She retired to her room and I was not allowed to see her because they said she was ill. It was only when they knew she was going to die that they allowed me in. She looked so pale and frail lying there on all her pillows. I . . . I told her I was sorry. I had never wanted to cause her unhappiness or hurt her. And she replied that it was not my fault, but I knew it was. I had spoken up and she had fallen ill. I begged her to get better and she promised that she would try, but we both knew she would not. She died a day later, and not long after that I was sent away to school."

"Poor little boy." Her eyes swimming with tears, Sophia

reached up and touched his cheek with her hand. "How miserable you must have been."

He took her hand in his. "I was. And it took me a long time to recover. But I did at last. Now I can live with the pain, and talking about it with you has made it easier to bear."

"Did you have no one in whom you could confide?"

He shook his head slowly, sadly.

"How very sad." She laid her head on his shoulder and the tears flowed unchecked down her cheeks.

Mark gathered her in his arms and held her quietly, his chin resting on her hair as she wept.

At last, sniffing, and wiping her eyes, she looked up. "I do not know what came over me. I am not usually such a watering pot, especially over something that happened to someone else years ago."

"You were sharing my loss as I wish to share yours. And yours is a terrible loss."

The hazel eyes filled again with tears. Her face crumpled. "I know. Whatever shall I do? How shall I ever bear it?" She covered her face with her hands and leaned against him sobbing.

"My poor, poor girl." He held her close, stroking her hair and murmuring, *my poor girl,* until the sobbing subsided. Then, reaching in his pocket, he pulled out a handkerchief and gently wiped her eyes. "You needed to do that, my love. You can not keep things bottled up forever, and it is better to cry now than to be suddenly overwhelmed by it later when you least expect it."

"I do apologize." She took the handkerchief from him and mopped her face with it. "I can not think when I have lost control of myself like that."

"Sophia." He laid his hands on her shoulders. "It would be far worse if you had not lost control, for then you would be an unfeeling automaton, and that you are not. You could not paint so superbly if you were that sort of person. You would not be beloved by so many people if you were that sort of person."

"Beloved, me?"

"Of course. You are the darling of every man here."

She shook her head slowly, incredulously.

"Believe me, you are. I have seen the men's faces when

you walk by. They light up. And it is not just because of your beauty. It is because you care about them, you are interested in what interests them. You share their hardships and their triumphs, and you are there with comfort and concern when they need it."

"Oh."

"Believe me, I know what I am talking about. You are very important, and much beloved by . . . by us all."

"Thank you." She glanced up at him and her breath caught in her throat. There was a look in his eyes that she had never seen before. She had caught a glimpse of it when he had comforted her after the death of Billy Barnes, but now there was an intensity that quite took her breath away

They stood gazing at one another, unaware of time or their surroundings, until a seagull screamed overhead and a large raindrop splashed on Sophia's forehead. Pulling her close, Mark kissed the drop away, retrieved her bonnet, settled it on her head, and tied the ribbons under her chin in a surprisingly expert bow.

"Come. I must take you home before you are soaked through." Throwing a protective arm around her shoulders, he hurried her toward sheltering trees and back to Sophia's quarters.

Fortunately, the rain, except for a few desultory drops, held off until they reached her door. Sophia reached for the latch, opened the door, and stepped across the threshold. Then, thinking better of it, she turned back. Frowning slightly with the effort of it, she tried to find just the right words to let him know what his sympathy and concern had meant to her, how they had filled some of the cold, hollow feeling inside her. But she could think of nothing. "I, ah, thank you. And you are right, I do feel better." Quickly ducking her head, as though ashamed of such an admission, she hastily shut the door behind her before Mark could frame a reply.

He remained motionless in front of the door for some minutes, smiling to himself. Then, still smiling, and oblivious to the rain now spattering on his shoulders, he headed down the street toward headquarters.

Chapter 29

The dark winter days dragged slowly by while both armies set about preparing their spring offensives. Mark, under the pretense of exercising Caesar every day, rode out of the city in all directions, getting the lay of the land and a sense of the quality of the roads. He also made a point to ride by the Hôtel de Brissac at roughly the same time of day he had seen the condesa riding toward Bayonne.

Hating himself for being suspicious, yet unable to banish the memory of the scornful expression in Sophia's eyes as she had alluded to the condesa's singular interest in British troop movements, he was torn between wondering if Sophia was jealous or if he was a complete fool. And what was the condesa? Mark could not be sure what he wanted the answer to be, but he was certain of one thing, and that was that he wanted some sort of solution to the puzzle, and soon.

The first day he rode by Diane's door all was quiet, and Mark was beginning to congratulate himself on the correctness of his own point of view when, returning to town after his invigorating gallop, he caught sight of one of the servants leaving the condesa's stables on horseback. This, coupled with the rider's nervous glances over his shoulder and the general direction in which he appeared to be heading made Mark halt Caesar in his tracks, turn him around, and follow at a safe distance. Once they had passed by the outskirts of town, it was quite easy for Mark to establish the man's destination as Bayonne, without being seen himself.

Having witnessed enough to decide that there was a pattern worth watching, Mark set his batman to keeping an eye on the activities at the Hôtel de Brissac and prepared to call more regularly on the lovely condesa.

Several days later, using the portrait as a pretense, Mark

knocked on the impressively carved door of the Hôtel de
Brissac. A serving girl answered the door. "Ah, monsieur,
le majeur, Madame has been hoping you . . . ah . . . pardon.
I shall inform Madame that you are here." She greeted him
in a most friendly fashion before leading him to the salon
where the condesa, elegant as usual, in a muslin morning
dress with a falling lace collar and Vandyke trimming, welcomed him warmly.

"Milord Adair, I am delighted to see you. This weather
has been so *affreux* that I have been confined to the house
until I am quite dull with boredom. And all of you English
are too busy to come brighten the hours of a poor widow."
Taking his arm, Diane led Mark to the sofa near the fire,
and disposing herself gracefully upon it, patted the seat
next to her in a most inviting fashion.

"Come now, tell me that it is the plans for Bayonne and
not my poor conversation that has kept you away." She
leaned forward with an enchanting smile that revealed just
a hint of the dimple at one corner of her mouth.

The smile, however, was lost on Mark, who looking into
her eyes, suffered an unpleasant frisson of recognition as
he recognized the sly expression from Sophia's portrait.
Stealing a glance over the condesa's shoulder to the easel
by the window where the portrait was now prominently
displayed, he was furnished ample verification of this impression. How could he have been so blind? Rapidly recalling his other encounters with the beautiful Frenchwoman,
Mark realized that every one of them had included some
pointed questions about the British troops.

". . . and when the rain lets up for more than three days
at a time, I suppose I shall have to steel myself to bid
you all adieu . . ." The condesa's words broke into Mark's
unwelcome reflections. That anyone should be taken in by
the Frenchwoman, no matter how lovely she was, was bad
enough, but that an exploring officer in particular, and
someone who was widely acknowledged for his skill at disguise, had been taken in by the oldest trick in the world—
a woman's flattery—was lowering in the extreme. The fact
that it all had been brought to his attention by another
young woman, one who was the complete opposite of the
condesa was almost more than he could bear.

"Ah, my dear condesa"—Mark leaned forward, allowing

the hand lying along the back of the sofa to slide imperceptibly until it rested on the lady's shoulder—"my time is not my own, else I would spend my days at your feet instead of on the endless paperwork the duke gives to me."

"Poor Major Adair." Diane leaned toward him so that the musky perfume clinging to her skin enveloped him in a seductive cloud. "All those maps to survey and battle plans to prepare." She thrust out her full lower lip into a delicious pout that would have driven anyone less suspicious than Mark to kiss the inviting red mouth right then and there.

"Nothing so exciting, I assure you. We have been so constantly on the move that no on has been able to make a comprehensive report of our last movements for our leaders in Parliament. The task has fallen to me, and I swear that I can tell you more now about what we have done in the last six months than you could ever want to know. The people at home are sticklers for detail—how many killed, how many wounded, how many taken prisoner, who is deserving of recognition."

"How very dull for you." The condesa's pout grew more pronounced.

"All the more reason that I crave the diversion of your charming company." The hand that had slipped to the condesa's shoulders now pulled her to him.

With a sigh, Diane slid both her arms around Mark's neck and gave herself up to his expert lovemaking.

The major emerged some hours later, physically satiated, but otherwise unsatisfied. While he had not given up any information to the condesa, he had not discovered any either, and the mission of an exploring officer was to do both, withhold and find out information. On the other hand, rendered acutely sensitive by both his own and Sophia's suspicions, he had been able to remain sufficiently detached during the passionate interlude to determine that the condesa's passion was as forced as his was.

Oh, he had enjoyed himself well enough. The condesa was a beautiful woman with a stunning body which she displayed to its best advantage and used with consummate skill—a skill, he noted wryly, that could not have been perfected by the young and faithful wife of an elderly Spanish conde who was often away with the army. It was obvious

to the major that at least one of the Frenchwoman's asser-
tions was patently false—she had not suffered years of
lonely widowhood.

And just how many other things about her were equally
untrue? In the next hour he was likely to discover, for he
knew that Finbury, his batman, was waiting back at their
quarters to give him a full report on the comings and goings
at the Hôtel de Brissac.

When he arrived at his quarters he learned just how duplicitous the lady was. "It is just like you said, sir," Finbury
reported, his grizzled countenance wrinkled more than
usual by his expression of disgust. "Every day at midmorn-
ing, a servant, or the lady herself, rides off in the direction
of Bayonne and then returns, regular as clockwork, two
hours later. Now I figure that no one could ride to Bayonne
and back in that short amount of time, especially a lady,
so it appears to me that they must be meeting someone
near our own forward posts at Barroilhet. Being on foot, I
could not follow, but it would not be too difficult for someone on horseback to track them down. The Bayonne–Saint
Jean road is the only one passable at the moment, the rest
being ankle deep in mud. And the fields are not much
better. A rider might avoid being seen by cutting across
the country a little bit of the way, but anyone who wanted
to cover any sort of a distance would be forced to use the
road at some point. So I say they are meeting someone
coming from Bayonne."

"Excellent work, Finbury. I appreciate your observations.
I shall take it from here."

"Very good, sir." Privately, Finbury thought it would
never have occurred to him to be anything but suspicious
of the Condesa de Gonsalvo y Coruna and her household
in the first place—she was a damned Frog, after all, lady
or no lady, Spanish husband or no Spanish husband—but
Finbury was the first to admit that the ways of the quality
were sometimes obscure. The major, despite being from the
best of the quality, was more comprehensible than most,
but even he sometimes behaved in ways that caused the
batman to scratch his head in puzzlement. Take this French
lady, for example. She seemed to have turned the heads of
all the officers, his master included, when it was as clear to

Finbury as the nose on his face that she cared nothing for any of them and was using them for all they were worth.

Shaking his head, the batman went off to brush the major's dress uniform, leaving the fate of the Condesa de Gonsalvo y Coruna in his master's hands.

Chapter 30

The very next day Mark decided to seal the lady's fate, one way or another. The high-flying clouds the evening before had promised another day without rain, a day fine enough that the lady herself might make the trip.

Having determined the direction in which she always rode, he felt confident enough to leave town well in advance of the hour that riders usually left the Hôtel de Brissac. He rode Caesar along the promenade and toward the headland where he had first seen the condesa and then, dismounting behind a rocky outcropping so he was hidden from view from the beach or on the road, he peered around the rock until he had good visibility of the road.

Within half an hour, Mark's vigil was rewarded as he observed a lone rider approaching from town. The rider paused, looking out toward the ocean as though enjoying the view and then, assuring herself the road was deserted, trotted swiftly off toward Bayonne.

Mark waited until horse and rider disappeared from view, threw himself on Caesar's back and galloped off in hot pursuit. The more powerful horse and more experienced rider reached the road in no time and soon had their quarry in their sights.

The flat coastal plain from Guethary to Bidart did not offer much cover, but fortunately the condesa—by now he had assured himself that it was the condesa—having made sure that she was not observed, did not turn around to reconnoiter a second time, but pressed on toward Bayonne.

Ready to leave the road at any moment and hide behind one of the hedges or clumps of trees that presented themselves along the way, Mark followed at a distance great enough not to be heard and near enough to keep the condesa within sight.

They rode on in this manner for the better part of an hour until suddenly, the condesa slowed to a walk. Sensing that she was nearing her destination, Mark hastily pulled Caesar off the road into a convenient copse and waited.

He had concealed himself not a moment too soon, for the condesa stopped, turned around to satisfy herself that she was unobserved, and then made a sharp turn to the right to pick her way carefully across the fields, heading in a northwesterly direction.

Mark waited a minute or two to make certain that all her attention was concentrated in front of her, then turned right himself, to follow a parallel path. Fortunately for him, he could keep just out of sight by sticking to a small ravine. Picking his way carefully, he emerged from the ravine every so often to assure himself that the condesa was continuing in the same direction.

At last he caught sight of a cottage surrounded by hedges. Sure that this was her goal, he pressed forward until he came to a point that he figured was directly in line with the building.

Emerging cautiously from the ravine, horse and rider made quickly for a small stand of trees near the cottage, arriving just in time to observe the condesa pulling her mount up next to another horse tied outside the cottage. The next minute a man emerged and, hurrying toward the lady, caught her in his arms as she slid from her horse, and led her into the cottage.

Still too far away to make out any detail, Mark dismounted, tied Caesar to a tree, and glancing swiftly in all directions, ran forward, keeping low enough to be out of sight.

Gaining the hedge near the cottage, he crouched down and strained to catch any sound of the activity inside, but he was too far away and the wind rattling the dry branches of the trees made it impossible to discern a thing.

Not being sure how long the interchange would last, but knowing from Finbury's reports that it probably would not be long, Mark did not dare move closer, but remained crouched uncomfortably behind the hedge until the creak of the door and the stamping of the horses warned him that the two occupants of the cottage were emerging.

Inching forward, Mark peered through the hedge.

Though much of his view was obscured by the horses and the hedge, he was just able to make out the skirt of the condesa's riding habit and legs encased in the green uniform of a French officer of the heavy dragoons. But now he was able to pick up snatches of their conversation.

"Au revoir, ma belle. Restes tranquil. Les Anglasis, they are stupid. They think that with winter here, and having beaten back Soult's surprise attack in December, they are safe to let down their guard. You worry too much because you can not yet discover their exact plans. Perhaps they are planning nothing, or, at most, to lay siege to Bayonne. This Wellington, he is not the strategist our emperor is, or Marshall Soult, for that matter. He can only react, so it is up to the French to plan."

"But it is so long. I wish to be with you, Étienne. *Ces Anglais,* they are gentlemen enough, but they know nothing of love. How much more must I wait, Étienne?"

"Patience, *chérie.* It will not be long now. But you must continue to send me reports regularly so that I may constantly feast my eyes on your charming face."

There was a long pause as the hem of Diane's riding skirt swirled around the officer's boots and Mark, crouched behind the bush, held his breath for fear he might call attention to himself. *You fool,* he chided himself cynically, *no one with his arms around the Condesa de Gonsalvo y Coruna would notice anything so mundane as the snapping of a twig or the crunch of dead leaves.*

At last the couple broke apart. Diane was hoisted into the saddle. She bent down for a final kiss and then trotted away, heading for the road to Saint Jean de Luz.

The French officer, only a lieutenant, Mark noted with some satisfaction, took a last look around, then he, too, mounted and headed across the fields toward Bayonne.

Once he had made certain that no one observed his movements, Mark walked back to the cluster of trees, untied Caesar, mounted him, and headed back toward the road, pondering what his next move was to be.

From the conversation that he had overheard it was clear that the condesa had not been able to gather any definitive information as to what the British Army's next move was to be, so it seemed that little actual damage had been done. Mark knew that only a few of Wellington's aides and Sir

John Hope were aware that the British were planning to cross the Adour below Bayonne instead of above it, and that Hope's corps were the only part of the army concentrating on the city while the rest were to bypass it.

He decided that the best thing to do would be to lull the condesa into a false sense of security, feeding her misinformation about the army's plans to lay siege to Bayonne, but he rejected this strategy almost immediately. If he been played for a fool, he wanted to know it for certain, and he wanted to know the reasons behind it. Was the condesa selling information to the highest bidder or was she acting out of loyalty to her country and her countrymen? Did she find the French officer more attractive than she found him? Was he a better lover?

Unable to stifle these thoughts, Mark urged Caesar to a gallop, hoping to catch the condesa and confront her before she reached Saint Jean and the Hôtel de Brissac. He wanted her alone, face-to-face, with no one else as an audience to lend her sympathy and support.

The faster he rode, the more angry Mark became, angry at the woman for her duplicity, angry at himself for having been so easily taken in, even angry at Sophia for having seen through the condesa and predicted the outcome of events with such stunning accuracy.

Catching sight of the lone rider ahead, he urged Caesar to greater speed. At first his quarry, hearing hoofbeats behind her, quickened her own pace, but then realizing as he gained on her that outrunning her pursuer was futile, she slackened her speed and, when he was within shouting distance, stopped altogether.

Diane turned around to identify the horseman behind her. "Why, Major, how delightful to see you. If I had known it was you behind me, I would have slowed long ago, but the weather looked threatening and I was trying to get home before it broke."

Mark raised one dark eyebrow in patent disbelief as he glanced at the clouds racing overhead. "Surely you were not away so long from your homeland as to forget that clouds moving so high and so fast never bring rain."

"Major, I am but a woman. What do I know of weather and clouds? You military men, on the other hand, are most astute about such things."

"*We* military men. Military men such as the French lieutenant you just met?"

The condesa's eyes flicked anxiously from his face toward Bayonne and back again. She licked her lips nervously. "Why, Major, what an absurd notion. What would a daughter of the de Brissacs have in common with one of those *sans-culottes*?" She tossed her head haughtily in the direction of Bayonne.

"Precisely what I was wondering myself. Does Étienne know that you consider him a *sans-culotte*? I would doubt it."

The color drained from the condesa's face. "Why, my lord, what are . . ."

"Cut line, my lady. I know you have been sending messages regularly to the French, if not in person, through your servant. I know that you can not wait to join your French lover Étienne who is a lieutenant in the heavy dragoons and though he may not be so much a gentleman as we English, is a better lover." Mark's mouth twisted into a bitter smile as he watched the stunned expression spread over the condesa's face. "Yes, I heard everything. There is no hope of denying it."

"What would you know about it," the condesa spat. "Years of enduring poverty, of being forced to marry a man who was over twice my age, all for what? *La Gloire*, and the pride of the de Brissacs? Pride, bah, stupidity more like. It is a stupidity that denies life. You think me a traitor. I am no traitor. I am a Frenchwoman and I am doing what I can to defend my country. So, do what you wish, I have a clear conscience. I at least am worthy of being called a daughter of those ancient warriors the de Brissacs for I have done what I could to defend my country against foreign invaders."

"The de Brissacs, a family whose aristocratic blindness you deplored just moments ago." Mark shook his head and turned Caesar toward Saint Jean.

"What? You are going to leave just like that? You are going to do nothing? Are you afraid to bring charges against a woman? What cowards you British are!"

"Your sex, madame, has nothing to do with it. Your effectiveness, or lack thereof does. Your precious information that you are passing along is nothing more than what any peasant working his farm between here and Bayonne or any fisherman selling his catch in the surrounding villages knows. Why should I do anything? It is a waste of my time." Mark dug his heels into Caesar's flanks and was out of earshot before the condesa, seething with frustration, could frame a reply.

Chapter 31

Though he might denounce to her face the condesa's efforts as being ineffective, Mark suffered the pangs of self-recrimination for his own blindness and inefficiency to such a degree that the only way he could answer his own bitter self-accusations was to throw himself into his duties and to encourage Wellington and Hope in their efforts to lull the French into believing that the British were preparing for a lengthy siege of Bayonne. Wrapped up in his work and his own unhappy thoughts, he kept close to headquarters, arriving early in the morning and leaving late at night, pausing only to eat or to sleep and to make sure that Caesar was properly looked after.

This rigorous regime also protected him from any accidental encounters with the woman who had been suspicious of the Condesa de Gonsalvo y Coruna from the very beginning. Still castigating himself for being all kinds of a dupe and a fool, Mark could not face the idea of seeing Sophia.

But Sophia was too preoccupied with her own affairs to waste much thought on the major or the condesa. With the prospect of improving weather, she knew the army would be planning a move deeper into the heart of France. She had already made some plans for this when the general called her into his study one evening.

"Sit down, my dear." He smiled kindly as he indicated a chair by the fire. "I am afraid that it may seem to you that I have not been sensitive to your circumstances since your beloved mother's death, and for that I do apologize. My only excuse is that I, too, have been coping with her very great loss."

"There is not the least need to apologize, sir." Indeed, there was not. Sophia was not the only one to think that the general had aged a great deal in the past few weeks. Everyone at headquarters had observed that the loss of his wife had obviously left its mark.

"I may have been remiss in my attentions to you, but I have not been remiss in my duties, and I have been concerning myself with your future welfare. In fact, I have here a letter, written in answer to mine, that arrived in the bag from the weekly packet boat this morning. It is from Lady Lydia Featherstonaugh, who writes to invite you to live with her in Brook Street."

"Lady Lydia? Brook Street?" Sophia was too stunned to do anything more than echo his words.

"Yes. I know that you have never had contact with your father's or your mother's families, but much as I regard you as the daughter I never had, the Edgehills and the Featherstonaughs are your true family. As the Featherstonaughs are more likely to be able to provide for you than the Edgehills, I wrote to the Duke of Broughton. The duke, no matter how much he might have disapproved of his brother, would never want it to be said that he had abandoned his orphaned niece. Lady Lydia writes, most kindly, that the duke, knowing of her wish for a companion, suggested she might invite you to live with her."

"A companion?" Sophia had seen enough of companions at some of the establishments in Lisbon to be less than enthusiastic over the proposition.

"I do not think, from the way that Lady Lydia writes, that she means for you to become one of those silent, long-suffering relatives of all work who spend their days at the beck and call of their more fortunate relatives. But here, see for yourself. She has enclosed a note to you."

Wordlessly, Sophia held out her hand for the letter.

My dear niece, it began, *if I may call you niece after all these years of shamefully neglecting you. General Sir Thornton Curtis has informed us of your sad loss, and though I can in no way ease that unhappiness, I do write to invite you to make your home with me. I realize that the prospect of sharing a home with someone who, along with the rest of the family, allowed her brother to live and die without any contact from her, is not the most encouraging, but I hope you will believe me when I say I*

*look forward to making amends for the family's treatment
of your parents. I do not know how your tastes run, but
my life here in London, though not so taken up with
amusements as many, is nevertheless pleasant. I keep myself busy with my studies, and lectures. I hope you will
join me. Though I was not in contact with your father, I
was always eager for news of him and his wife, who, by
all reports, was a woman of sense, a woman he was lucky
enough to marry. I trust that being raised by such a
woman that you are also a young woman of sense, else I
would not extend this invitation to you. I look forward to
a favorable reply. Sincerely, Lydia Featherstonaugh.*

"Well?"

"Her invitation is kindly enough meant, and she does
sound as though she has given it serious consideration. As
I remember it, she was Papa's favorite sister, but that was
long ago, and he spoke so little of his family that I can not
say for certain. I believe she was a good deal younger."
Sophia paused, and staring into the fire, folded and unfolded the letter abstractedly until she at last burst out,
"But may I not stay with you, sir? You are my family now.
And who will keep house for you now that Mama is gone?
I may not be Mama, but I have spent so many years helping
her that I am sure I am equal to the task."

Sir Thornton smiled at her fondly. "I know you are, but
that is not the issue. The issue is your future. I am a rough
old soldier, and it would be unfair, nay, selfish, of me to
give my own comfort a moment's thought where your future is concerned. No"—he held up a hand to forestall the
protest she was about to make—"hear me out. I shall miss
you, more than you might imagine. Your presence has been
such a comfort to me since your mother passed away." The
general paused and blinked rapidly once or twice before
continuing. "But I could never offer you the opportunities
that the Featherstonaughs can. Your father was a harum-
scarum lad who perhaps did not deserve his birthright, but
that is no reason to deprive you of yours."

"But I do not wish to live that sort of life—fashionable,
frivolous, and empty."

"I know, my dear. But believe me, you will never be
that, no matter what sort of society you are thrown into.

But, from what I can tell of Lady Lydia, you will not be asked to become one. It appears to me as though you are in far greater danger of becoming a ferocious bluestocking, for it sounds as though your Aunt Lydia is a lady of strong opinions and fearsome intellect. There, you see, it may not be so bad." The general was encouraged by the wan smile that flitted across the sad face in front of him. "Besides, the Allies have crossed the Rhine and if this warm spell holds, we shall be on the move soon. With the Austrians in Switzerland and the Russians and Prussians progressing toward Nancy, I truly do not think that the French will be able to resist us much longer. I expect to be in England myself before the year is out."

"Truly?"

"Truly. And you can be certain that the first thing I shall do upon returning home is to call on you. I know that you are not happy about this, Sophia, but believe me, it is the only way. I shall have to devote all my attention to my work in the next few months as we move into France. Keeping our armies well supplied so that they do not plunder the countryside is more critical than ever."

Sophia, sensing that, in his own kindly way the general was doing his best to tell her that he would be glad to be rid of responsibility for a young lady who had only a Portuguese peasant to look after her, nodded slowly. "I understand."

"There's my girl." The general laid a firm hand on her shoulder. "I know you would rather be joining the cavalry than retreating to London, but sometimes, in order to help win a war, we are asked to do things we do not wish to do."

The wealth of sympathy in the general's eyes brought tears to her own. Sophia gulped and nodded. "I know, sir." The interview was at an end and she rose to go, but halted before she reached the door. "Thank you for understanding."

"No thanks is necessary. You are a good soldier. You know that your duty lies in what is best for many of us. Your mother would be proud." *And your father would not have the least conception,* he muttered to himself. "There is a boat returning to England at the end of the week that has room for a passenger. I know it seems very soon, but events are unfolding rapidly and there may not be another opportunity.

Doing her best to hide her dismay, Sophia nodded and fled to her bedchamber.

Chapter 32

Sophia began packing the next day. Trying not to think about the familiar way of life she was leaving behind, she once again began laying her few treasures in the well-worn trunks that had accompanied her and her mother from England to Portugal, Portugal to Spain, and Spain to France. This time, however, she would be moving on alone.

Placing her mother's sewing basket in the corner of one trunk and proceeding to fill it with a few of her favorite books—Pope's poems, a volume of Shakespeare, Addison's essays—Sophia was fighting back the tears when she heard a timid knock on the door.

It was Jeanne. "If you please, mademoiselle, there is a gentleman here to see you."

"A gentleman?"

"Yes, mademoiselle. Major Adair."

"Major Adair? Oh, yes, thank you, Jeanne." Taking a quick glance in the looking glass, which, fortunately, she had not yet packed, Sophia tidied her hair and wiped a smudge of dust off her nose. She looked pale and tired in the black bombazine mourning dress of her mother's that had been taken apart and refitted for her, a complete contrast to the condesa, she thought wryly as she pulled down the sleeves that had ridden up her arms as she packed.

Slowly she descended the stairs, trying to guess what possible reason the major could have for paying a visit.

He was leaning against the mantel when she entered the parlor, and as he turned to greet her, she was struck by his air of fatigue. His face was drawn and tired and the dark eyes seemed even more deep-set than usual.

"You look exhausted, Major. You must be working very hard." Her hand flew to her mouth. "I do apologize. How ill-bred of me to blurt out such a thing without even thanking you for calling or offering you a chair."

A half smile tugged at his mouth as he took the proffered seat. "Ever the forthright Miss Featherstonaugh. Actually, it is refreshing to know one woman at least, who speaks her mind." The sarcastic note in his voice clearly indicated that this was not just a general observation.

"Oh? I am flattered, I think."

"You were right about the condesa." It was Mark's turn to blurt out his thoughts. "She is utterly false."

"I am sorry."

"Why should you be sorry? She is precisely what you said she was—cold, scheming, duplicitous . . ."

"Goodness, how did you come to this conclusion?"

"By following her."

"Ah." So he had believed her after all! The warm feeling that flooded through her at this admission took Sophia by surprise. She had not realized to what extent she valued the major's good opinion or how unhappy she had been made by their disagreement. "What happened?"

"I caught her giving information to her French lover."

"A French lover! If her heart was engaged, it is understandable I suppose, and she is French, after all."

"How can you defend her after you told me in so many ways not to trust her?"

"I never said that she was dishonorable, I just thought she was hiding something. But according to her way of seeing it, she might have been acting in the most honorable way she could think of."

"Like any exploring officer, I suppose."

The bitter tone in his voice tore at Sophia's heart. "No, you must not think . . ." She rose and crossed over to his chair to lay a comforting hand on his arm. "You are not like that."

"How am I different?"

"You would not deceive . . ."

"I have deceived many times. You know that. You have even seen me trying to deceive the world as a priest, as a peasant . . ."

"But you would not deceive someone when it was a matter of the heart."

"Heart? This was not a matter of the heart."

The relief that washed over her was another complete surprise to Sophia. So he had not cared about Diane de Gonsalvo y Coruna in *that* sort of way. "Oh, but you would never use a member of the female sex in such a way. If you have deceived people, it has been those who are waging a war just as you are waging a war."

The hazel eyes looking up at him shone with conviction. He clasped the slender fingers gripping his arm. How he was going to miss her when she was gone. "Thank you. You make it all seem right somehow, Sophia. I shall miss you when you are gone." He rose and took her other hand in his. "Actually, that is why I am here. I heard at headquarters that you are leaving soon. I have orders to ride over to Hill's corps near Urrcarray today and I may not return before you go so I have come to say good-bye."

"Thank you. That is very kind of you," she whispered. In spite of her best efforts, her eyes filled with tears.

"My poor girl." Mark pulled her into his arms and held her tight, wishing desperately that he could say something that would lift her spirits during what was bound to be a lonely journey to a place where she knew no one. "I wish I could help."

"You have." She smiled tremulously. "Just knowing that I have you as a friend . . ."

"A friend you may always call upon if you need him." Mark bent his head to press his lips to hers. He had meant the kiss to seal his pledge of friendship, but as his lips touched hers, something happened. He became acutely aware of the softness of her skin, the delicate scent of lavender, the slenderness of her waist beneath his hands, the long, slim line of her thigh pressed against his, and he found himself kissing her hungrily, desperately, fueled by a desire he had not thought possible.

For a brief moment he gave himself up to the passion that rose within him. Just for a moment, he savored the exquisite ache of longing, and then his sense reasserted itself. How could he be thinking such things, feeling such things toward a woman he had just assured of his help should she ever need it? How could he be thinking of making passionate love to her and coming to her defense at the same time? How could he wish so intensely at this moment to be her lover while he was pledging himself to be her protector?

Gently Mark thrust Sophia away from him. Drawing a deep breath, he tried to get hold of himself. The big eyes still gazed trustingly into his. Good. Perhaps she had not felt it, the desire, his body's craving for her. Perhaps she did not know how close he had come . . . to what? To treating her as a woman instead of a friend? Forcing his own confused thoughts from his mind, Mark tried to focus on Sophia. "You will be all right, believe me, you will. At the moment you do not think so, but I know you. You are strong. You are resourceful. You will do well. And when I return to London . . ." For some inexplicable reason, he discovered that he could not go on. His throat was tight, as though the damp weather had finally given him the sore throat and cough that everyone in Saint Jean seemed to suffer.

He grabbed Sophia's hand again, raised it to his lips, and was gone before she could begin to frame a reply.

Sophia remained rooted where she stood in the middle of the room, transfixed by what had just occurred. Then, slowly she sank into the nearest chair and, staring into the fire, tried to make sense of all that had just happened, trying to sort through her disordered thoughts and feelings, but she could not. At the moment she was too overwhelmed with everything—her mother's death, her packing, her impending departure, an unknown life before her—to deal with anything, to comprehend anything. Resolutely she put all the jumbled impressions and emotions out of her mind and returned to her bedchamber and the task at hand-packing. She could not bear to think of the farewells she would have to endure.

It was not until the end of the week, after she had boarded a brig bound for Portsmouth, that she was able to relive the major's good-bye and wonder at it.

One thing seemed clear, however, and that was that whatever Major Lord Mark Adair's relationship with the Condesa de Gonsalvo y Coruna had been, it was now most definitively at an end.

At last Sophia could admit to herself the constraint this relationship had put on her own friendship with the major. Until the appearance of Diane de Gonsalvo y Coruna, Sophia had felt closer to Major Lord Mark Adair than she had ever felt toward anyone else except her mother. With the appearance of the condesa, he had seemed to withdraw, or maybe she herself had withdrawn, especially after their disagreement over the condesa's portrait. She had thought, especially after their discussion of losing their mothers, that they had regained some of their original intimacy. Certainly there had been a naked vulnerability in the major's eyes when he had confessed to his feelings of guilt over his mother's death that made Sophia believe he had never confided it to anyone except her, but at the same time, he also seemed to be perfectly capable of being intimate in other ways with Diane de Gonsalvo y Coruna, ways in which he was not intimate with Sophia.

As Sophia paced the brig's deck or leaned over its rails to gaze at the gray swells all around her, she thought again and again of the look in his eyes as he had assured her that he was *a friend you may always call upon if you need me.* There had been an intensity in that look, an insistent note in his voice that made it seem as though there were some other message he had been trying to convey to her.

Not only did she think about the major's looks and words, but about her own reaction to them, how his farewell kiss had evoked feelings in her she did not know existed. Until that moment, she had not understood the hunger she had observed in the condesa's eyes when they rested on the major, a hunger she had seen in the eyes of other women when she had caught them gazing at some of the more dashing officers.

Until that parting moment with the major, she had thought herself immune to such things, but now she knew that she was not. The attraction she felt toward Mark Adair, the lean, tanned face with the high cheekbones and mobile mouth, the straight dark brows over penetrating eyes that missed nothing, the broad shoulders and long legs that made him tower over other men, was an attraction she had never felt toward anyone else.

It was not that he had kissed her or held her in his arms, she knew that now. The kiss had just forced her to realize that she had been attracted to him for a long, long time— since the first day he had come pounding over the hill on Caesar's back and scolded her for sketching in the middle of a war. And as his lips had come down on hers, as he crushed her to him so that she was close enough to feel his heart beat, Sophia had discovered that she had also wanted that kiss for a long, long time.

Chapter 33

The winds were favorable, and within a little over a week they arrived at Portsmouth. She spent the night at the George Hotel, and the next day, following the general's instructions, allowed Colonel Potter to hire a post chaise for her.

Lost in her thoughts of those she had left behind, Sophia paid little attention to the rolling fields of Hampshire or the high, wide sweep of the downs as they crossed into Surrey, nor did she notice much about the neat little villages and towns they passed through—Buriton, Petersfield, Farnham.

Finally, late in the evening, they arrived in the metropolis seething with such activity that it reminded Sophia of nothing so much as the army on the march—horses, carts, oxen, all crowded into the streets. At long last they pulled up in front of a slim, elegant house in Brook Street where the door was immediately thrown open by a grizzled butler who nodded affably at Sophia and led her upstairs to the drawing room.

Pausing anxiously on the threshold, she drew a deep breath and plunged into what was to be her new life. A fire was burning cheerily and the room, whose delicate shade of blue with graceful white pilasters clearly declared its decorations to be inspired by Adam. Her first impression was that she had stepped into a Greek temple or a museum, for in addition to the neoclassical design, there were marble busts and statues placed in every available alcove and on every available surface.

Sophia's attention was so absorbed by the exquisite statuary that for a moment she was unaware of the tall, thin woman who rose to greet her.

"My dear, you must be worn to the bone. Do come sit by the fire and let me ring for refreshment."

With some trepidation, Sophia examined the woman in front of her. Yes, there were her father's bright blue eyes and long nose, but the eyes were piercing and intelligent rather than laughing. The finely shaped mouth and chiseled chin exhibited a great deal more resolution than her father's ever had. All in all, it was a face that showed character where, at the best of times, her father's had shown charm, but mostly, amiable weakness.

"Thank heavens you appear to look more like your mother, who must have been a beauty. The Featherstonaugh women tend toward horsiness." It was clear that Sophia was being observed as critically as she had been observing. "But that is neither here nor there. I am delighted to have you here, though I realize that you probably can not say the same thing, for London must be decidedly flat after the Continent."

"I am grateful for your hospitality." Sophia sank wearily into the proffered chair as her hostess turned to give instructions to the servant who had appeared in response to her summons.

"I expect that that is mostly nonsense, though kindly meant, for who would willingly leave friends and a familiar atmosphere, no matter how uncomfortable it might be, for a totally unknown accommodation among the family that disinherited your father and behaved so badly to your mother. Now tell me, child, what are your interests and what you would like to do in London?"

"I hardly know, I . . ."

"You look like a young woman of sense and though every young woman naturally wishes to meet some society, I expect that there are things you would like to do besides that."

"Well . . ." Sophia paused. She had never really given much thought to such things, for she had always known that she wanted a life with more meaning in it than an endless round of social calls, routs, balls, and all the other diversions of a fashionable existence. If she had dreamed of anything at all, it was to be recognized as an artist, though she could hardly confide something as personal as that to the woman sitting opposite her in spite of being told she looked as though she had sense. And Sophia could not help wondering what it was about her that made Lady Lydia think she had sense.

"It is obvious that you are not one of those flighty young misses who wishes to flit from one crush to another. You do not simper, your countenance shows you to be a thoughtful person, and your attire, while it is appropriate and of excellent quality, is not the latest kick of fashion." Her aunt volunteered these observations as if reading her niece's thoughts. "But you still have not answered me."

"I never expected to come to London, but if I had, I would have dreamed of seeing the exhibition at the Royal Academy."

Lady Lydia nodding approvingly. "So you shall, and also the exhibition at the British Institution for the Development of Fine Arts which this year is showing the works of Hogarth, Wilson, Gainsborough, and Zoffany. General Curtis wrote that you are something of an artist which is why I have put you in a bedchamber at the front of the house where the windows afford the most light and there is ample room to set up an easel. I spend my mornings studying and I daresay that you would like time to work alone."

Sophia's eyes stung with grateful tears. Perhaps life in London would not be so miserable after all. Incredible as it might be, Lord Harry's sister appeared to be a woman after his daughter's own heart. "I . . . I do not know what to say except that I am very grateful . . . thank you."

"You need say nothing at all. It is my own selfish wish for quiet moments that prompts this suggestion. Now, I expect that you need rest more than anything. I shall show you to your chamber and will send the maid with hot water and some supper. I shall not expect to see you before tomorrow noon at the earliest."

Lady Lydia led her up the stairs to a large bedchamber hung with blue damask. A space had been cleared by one window, and a comfortable chair had been placed next to a fire whose cheering blaze welcomed her. Observing these thoughtful arrangements, Sophia once again blinked back tears of relief and exhaustion.

"There, now. I leave you to your own devices for I am sure you are quite fatigued." Lady Lydia paused in the doorway. "You know, I was quite worried about his change, but I expect we shall rub along tolerably well together." With an impish smile that made her appear nearly as young as Sophia, she closed the door gently behind her, leaving her niece alone with her thoughts.

Chapter 34

Lady Lydia was as good as her word, leaving Sophia alone to paint, read, write letters, or amuse herself however she wished every morning. They would then meet over a light luncheon and discuss plans for the rest of the day.

While the exhibition at the Royal Academy was still more than a month away, Lady Lydia did arrange for her niece to view some of the best private collections belonging to acquaintances, and they went to Spring Gardens to see the annual watercolor exhibition.

Lady Lydia allowed her niece time to settle in and feel comfortable in her new life before thrusting her into any social events, though naturally she had introduced Sophia to acquaintances encountered at the various exhibitions they attended. To Sophia's infinite relief these acquaintances were, for the most part, as erudite and serious as Lady Lydia herself. Lady Lydia, who confessed to her niece that she did have the reputation of being a bluestocking and something of a dragon as well, did not have many callers, so they were left to pursue their interests and their sedate life in relative peace and quiet.

One caller, however, did venture to break this pleasant routine. Aunt and niece were each contentedly poring over a page of the *Times,* which they had divided between them, when the butler came to announce a visitor. He barely had the opportunity to pronounce the words *Lady Arabella Featherstonaugh* before the young lady herself came bouncing into the room.

"Dearest Aunt Lydia, I know that you like your privacy, but it is past noon and we have just arrived in town and I am dying to see my new cousin. What is she like?"

"See for yourself," her aunt responded calmly. "Though

it would be nice if you could make her feel a little less like some animal in a zoo."

The young lady was fashionably dressed in a bonnet and pelisse that were in the height of elegance, but her sophisticated appearance was belied by the sparkling eyes, mischievous expression, and enthusiasm of a young miss just out of the schoolroom. "Oh." She raised a hand encased in a lemon-colored kid glove to her lips in dismay. "I *do* beg your pardon, but when Papa told me that Lord Harry's daughter was staying with Aunt Lydia in London, I just had to come see you."

"Ah, that is very, er, kind of you." Sophia was still reeling from the young lady's eruption into the peaceful sitting room.

"You must forgive me." Lady Arabella plopped into the nearest chair and stripped off her gloves. "But our family is so dreadfully straitlaced and dull, Papa especially, that I just *had* to introduce myself to the only interesting relative I have. Aunt Lydia says your father was so naughty that Grandfather cast him off without a penny. And then he married your mama. I think it is all too thrillingly romantic."

Sophia could not help smiling at the notion that being disinherited warranted the instant respect of a strictly brought-up young lady. "The *thrillingly romantic* part seemed to have disappeared before I came along, but I admit that life was certainly never dull where Papa was concerned."

"Oh do tell me all about it and about life with the army. How exciting it must be to follow the drum. You must know ever so many interesting me . . . er, people."

Sophia suspected that it was handsome young men in scarlet coats that were the chief attraction for Lady Arabella, but she was more than willing to beguile her with tales of army life. It had been so long since she had talked of such things that it was almost a relief to speak of them, though she did feel a lump rise in her throat more than once.

Lady Arabella felt a good deal later, but not until she had extracted a promise from Sophia and her aunt to go driving with her and her mother in the park the very next day.

As the door closed behind her lively niece, Lady Lydia smiled ruefully. "I am afraid that your quiet existence has come to an end, for Arabella will not stop until she has bullied you into attending all the most fashionable squeezes in town. But she is a good girl. You are fortunate you are still in mourning for you can excuse yourself from anything you do not wish to be part of."

But that evening as Sophia lay staring up at the hangings on her bed, she was thinking not of balls and routs, but soldiers marching and fighting, and of one soldier in particular.

Sophia fought against the tears that choked her. She told herself that homesickness was natural, that the pain of losing her mother and missing old friends would be softened in time, but deep inside her, a voice so faint that she was almost unaware of it, suggested that the feelings overwhelming her were not just those of unfamiliarity and loss, but that some emotion even more compelling was affecting her in ways she could barely identify.

The reflections of the night were soon banished by the concerns of the day as Sophia prepared to meet the Duchess of Broughton, whose footman had brought around a note inviting them to join her in her afternoon drive.

Sophia had suffered a good deal of misgiving over meeting the wife of *my starched-up prig of a brother,* as Lord Harry had always referred to him, but Arabella's ingenuousness and Aunt Lydia's kindness had gone a long way toward dispelling her worries. Indeed, the duchess appeared to be an older, plumper version of her daughter and though less forthright, welcomed Sophia graciously, even going so far as to point out all the notables as they proceeded in a stately parade around the park.

Sophia was relieved to discover that the duchess seemed to bear not the slightest ill will toward Lord Harry or Lord Harry's daughter, and beyond expressing her condolences at the loss of both Sophia's father and her mother, she evinced no further interest in either of them.

There were others, however, who did speak of Lord Harry Featherstonaugh. Lady Louisa Cathcart, who had greeted the duchess and her daughter fondly as her barouche paused next to theirs, was happy to meet Sophia. "Lord Harry's daughter, is it? I am delighted to make your acquaintance. Such a charming scapegrace your father was." Lady Louisa scrutinized Sophia for a moment. "Though you do not have the look of him, you know."

"No, ma'am. I believe I take after my mother though I am not quite so beautiful as she was."

"Ah yes, your mother. We were quite wild to meet the woman who captured Lord Harry's heart and hand, but we were destined to be disappointed. However, I am glad to meet you at last. Welcome to London, Miss Featherstonaugh, though I imagine London must seem sadly flat after your adventurous life in the Peninsula."

Sophia had no answer, for she *did* find London to be sadly flat, but for other reasons than those Lady Louisa assumed. And as it would have been highly impolite to acknowledge such a thing, she merely smiled and replied, "Thank you."

Not that Sophia regretted the unusual life she had led. As she sat in various salons and ballrooms watching couples whirl around the floor, glad to have the excuse of her mourning to keep her quietly on the sidelines with the dowagers, she often thought how interesting and enlivening her life had been compared to the lives of those who were laughing and flirting, trading the same *on-dits* this year as they had traded the last.

How trivial it all seemed compared to marching and fighting across inhospitable terrain. And how insipid the men appeared after those she had been accustomed to. The best of them were intelligent and respectful enough, but beyond that, they seemed hopelessly dull.

What was happening to those back in France, risking their lives? Sophia continued to wonder this and to scrounge for every scrap of information she could discover about the British forces in Europe until one day in early April her aunt looked up from the *Times* to remark. "It has ended."

"What has ended?"

"*What has ended?* How can you ask, child, when you have been fretting over them since you have arrived. *It,* the war. Paris has surrendered to the Allies and Napoleon has abdicated."

"Thank God!" Until she uttered the words, Sophia did not realize how worried she had been. He was safe then.

At least, she was mostly certain he was safe. She had constantly scanned the lists of dead and wounded for one name in particular and his had never appeared. Now at last she dared to hope that he had come through unscathed. Offering a silent prayer of thanks, Sophia went off to a concert at the Hanover Square Rooms with her aunt and Lady Arabella with a lighter heart than she had had in months.

Chapter 35

It was not until nearly two months later, however, that Sophia was able to assure herself thoroughly and completely of Major Lord Mark Adair's survival. She was attending Lady Montmorency's ball, a splendid crush, and she had just taken her usual seat among the dowagers on one side of the room when her eye was caught by a dark head and a lean tanned face that rose above the rest of the crowd that was pushing its way into the brilliantly lit ballroom.

Even before her mind had consciously recognized the major, her ragged breathing and the rush of blood to her cheeks told her that he had arrived, for no other person in the world was capable of making her feel light-headed and exhilarated in that same way. Sophia told herself that the weakness in her knees and the trembling that seemed to affect the hands she gripped together in her lap were merely a reaction to the natural anxiety she had felt for his and everyone else's safety. But some minutes later as she viewed with perfect equanimity the arrival of Andrew Leith Hay along with Frederick Ponsonby, she knew that her happiness at seeing the major was more than relief at his safe return.

The room seemed to grow brighter after that. Conversations seemed wittier, people friendlier, and in general, Sophia found herself enjoying this particular ball more than any other one so far. Even the self-congratulatory air of the foppish and fashionable Lord Wardale or the pedantic pronouncements of Sir Ernest Tudway were less irritating than usual. In fact, Sophia hardly heard them at all, but nodded and smiled at the appropriate places as her eyes followed a tall figure in uniform around the room.

Would he notice her? Would he still wish to be friends

with her now that she was not one of the few young women available to talk to? Would there still be that special undercurrent of sympathy and understanding or would it degenerate into mere polite acquaintance? Sophia tried to put such anxious speculations out of her mind, but she could not. What did it matter, after all, how Major Lord Mark Adair conducted himself? For the first time since her mother had died, she felt fully alive.

She would have been astounded to learn that the major, casually greeting acquaintances and accepting congratulations on his safe and victorious return, was scanning the ballroom as intently and eagerly as she was, searching for one particular face, whose eyes sparkled with intelligence and humor. A face that scorned coquetry and flirtatiousness. Would she still be the same forthright Sophia or would she have become just another fashionable beauty? To those around him, the major looked appropriately bored by the brilliant throng around him. Long years as an exploring officer had taught him to conceal all thoughts and emotions with extraordinary skill, but at the moment he felt as though in some odd, inexplicable way his entire life hung in balance.

At last he caught sight of her sitting on the edge of the crowd, listening politely, if without any great enthusiasm, to a young buck holding forth. It was not until he felt his heart pounding and his breath strangled in his throat, that Mark realized just how very much he had missed her.

The long hours of hard riding, drawing maps of roads, hills, marshes, and French pickets while avoiding foraging parties and peasants ready to sell him out to their compatriots had been a blur for him since she had left. He had carried out his duties to the best of his abilities, even participating in a final cavalry charge at Toulouse, but the excitement had gone out of it all for him. At the time, he had attributed it to having been a soldier too long, but now he knew it had been because he had not had Sophia to share it with.

Over the months he had come to know Sophia, he had grown accustomed to sharing everything with her, and knowing that he would be sharing it with her had made him exert himself all the more so that he could report a job well done. Without her as an audience, the challenge seemed to have gone out of it all and it had become routine. Of course he had had his fellow officers, but Sophia had brought a unique perspective to things that increased his own appreciation and understanding. And she also accepted and sympathized with the difficulties he had with his role as an exploring officer while the others could never quite get over their disdain for the covert nature of his duties even though their lives depended on the information he brought to them.

When Mark finally pushed his way through the crowd of eager young misses and self-important bucks, Sophia looked up immediately, as though some sixth sense had told her he was there.

He heaved a sigh of relief at the welcoming smile that lit up her face. At last he would have someone to talk to, someone intelligent and sympathetic, someone who did not have to have every detail explained to the fullest degree so they could comprehend what he was discussing.

"Major Adair!" She greeted him happily and then turned to the older woman next to her. "Aunt Lydia, this is Major Lord Mark Adair, a friend of mine from the Peninsula."

Not *a* friend, Aunt Lydia amended silently as she saw the glow in her niece's eyes, but *THE FRIEND*. "Happy to meet you, Major. My niece has spoken of you."

"She has? Nothing bad, I hope." Mark tried desperately to read the older woman's expression, but the sharp eyes and angular features revealed nothing beyond a lively intelligence. Before Mark could question her further, her attention was demanded by a portly gentleman with spectacles.

"I'm delighted to see you back in one piece. How did the Spaniards hold up? I saw from the papers that once he left the Seventh Division at Bordeaux, Wellington was forced to rely on the Spanish infantry to support him."

Mark grinned. "How well you guess the difficulties involved in *that* maneuver. They were paid and given rations as well which kept them from plundering, thank goodness, but you know how the Spanish are. They followed Freyre in double quick time before Beresford even began his attack, so they were somewhat tired when they reached the French entrenchments on the hillside. And once they found cover they did not move. Naturally the French *voltigeurs* moved down among them and sent them running back down the hill. It was only the, ah, *encouragement*, of the heavy dragoons at their back that rallied them."

"Ah yes. They do not lack for bravery, but they are easily discouraged."

"Precisely."

As he talked, Sophia felt as though she were once again back in the old life. It was a relief to discuss something, really discuss it, with a man who actually paid attention to her opinion and respected it instead of expecting her to sit quietly, nodding and approving, while he did all the talking. Unlike other men, Mark would pause to watch her reaction or ask her what she thought of some particular detail. Having experienced what passed for polite conversation, Sophia was more appreciative than ever before of his willingness to listen to her.

However, as he spoke, she could not help noticing that some of his old energy, his exuberance and brashness, had disappeared to be replaced by something more cynical. What had caused it? When she had first met him, he had already been in the Peninsula for over three years and though he had spoken ironically of his role as an exploring officer, there had not been the world-weary, self-mocking, and satirical air that now seemed to hang over him. She hated to think that he might have changed and lost the sensitivity that had made him special to her.

Sophia rode home to Brook Street that night in a reflective mood, both relieved and disturbed by their reunion— relieved that he was safe, but disturbed by the change she sensed in him.

Chapter 36

Sophia was not the only one suffering from conflicting emotions. As Mark headed back to his brother's mansion in Grosvenor Square, his temporary quarters until he found his own, he hoped that the cool night air and the relative emptiness of the streets would help him sort through the feelings that had overwhelmed him the moment he saw Sophia again.

Much as he had resisted doing so, he had admitted to himself several months ago that there had been an empty spot in his life after Sophia left the Continent, but he had not realized how empty it had been until the moment he had seen her that evening, sitting calmly at the ball, watching the crowd with that bright, observant, half-amused, half-deprecatory expression on her face. She was an oasis of calm good sense in a desert of purposeless vanity.

What had also surprised him was his own lack of self-assurance as to her feelings. Until now, Mark had never really stopped to consider his effect on women. He had always been assiduously pursued by attractive matrons in search of a dashing antidote to their boring husbands and young misses who sought a husband of suitable wealth and rank. How they felt about him personally had never really entered into the picture before because he had never really cared. He had decided long ago that any marriage he made would have nothing to do with feelings and everything to do with logic. Even his passionate relationships with women were about desire, not tenderness. Now, however, he found himself caring tremendously what Sophia felt about him.

There was no doubt that she had been glad to see him. Her smile had been warm and welcoming. But would she have been just as welcoming to any other friend she had not seen for some time, Andrew Leith Hay or Fitzroy Somerset, for example? For the first time in his life Mark felt a strong attraction to one woman above all others, and he wanted Sophia to feel the same way about him.

But did she? When he had held her in his arms in her quarters at Saint Jean de Luz, Mark had been ready to swear that she cared for him as much as he cared for her. Her eyes had glowed with a warmth and tenderness that spoke only to him. He had felt her heart beat faster as he had pulled her to him and her lips had responded with a passion that matched his. But perhaps he had been wrong. Perhaps the strength of his own feelings had projected itself onto hers.

Perhaps in London she had found someone else with whom she shared things, someone who was less reckless, someone more stable and dependable than her father had been, than any cavalry officer could be. She had lived among them all her life. What could one cavalry officer offer her that would make him mean more to her than all the other men in London, men whose variety of experience would make her life more exciting than it ever had been?

Entering Cranleigh House, Mark hurried up to his bed-chamber, where he allowed Finbury to help him out of his coat, poured himself a large measure of brandy from the decanter on his dressing table, and threw himself into a chair in front of the fire.

What was he to do? How was he to proceed? Any exploring officer worth his salt ought to be able to discover a lady's state of mind and heart on any topic, but how was he to do so without Sophia's being aware of it?

Mark tossed off another glass, and then another. Life had been more dangerous, but a good deal simpler in the Peninsula.

Life at home was a different thing altogether and it hit Mark full force the next morning in the breakfast room. Ordinarily, by the time he returned for breakfast after his early morning ride, the room was empty, his brother having eaten while he was out riding, and his sister-in-law and nephew taking chocolate in their bedchambers considerably later.

This time, however, not only the duke, but the duchess, awaited him. From the unmistakably determined expressions on their faces it was clear that they were bent on

having *a talk*. Mark swore softly under his breath. He had
taken up residence in the Duke of Cranleigh's town house
against his better judgment, but after years of soldiering,
he had no desire to live in the barracks, nor had he had
time yet to find himself suitable lodgings. It was now brutally obvious that this had been a serious lapse in judgment
on his part.

"Ah, good morning, Mark. This encounter is fortunate
indeed, for we are all so busy that our paths rarely cross."

"Did you have something particular you wished to say
to me, Richard?"

The Duke of Cranleigh cleared his throat uncomfortably.
Five years ago he would not have hesitated to point out
familial duties to his younger brother, but facing this lean,
tanned stranger with the cool air and eyes that looked right
through one was quite another matter. "No, dear boy, just
happy for the opportunity to talk."

The duchess stole a quick glance at her husband. It was
not like him to lose any opportunity to hold forth on his
favorite topic—what every family member owed to the illustrious name. "What Richard means"—she leaned forward to smile encouragingly at her brother-in-law—"is that
you have been off fighting that dreadful war for so long
that now you are safely returned you must want to settle
down to a home of your own and forget all the miseries
and discomforts of the last five years.

*Not nearly so dreadful as kicking one's heels in one ball-
room after another with nothing more exciting to do than
gamble away one's fortune for high stakes,* Mark could not
help thinking. "Why, Letitia, am I to infer that you have
selected some delightful young lady to share this domestic
bliss with me?"

"Oh no." The duchess tittered nervously. Really, Mark
was far too acute. She had warned Richard that he would
know what they were about the instant he walked into the
breakfast room, and he had. She glanced uneasily into the
dark brown eyes that bored into hers. "Well, yes. Richard
thinks it is time you settled down. It is wonderful that you
have been out defending your country, but it is time now
to think of your family, you know."

With an effort, Mark refrained from pointing out that to
some people, duty to one's country outweighed all other

duties. "I see. And who are these paragons that you have chosen as being worthy of an alliance with the illustrious Adairs?"

The duchess glanced pleadingly at her husband.

"Ahem. Well, I am sure you are aware that Father and I always considered Lady Laura Carlow to be the most advantageous match for you. Her family goes back nearly as far as the Adairs. Their lands are considerable and it has always been understood that his daughter would be an excellent wife for you."

"But of course, if you find you can not like Lady Laura, who is quite lovely, there is also Lady Cecilia Warburton, who is most unexceptionable," the duchess added with an encouraging smile.

"Thank you for arranging my future so carefully for me. I gather that I shall encounter both of these paragons at the Countess of Roxley's rout this evening, to which you seem to have committed me."

Husband and wife exchanged a congratulatory look at a job well done. Richard was the first to respond. "Naturally. All the most important members of the *ton* will be there."

"And what else would you be doing now that the army's services are no longer needed?" Long inured to her husband's overbearing ways, the duchess sympathized with her brother-in-law's annoyance.

"What else indeed?" Mark tossed off a cup of coffee and strode from the room, too furious to remain in their company a moment longer.

Still seething, he headed over to Gentleman Jackson's boxing saloon to wear off his annoyance and keep himself in fighting trim. In the back of his mind, he had known it was coming. Even before he had left for the Peninsula, his brother had been urging him to set up his own establishment, and the name of Lady Laura Carlow was frequently mentioned in these conversations.

When he considered it rationally, divorcing it from his brother's irritating tendency to run everyone else's life, it was not such a surprising suggestion. Mark had always known that he must marry, and to a woman such as Lady Laura. Marriages among people of his station in life had everything to do with family and connections, and nothing to do with love. Love had led his mother into an ill-advised and unhappy marriage, and her son had resolved never to make such a mistake. Even attraction to his wife seemed problematic to a man who had been so recently betrayed by the Condesa de Gonsalvo y Coruna. At least someone like Lady Laura would scorn to act as the condesa had acted. A lady such as Lady Laura would consider seduction and deception unworthy of her. She knew the rules as well as he. She would never stoop to embarrassing them both by pretending to be attracted to him. And with a wife such as those his brother suggested, Mark would be protected from the designs of any other women he might be attracted to.

Would Lady Laura be the most reliable, most trustworthy candidate for the position of Lady Mark Adair? Not caring a whit about Lady Laura or Lady Cecilia, and recalling from the dim recesses of his memory that the physical charms of both of them were about equal, Mark found himself wondering how he was to choose between them.

As he mounted the steps to the boxing saloon, he decided that he would just have to hope that something would occur to give him a preference for one of them over the other. Ruthlessly he squelched a picture that flashed across his mind, a picture of the one woman who did not flirt or act the coquette, a woman with whom a man could enjoy an intelligent conversation, a woman who observed the foibles of the fashionable world instead of participating in them.

Chapter 37

The evening, however, brought him no closer to enlightenment. Both Lady Laura and Lady Cecilia were fashionably fair with the requisite rosebud lips and retroussée noses. Both were graceful dancers and amusing companions with an inexhaustible flow of clever remarks and *on-dits*. Both were becomingly attentive, though the minute he spoke of anything serious he could see their eyes begin to glaze over in spite their well-bred attempts to keep the smiles pasted to their lips and to nod in the appropriate places. And it was clear from his brother's approving smiles that selecting Lady Laura or Lady Cecilia would permanently insure him against the duke's ponderous attempts to direct his life. That in and of itself was worth a good deal to Mark.

Why, then, did he feel the leaden weight of his life closing in on him? Why did this safe, secure future fill him with more foreboding than even the most horrific day in the Peninsula? Overcome with a vague distaste for life in general, Mark left the rout early to wander the streets for hours, feeling more alone than he could ever remember. He considered going to the barracks and reminiscing over a bottle of port with his fellow officers, but most of them would congratulate him rather than commiserate with him on the prospect of marrying an attractive, wealthy woman.

No one would understand how utterly bored he was at the thought of a comfortable life devoid of danger and empty of challenge. That was it, he needed a new challenge. And the thought of challenge brought with it the memory of someone else who could not exist without a challenge— Sophia Featherstonaugh.

The pall of dullness and boredom that had hung over him all day vanished as quickly as if the sun had broken

through the clouds. He could talk to her. She would understand how he felt.

The tide of happiness that washed over him, the sense
of relief that flooded through him as he thought of Sophia,
were miraculous. But then followed the inevitable question.
Did she feel that way about him? And how was he to
discover whether or not she did?

Almost as quickly as the question arose, it was answered.
He would ask her to draw portraits of his two possible
fiancées. Not only would she be able to show him the subtle
differences between the two that he had been unable to
detect, but her reaction to his request would tell him something about her own feelings for him. Despite Sophia's
angry disavowal of the slightest jealousy of the Condesa de
Gonsalvo y Coruna, Mark still believed that some of her
distaste for the condesa *had* sprung from feelings of jealousy. Surely he was right about that. Sophia for all her
intelligence and unusual upbringing was still a human being
after all, still a woman.

Mark was so relieved and delighted by his idea that he
could hardly wait to put it to the test. Not only would the
commissioning of the two portraits provide an excuse to
call on Sophia, it would give him the opportunity to discover how much she cared for him, if she cared for him at
all. Now all he had to do was to decide whether or not he
really wanted to know.

The next afternoon Sophia was reading the *Times* when
Lady Lydia's butler came to announce that there was a
gentleman below to see her. "A gentleman?" Sophia remembered with a sinking feeling that Sir Ernest Tudway
had been promising to stop by and leave another of his
learned and unintelligible treatises on an obscure topic for
her to read.

"It is a Major Lord Mark Adair. Am I to tell him that
you are at home?"

"Oh yes, certainly. By all means. Thank you, Mackworth."

Observing the major as he followed Mackworth into the
room, Sophia could not help but be struck all over again
by the way his powerful figure infused the room with energy and excitement.

"Good day, Major." She rose to greet him. "I am sorry that my aunt has gone to call on a friend of hers who is very ill."

"Will you take it amiss if I tell you that I am not calling upon her, but upon you?" Mark raised a quizzical brow.

"Not at all. You mistake my meaning. It is just that I should like her to become better acquainted with you."

"Am I to take it, then, that you value her opinion? She must have made you feel welcome here after all."

"Yes. She has been most kind to me. She has done a great deal to make me feel at home here and she has introduced me to many of her acquaintances, who are more sensible than I could have hoped."

"That must be a great relief to you." Mark could not help feeling vaguely disappointed as he realized that in some odd sort of way he had hoped she would welcome him as the only person with whom she could truly share her thoughts and feelings, the way he had welcomed the sight of her bright, intelligent face among the fashionable throng at Lady Montmorency's ball.

"Yes. And I expect you can guess just how great a relief it is." She smiled at him shyly.

"Sophia . . . I mean, Miss Featherstonaugh."

"Yes?"

"This is not purely a social call. I have come to ask a favor of you."

"Yes?" He seemed oddly ill at ease and Sophia could not imagine what was coming next.

"Once again, I find myself in need of your skills." When he had first come up with the notion of having her draw pictures of Lady Laura and Lady Ceclia, it had seemed easy enough to ask her to do a simple sketch of the two young ladies, but now, for some reason, he was having great difficulty articulating his request. "I need your help deciding . . . I mean, I need your skill at reading character . . . well, what it is, is that there are two young woman I am thinking of . . . in short, I am trying to decide which one to ask to become my wife."

Even as he said it, he could hear how absurd it must sound, but Sophia did not evince the slightest reaction. In fact, she betrayed no emotion at all, not even the flicker of an eyelash, but sat, an expression of polite interest frozen

on her face. "I was wondering"—he tugged uncomfortably
at his cravat—"if you would be so good as to draw a portrait of each one of them—a sketch, nothing more. You
always see so much, and I thought you might distinguish a
difference between the two that I had missed, a difference
that might help me to choose one over the other."

For a moment Sophia could not speak. She felt as she
once had when as a small girl she had walked too close
behind a horse and been kicked in the stomach. Then, with
a valiant effort, she summoned her wits about her. "These
two women are so interchangeable, they mean so little to
you that you can not choose between them?" she asked
incredulously. "I have never heard of anything so cynical
in my entire life!"

"Cynical? Is it cynical or is it rational? I assure you that
neither one of them cares a whit for *me* as a person, but
they both care a great deal for what I represent, a husband
who is of an equal station in society and wealthy enough
to provide for them. Surely you do not pretend that I
should marry for love. After all, *you* would never be so
reckless as to marry for love."

"Yes, I . . . ." The image of her careworn mother scrimp-
ing and saving the little left over for them after her father
had lost yet another sum on some ridiculous wager rose
before Sophia, and she thought of the endless nights they
had sat up waiting for him to stagger home from the arms
of some woman, or an evening drinking with the lads. "No,
I would *not* marry for love." But even as she uttered the
words, another picture of her mother smiling fondly at the
general flitted through her mind. At first Sophia had assumed that the general and her mother, both widowed and
mature, had married merely out of mutual respect and a
wish for companionship, but she had, over time, revised her
opinion as she had watched the two of them together. Perhaps their maturity had given them the freedom and the
confidence to follow their hearts. Certainly the affection
she had witnessed between them had often made her feel
left out and just the tiniest bit jealous of their obvious delight in one another and their very real happiness. "I mean,
I do not know," she concluded lamely.

Mark heaved a sigh of relief. There was hope after all.
"Then could you help me? You must consider this as you

would any other commission, as an opportunity to advance your career, except that you will know I am counting on you for so much more."

She opened her mouth to refuse, but shut it again when she realized how churlish it would sound. After all, he was only trying to promote what she had often expressed as her dearest wish. It would be most ungrateful of her to reject such an offer on the grounds that she disapproved of his behavior, and it would be even worse to condemn that behavior if she could not counter his logic with her own strong arguments against it. He was only doing what every one of his acquaintances would do or had done. Why then did she feel so dreadfully disappointed in him? "Very well."

Mark rose and took both her hands in his. "Thank you so much. I shall be forever in your debt. You will hear from me as soon as I have spoken to Lady Laura and Lady Cecilia."

Another bow and he was gone, leaving Sophia to wonder if she had gone stark, raving mad. Here he was offering support and encouragement for her career and she wished to have nothing to do with any of it, or with the two young women whom she had never seen before, but already detested.

Chapter 38

In fact, it turned out that neither lady was particularly detestable. Each one was far more charming and far less self-serving than the Condesa de Gonsalvo y Coruna had been. During her session at the family's town residence in Portman Square, Lady Laura confided to Sophia that she hoped to do everything in her power to make Lord Mark Adair a suitable wife. "His papa and mine were friends since Eton and Mark is so much more charming than the Marquess of Ashworth, who is Papa's other choice for me. The marquess is years older than I and though Mark is only a second son, Papa feels it incumbent upon him to honor a promise he made to Mark's papa when I was in the cradle, which is most fortunate. I do think the major is quite handsome, do you not, Miss Featherstonaugh?"

Sophia, intent upon her sketch, was able to mumble a reply that neither confirmed nor denied this opinion and her subject chattered gaily on, never noticing that her portraitist, while appearing to listen with great seriousness to everything she said, never actually responded to any of it.

It took the entire afternoon, but Sophia, bound and determined to have as little contact with either one of the prospective fiancées, was able to sketch in enough detail that she required only one sitting with each of them.

Lady Cecilia, though slightly more reserved and less forthcoming than Lady Laura, welcomed Sophia graciously and sat uncomplainingly in her Berkeley Square drawing room for the entire session. When it was over she begged to see Sophia's work. "Why, you are vastly clever, are you not? Lord Mark told me that you were. He says that you are good enough to become the next Angelica Kauffmann, and that he is determined to see to it that you do. He is such a forceful gentleman. Tell me, Miss Featherstonaugh,

since you, too, were in the Peninsula, do you think he will
find living in the country quite dull after all his travels? I
myself prefer a quiet life and I look forward to returning
to Kent. It would be such a relief after the rigors of the
Season. Mama quite adores all these routs and balls, but I
prefer a quiet evening by the fire—so much more enjoy-
able, do you not agree?"

Once again Sophia, putting the final touches on the
sketch, was able to avoid responding. She could not help
feeling pleased that Mark had spoken of her in such a complimentary fashion, but in truth, she found little to decide
between the two ladies. Both women appeared to be
equally unsuited to a man who craved activity and constant
challenge. She as much as told the major this several days
later when he came to collect the sketches.

Mark crossed over to the windows of Lady Lydia's drawing room that looked out over Brook Street. Holding them
to the light, he examined first one sketch and then the
other. "But these are no help. They are both lovely, but
virtually indistinguishable."

"So are the ladies."

"This is not like you, Miss Featherstonaugh." Mark con-
gratulated himself on his carefully noncommittal tone of
voice. So she did not care for either of his worthy pros-
pects—that was most encouraging. "Ordinarily you have
a decided opinion on everything. You never fail to pick
up some clue as to the personality beneath the outward
facade."

Perhaps in this case, there is none, Sophia longed to reply,
but she held her tongue.

"Then whom do *you* think I should marry?"

"Why marry at all?"

"Why indeed? A very good question, Miss Featherstonaugh. But, tell me, even though you might not believe it
possible, do you not secretly hope to marry, to find someone with whom you could share the rest of your life, someone to whom you could confide your deepest thoughts, your
most cherished dreams? Do you not have worries and fears
that would dwindle into nothing if someone could share
them with you?

"I never thought of marriage." That part, at least, was
true. As to the rest of it, she had pictured it almost con-

stantly since the day they had said good-bye in Saint Jean. While it was true that her aunt had been very kind and they possessed similar tastes and intellectual interests, no one, not even her mother, had shared things with her so intimately as Major Lord Mark Adair had. And when she had left him in France, it had felt as though she had left half of herself behind.

Watching her closely, Mark wondered what brought the color rushing into her cheeks. Was she remembering the way her lips had responded to his kiss, the way her body had molded itself to his?

"I am sorry, Major, that my pictures did not help you with your decision." Unable to bear his scrutiny any longer, Sophia turned and walked briskly away from the window toward the sofa in front of the fire.

"No matter. They are excellently done. I am sure that both ladies will be pleased to receive them, and you have proven to me that I can not commit myself to spending my life with either one of them."

The relief was so great that Sophia's knees almost buckled underneath her. She grabbed the back of the sofa to steady herself. "Then if I have been able to help you in any way, I am pleased."

"Yes, you certainly have helped me. You always do." He came to stand next to her, looking deep into her eyes, searching for some clue, something that would tell him for certain that she wanted him as much as he wanted her. His eyes remained steady on her face for some time, then, raising her hand to his lips, he kissed it, turned, and was gone.

Walking back down Brook Street, Mark asked himself, *What next?* The wind ruffled the paper that Sophia had wrapped around the pictures. He looked down at the package in his hand. What a fool he had been! It seemed so simple now; how could it have been so complicated before? *Why marry at all?* he heard her asking. Why indeed? For the reasons he had just given her. He did not wish to marry Lady Laura or Lady Cecilia, not so much because he had anything against either lady, or against marriage, for that matter, but because he wished to marry Sophia! The vague feeling of unrest and dissatisfaction that had been hanging over him since she had left Saint Jean vanished in an instant and once again his life felt full of possibility and, yes, challenge. For how was he to convince Sophia Featherstonaugh that she wished to marry him?

I never thought of marriage, she had said. That, given her father's example, he could well believe, but what did she think of love? There was the challenge. He could not say to a woman like Sophia, *I love you, I want to marry you,* just like that with no preparation, no warning, nothing. She would not believe him for an instant. Her natural distrust for dashing cavalry officers in general, and one who had been involved with the Condesa de Gonsalvo y Coruna in particular, would make her inclined to distrust anything he might say. So how was he to convince her? What was he to do? Somehow he would have to come up with something.

But the moment Mark entered his brother's impressive marble hall, his attention was distracted by a more immediate problem. As he crossed the black and white tiles and headed for the imposing marble staircase, he heard his name being called.

"Uncle Mark?" His nephew, Richard, appeared in the doorway of the library and glanced anxiously around to assure himself that they were unobserved. "Might I have a word with you?"

Something was seriously amiss. It took no great powers of observation to see that his ordinarily blithe nephew was greatly worried about something. His customarily sunny countenance was drawn and haggard and the unnatural pallor of his skin only made the dark circles under his eyes all the more pronounced. "What is up, lad? You look as though you are in a devil of a coil. Mark poured a glass of brandy, handed it to his nephew, and pointed to a chair on one side of the fireplace. "Now, out with it."

"Well, you see, the last few nights at Watier's"—Richard tugged nervously at his cravat as his uncle's eyebrows rose—"and, no, Papa has not the slightest notion that I frequent the establishment. He does not approve of any game of chance, but that is because he does not understand. It is the opportunity to test one's wits against someone else's. Not all of us are lucky enough to prove ourselves in the Peninsula, and a man must do *something.*"

Mark nodded encouragingly.

"You see, the thing of it is, everyone does it, and one does not want to be thought of as hen-hearted so one has to play a little to keep up one's reputation. And, if one does not want to be thought of as a nip-cheese, one has to wager a decent sum. All the really choice spirits go to Watier's these days and there is no harm in a friendly game of whist, is there?"

"Except that . . ."

"Except that last night and the night before I lost nearly one thousand pounds. I know, I know, that does not seem such a princely sum compared to many, but Papa is so clutch-fisted he would be horrified if he found out and I do not have the ready to pay my debts, which, of course, must be paid."

"So you would like a draft on my bank for one thousand pounds."

"Oh, no, nothing like that." Richard ran his fingers distractedly through his hair. "It is just that I think, I mean, I feel fairly certain that I was cheated."

"That is a serious accusation, lad."

"I know, I know. And I know that anyone who is at Watier's is a gentleman and that every greenhorn who loses thinks he has been beaten by a Captain Sharp, but I *am* more than seven, you know, and I *do* play a fair game of whist. I have not ever lost before. Oh, a game here and there over the years, but nothing to signify. However, these last few nights, I could do nothing *but* lose and each time, I was playing with the same people. So that is why I think that there is something havey-cavey about it. But I do not know who it is nor what to do. One simply can not accuse one's enemies, much less one's friends, of cheating at cards, particularly if one does not know which one is doing it. Whatever shall I do?" He groaned and buried his head in his hands.

"It is always the same group of people, you say."

"Yes. Fenton Crawthorne, Calverly Berwick, and Digby Northcote."

"Friends of yours?"

"Yes. Er, well, that is, since I have come to town, but they are all perfectly unexceptionable. Berwick and I were at Eton together, and everyone knows that Northcote is rich as the Golden Ball so he has no need to do such a thing. And Berwick has known Crawthorne this age—their families have neighboring estates in Oxfordshire, or some such thing—so it is not as though any one of them is not a gentleman."

"No? Hmmm." Mark thought for a while. "And are you being pressed for the money?"

"No. Crawthorne is being most gentlemanlike about it. They all say that my luck will turn, I just need to play a little more to win it all back, but I have never had a losing streak before. It is not as though it were E.O. or hazard, which *are* a matter of luck."

"I agree." Mark rose and laid a comforting hand on the young man's shoulder. "Let me think about it a bit, lad, and I shall see what I can come up with. Let us talk again tomorrow."

Richard rose, smiling shyly at his uncle. "You are a great gun, Uncle Mark. Papa knows about a great many things, of course, but he is such a stickler for propriety, and he can make one feel so . . . feel so . . ."

"Believe me, lad, I know precisely what you mean. Now you go out and get some fresh air and exercise. Your father is not noted for being sensitive, but he will notice if his son and heir walks around looking like a ghost."

Then, following his own advice, Mark ordered Caesar to be saddled up and brought around for a ride in the park. Fresh air and exercise always cleared his mind as well and helped him to think.

And just as he had hoped, after a few turns around the park he had come up with a possible solution not only for his nephew's difficulties, but his own.

Chapter 39

The very next afternoon, Mark unveiled his plan to Sophia and her aunt. "I know that it is difficult to credit, but I believe Richard. He is not a genius, but he is a clever lad, and if he thinks he is being cheated, then he is. The devilish part is to catch the one doing it, and that can not be done in public. Doubting a man's honor is the worst insult one can offer a gentleman, and one must be extremely circumspect. Therefore, I think it is best to arrange for the unmasking, if there is to be one, someplace away from London and the possibility of gossip.

With that in mind, I have arranged for a small house party at Cranleigh. Buckinghamshire is close enough to town that no one will object to a few days in the country, especially with access to Cranleigh's stables and its cellar. My brother is not a connoisseur of either horses or wine, but familial pride forces him to employ those who are, so the family estate is as famous now as it was in my grandfather's day. Now, however, we come to the part where I must ask for the assistance of you two ladies."

Mark turned to Lady Lydia. "I expect that by now you realize what a talented artist your niece is, but I am not sure you know of her almost magical powers in reading character. She has saved me from the disastrous consequences of my own mistaken impressions more than once, for which I am most grateful, I assure you.

"Miss Featherstonaugh, I know that I am always asking for your help and doing very little to repay it, but if you could join us at Cranleigh and spend a few days sketching my nephew and his friends playing cards, my nieces performing on the pianoforte or reading aloud, I feel certain that you will be able to tell in no time who is the scoundrel among us." Mark smiled at Sophia in a way that made her bones turn to water. "I can not offer you much in return except some magnificent countryside for riding and a collection of family portraits done by the masters of the day—Holbein, Vandyke, Hilliard, Kneller. My nieces, Caroline and Maria, will hang on your every word. Caroline is sixteen, Maria fourteen. They consider themselves to be very grown up and are furious at their Papa for refusing to allow them to come to town. My brother, however, knows what a handful they are and says they will have ample opportunity to cause trouble when they have their first Seasons. Until then, they are not being given the slightest chance to risk their reputations. As for you, Lady Lydia, I offer an excellent library. Once again, my brother's pride has insured that he has built the collections of my ancestors. What do you say, ladies? Will you come to my rescue?"

Observing the delicate flush that rose to her niece's cheeks and the sudden sparkle in her eyes, Lady Lydia did not have the heart to refuse. "I have not been to the country in some time. Yorkshire is too long a trip for me, and Broughton Castle is as drafty and uncomfortable an old pile as one could ever hope to see. What do you say, Sophia, to a few days in the country?"

"I . . . ah . . ."

Mark hurried to press his advantage. "Of course, Atalanta is also invited. I am sure she would wish to encourage you to take advantage of the opportunity to leave behind crowded city streets. I shall even give you a chance to beat me in a proper race."

Sophia chuckled. "In the face of such shameless manipulation, what can I do, but say yes?" Her own heart already beat faster at the prospect of gallops in the countryside and the easy camaraderie she had shared with the major in the Peninsula.

So, one bright spring day a little over a week later, Lady Lydia's ancient traveling coach lumbered down Brook Street toward Paddington and then to Buckinghamshire.

Mark and Richard led the way in a shiny new curricle that Mark had purchased, along with a magnificent team of grays, the week before.

The weather promised to be fair for some time and Sophia's spirits, lighter than they had been since her mother's death, rose considerably as they left the busy streets of town behind them and proceeded toward the rich, rolling green of the Chiltern Hills.

Cranleigh was a relatively modern house, constructed during Queen Anne's reign on the ruins of the original Tudor palace built for the Dukes of Cranleigh. It had been designed by Vanbrugh, though on a smaller, more commodious scale than either Blenheim or Castle Howard, and it was situated in a spacious park, surrounded by gardens and grounds laid out by William Kent.

Lady Lydia and Sophia were greeted on their arrival by Caroline and Maria, who were ecstatic at the thought of company besides their governess. "You have no notion how dull it is here," Caroline confided to Sophia as she led them to their chambers. "Miss Priestly does her best to keep us amused, but really Maria and I are quite beyond the schoolroom now and there is not a great deal more for her to teach us. So it is excessively exciting to have visitors. Uncle Mark says that you have spent most of your life on the Continent. I am sure you have had perfectly splendid adventures and know everything that there is to know about the latest fashions. Of course we have been at war with France, but war or not, everyone always looks to Paris for a true à la modality. And Uncle Mark says that you are a most accomplished artist. Surely you can draw some of the gowns they are wearing in France this year."

Sophia thought of the condesa and smiled ironically. "I expect that I can."

"Oh, could you? Maria and I would simply adore that. We could have them made up in the village. How that would make Lady Lewis and those odious daughters of hers stare!"

Despite her own lack of interest in the fashionable world, Sophia could not help but laugh and promise to do her best. There was something so appealing and infectious about Lady Caroline's absolute conviction that Sophia, who had spent her life in army camps, could give the Duke of Cranleigh's daughters enough fashion to compete with the reigning belles of the countryside.

The days passed quickly enough. Sophia had never really been part of a group of carefree young people, and she found herself thoroughly enjoying the youthful spirits of Maria, Caroline, Richard, and his friends. Watching them all laugh at the antics of the young men as they strove to amuse the girls and Sophia with donkey races and games of battledore, Mark could not help feeling a hundred years old and somewhat out of place. He had been able to comfort Sophia, even make her smile, but he could not ever remember having made her laugh as she did at these childish games.

In the evenings they repaired to the drawing room where Richard and his friends played cards, Caroline practiced the pianoforte, Aunt Lydia read, Sophia sketched, and Mark observed.

After several such evenings he approached Sophia one morning as she was examining the dizzying array of titles in the library. "Do you think you have been able to capture the gamesters accurately enough for us to guess the one we should be wary of?"

"I think so."

"Good. Let me call Richard and you bring your sketchbook."

"Very well." Sophia ran to retrieve her sketchbook and returned to the library, where Richard and his uncle awaited her. "Here."

"Why, Miss Featherstonaugh, these are magnificent!" Richard bent over to look at the sketchbook. "You are a true artist, and far more talented than Uncle Mark led us to believe."

"Why thank you." Sophia blushed with pleasure.

"Indeed she is, but let us have a look at what she has done." Mark reached over to take the sketches from her and examine them. "Hmmm." He glanced at first one and then another and then another. "What do you think, Richard?"

"Well, sir, look at the hands. They seem to be held so oddly. And the shoulders. They are tensed as though he is watching for something."

"Precisely. What do you say? I think we have our man."

"I suppose so, but Sir Fenton? It hardly seems possible. He is so plump in the pocket, one can not imagine he would cheat."

"But look at the way he chews his lip, lad. Could anything be more indicative of an uneasy state of mind?"

"I quite agree, but it is so incredible. Why would . . ."

"Let us put it to the touch. Play again tonight at your usual card game and I shall watch most carefully."

"You, Uncle? But what can you see? I have been playing cards with this man for over a month now and I have not seen anything amiss."

"Tut, tut, man. I used to be an exploring officer. Give me some credit for knowing what I am about."

"Very well, sir. I hope you can see what I have failed to detect this age."

"Trust your uncle, Lord Richard, he *does* know what he is about." Sophia could not keep herself from defending Mark.

"If *you* say so, Miss Featherstonaugh, then I shall. But I must say the we, none of us, would be any closer to the truth without your sketches. Your perspicacity is astounding."

"You are too kind."

"No. Truly, I mean that. And how you can be such a talented artist and a magnificent horsewoman besides is something quite out of the ordinary. Anyone can see that Atalanta is a handful, yet you make her perform as though she were a member of Astley's troupe."

"You give me far too much credit."

"Not at all." Richard's blue eyes glowed with admiration and enthusiasm. "Sir Fenton, Berwick, Northcote, all of them say they have never known a woman to ride so well."

"I thank you all." Sophia smiled indulgently. His boyish admiration was truly charming, as well as infectious.

Later that afternoon, as they galloped across the fields, she could not help reveling in the almost worshipful way all the young men praised her equestrian abilities. Indeed, the only dark spot in an otherwise perfect day was the cynical smile that twisted the major's lips as he listened to their effusive compliments. Well, he was accustomed to riding with cavalry officers, which naturally left him unimpressed. Let him smile as cynically as he wished, these men, at least, could appreciate the hours she had spent listening to her father's instructions and practicing endlessly under the watchful eye of Sergeant Mapplethorpe.

That evening after only an hour's play, Mark suggested that they break for some refreshment. While the others were listening to Caroline perform a set of lively country airs on the pianoforte, he and Richard called Sir Fenton into the library.

"Crawthorne," Mark began sternly, "it has come to my attention that you have been enjoying almost unbelievable success at the card table."

"Why yes. I am accounted something of an expert at whist."

"So is my nephew, sir."

Closely observing his uncle, Richard could not remember when he had seen him look so forbidding.

"Ah, but I have made a science of it."

"And I a science of observing. You may have heard of my experiences in the Peninsula. There, I observed men whose lives depended on their skills of deception."

Sir Fenton licked his lips nervously. "I am sure you did. It is said that you are a great hero."

"Enough of a hero, at any rate, to be appalled by a man who would seek to take advantage of his friends."

"How dare you, sir!"

"No. How dare *you*, a gentleman born and bred, seek to defraud your friends like some common Captain Sharp?"

"You are out of order, sir."

"Am I? Then what about the card you have in your left sleeve, or do I have to pull it out for you?"

The unhappy young man collapsed in a heap on the sofa. "Please. You do not understand. I shall be utterly ruined."

"As you sought to ruin my nephew, sir. What possible explanation could you have to offer for such behavior?"

"It was Newmarket, sir. I went there with some fellows from university. We bet on several horses and I was doing well until the last when, intoxicated by my successes, I bet everything and lost. I lost more than I could possibly pay and I was in utter despair until they suggested a round of cards so I could earn some of it back. They were drunk as lords and flushed with their own success so they did not notice when I switched one card for another. I won easily then, and in no time at all I had won it all back. I deserved to win from them. Had it not been for them I should never have been encouraged to bet it all in the first place. But it was so easy and I had been so successful that I could not stop. It added to the challenge of the game to see if not only could I win, but could deceive them as well. Of course I won fabulous sums. And that was that. Of course I won fabulous sums. And that was that. Soon I could not stop, but I hated myself. I am almost relieved to have been caught. But I beg you, do not expose me. It would kill my father."

"You should have thought of your father in the first place. Now you will pay my nephew and his partner back everything they have lost to you and you will not darken the doors of Watier's, or any other gaming establishment ever again. And believe me, I shall know it if you do."

"But how am I . . . yes, sir. You are quite right, sir."

"Now, once you have written vowels for my nephew and his partner you will discover pressing reasons for returning to town."

"Yes, sir. I am sorry, sir, so sorry," the young man babbled as he hurried from the room.

"There, you see." Mark turned to his nephew. "You were absolutely right. He was not to be trusted."

Richard wrung his uncle's hand. "Yes, though I still can not believe it. Thank you, sir."

"Do not thank me. Thank Miss Featherstonaugh."

"Indeed, sir. She is a wonder, is she not? So talented, so clever. It is hard to believe she is quite real, isn't it, sir?"

"Yes, Richard, it is," his uncle replied softly under his breath as the young man dashed from the room to go in search of his partner with the good news. "Hard to believe it at all, but true."

Chapter 40

True to their agreement, Sir Fenton excused himself from their party the next day. The rest of them spent the morning rowing on the ornamental water and playing croquet. Watching the younger set, Mark came to the unnerving conclusion that instead of being amused by his nephew's endearingly obvious admiration, Sophia appeared to be flattered by it. He found it difficult to believe that a young woman who had grown up among young men should find this one any different or any more intriguing than the hundreds of young officers she had known all her life, but apparently she did, for she spent nearly the entire day in Richard's company and it seemed to Mark that every time he turned around, Sophia was laughing at something his nephew had said.

Mark had known Richard since he had been in short coats, and though he considered him pleasant enough, he would never in a thousand lifetimes have called him amusing. That someone as clever as Sophia should enjoy the company of his unsophisticated nephew after having known Wellington and his staff was ludicrous in the extreme. Surely she was not attracted to him?

Mark knew that Richard's fair hair, open countenance, and bright blue eyes were accounted handsome by many young women, but surely not Sophia. Surely she had known too many men of real character to be drawn to his exuberant, hail-fellow-well-met air and undiscriminating enjoyment of everything and everyone.

If she could not possibly be attracted to Richard's person or his mind, did it mean that she was attracted to his station? It hardly seemed likely that the prospect of becoming the Duchess of Cranleigh could influence someone as independent as Miss Sophia Featherstonaugh, but perhaps

Mark was wrong to think that. God knows he had been wrong about a woman before, and not so very long ago.

By the time afternoon rolled around, Mark was in a thoroughly bad humor, and it did not help matters to overhear Richard and his sisters begging Sophia to show them her other pictures as she sat sketching in the rose garden. Hating himself for not being able to ignore it, Mark edged closer to the group as they leafed through the sketchbook and exclaimed over the remarkable likenesses of the portraits she had drawn during the evenings.

"Why, Uncle Mark, here is one of you," Richard called out. "I say, you do look rather a cold, dangerous fellow."

"Oh I would not say that." Mark strolled over to look at the picture he remembered from Saint Jean, but it was not the same picture, not the same one at all. Eyes that had appeared to glow with passion now looked bored under drooping lids. Lips that previously had seemed to urge men to follow him into battle, now twisted cynically into a smile that was closer to a sneer. Mark felt the cold shock of recognition as though someone had tossed a bucket of water in his face. Too stunned to speak, he could only stare at the sketch in front of him.

At last he found his voice. "Do I . . . do I really look like that?"

Sophia flushed uncomfortably. "You are a good deal changed, you know," she temporized before turning to answer a question of Maria's about perspective and landscapes.

Ignored once again by the young people, Mark snorted bitterly and turned away. He had been deceived again. The woman he had trusted to be more true, more honest than most of his fellow men, had turned out to be no better than the rest of her sex.

Disgusted with the entire world, but most of all himself, Mark strode off in the direction of the stables. At least Caesar remained loyal. He needed a long ride to clear his head of all thoughts of a woman over whom he had almost made a bigger fool of himself than any other women in his life, even the condesa.

Returning from his ride, less angry, but no less disillusioned, Mark resolved not to seek out Sophia's company anymore, a resolution he broke the moment she stepped onto the terrace before they gathered for dinner. The others, involved in a noisy game of jackstraws, were completely oblivious to the absence of two members of the party.

Sophia strolled over to the edge of the terrace to look down at the ornamental water. She wanted to be alone with her thoughts that evening. The past few days, trying to fulfill the major's expectations and identify the scoundrel in their midst, had been something of a strain. Besides that, she had been troubled by the major's attitude toward her for the past day or so. Gone was that special smile that he reserved only for her. Whenever he glanced in her direction, his eyes had seemed as cold as slate, his expression hard and unyielding as though he were angry at her. She could not think what she had done to offend him, but it was obvious that something was amiss, and it made her feel, she admitted unhappily to herself, absolutely miserable.

A footstep behind her made Sophia whirl around to find herself looking into the very eyes she had been thinking of. "Major, I did not expect you."

"Expecting someone else, were you?"

"Someone else?" She looked genuinely puzzled.

"Richard, perhaps?"

"Your nephew? Why would I be expecting him?"

"You tell me."

Her expression remained completely blank. Either she was a very good actress or completely innocent of any of the designs on his nephew that he had been imagining.

"You and he seemed to have reached an excellent degree of understanding."

"Richard?" Sophia began incredulously. Then with dawning anger, she continued. "How dare you insinuate such a thing! Richard is a nice boy. I grew up with hundreds of nice boys like him, too many of them not to recognize a genial weakling when I see one. How you could think I would be so blind or so stupid as to . . . oh, it goes beyond all credibility. I have never been so insulted in my life! And by you of all people!"

She whirled around and ran angrily away from him toward the French windows that opened onto the terrace, but he caught her before she reached them and pulled her away from the view of the others.

"Miss Feather . . . Sophia, I did not mean it. Please, you must understand."

He turned her around to face him. Tears filled her eyes and one glistened on her cheek. Gently, he wiped it away with one finger. "Please let me explain. I never would have said such a thing if I had not been crazy with anger. There was that picture. How could you think I had turned into such a man as that? And in addition to seeing me as cold and cynical, you seemed to hang on every word of his. What was I to think?"

"At least he enjoys life. He does not sneer at it. It is refreshing to be with someone like that."

"Refreshing, perhaps, but you would be bored within a week. He is not the man for you."

"How dare you!"

Sophia raised her hand as if to slap him, but Mark caught it and pulled her roughly to him. "Because *I* am." His lips came down on hers, hard and demanding, forcing her to acknowledge the truth of what he said.

For an instant she yielded, kissing him back with all the passion that he had known was in her. Then she wrenched herself away. "How dare you!" she hissed again, and then she was gone, through the French doors and into the house.

Sophia did not reappear that evening. It was obvious that she had gone to bed, and Mark, not wishing to see or to speak to anyone else, soon retired to his own chamber, where he downed multiple glasses of brandy and then threw himself fully clothed on the bed waiting, hoping, for oblivion to come.

Sophia barely made it up the stairs and to her chamber before she was overcome by tears of anger and outrage. She had thought he was her friend, that he respected her, even admired her, but now he had grabbed her and kissed her like any other woman who threw herself at him, like Diane de Gonsalvo y Coruna. The fact that she had kissed him back was something she refused to acknowledge or deal with at that particular moment. She had though that Mark was different, that he was sensitive, understanding, sympathetic even, but he had turned out to be as self-centered as other men, as self-centered and unreliable as her father. Furiously she undressed and climbed into bed, where she cried herself to sleep.

Awake before dawn the next morning, Sophia lay in bed until it was light and then she arose, donned her riding habit and her boots, snatched up her hat and gloves, and went to the stable to find Atalanta.

The horse whickered a greeting as Sophia threw on her saddle and bridle and dug in her pocket for lumps of sugar, which the mare devoured eagerly. Leading her from the stall, Sophia climbed the mounting block and threw herself on the horse's back and they were off, galloping across the park as Sophia tried to put all thoughts of Major Lord Mark Adair out of her mind.

She was successful at this for a few moments only, then the pounding of hooves told her that she was being followed, and followed by a rider good enough to catch up to her. There was only one such rider she knew of.

Sophia dug in her heels, but it was no use. Caesar was soon upon them and a powerful hand reached out to grab her reins. Atalanta struggled to keep her head, but it was no use. She was no match for a determined cavalry officer.

The horses slowed to a halt. Mark jumped down and came around to help Sophia dismount. Ignoring his outstretched hands, she slid off herself, but the instant her feet touched the ground he caught both her wrists and pulled her to him.

"Sophia, look at me. Listen to me. I apologize for last night, but . . . no, actually, I do not apologize. I only beg your pardon for thinking ill of you. For the rest of it, I do not apologize. I was crazy with jealousy. I know that does not excuse my behavior, but perhaps it explains it. I have missed you horribly for months. Not having you to talk to, to share things with, has been miserable. I did not know how miserable I was until I returned home and saw you sitting in the ballroom, smiling at me, giving me a place in the world where I belonged, where I was understood and appreciated. I thought, I mean I hoped, that maybe I did the same thing for you, but now I am not so sure. The general said you knew too much about cavalry officers to fall in love with one, and there are so many men who can offer you a life that is the complete opposite of all that, but none of them can care so much about your happiness, none of them can possibly love you as much as I do."

Unable to think or speak, or even to breathe, Sophia

gazed up at him. The look in his eyes, pleading, loving, was
almost more than she could bear. She closed her eyes, felt
his lips on hers, tender, caressing at first, and then more
demanding as he pressed her to him, planting kisses along
the line of her chin and down her neck. She gave herself
up to the ecstasy of being wanted by the man she had
ached for for so many months. But then, the memory of
another cavalry officer, and a woman who had given herself
to him so recklessly many years ago, came to her mind.
"No, I can not."

"Why, Sophia? I love you. I want you. You love me. I
know you do. Your kisses betray you."

"I can not. It is madness to give in to such a thing."

"Is it madness to spend the rest of our lives together?"

"It will not last. Papa . . ."

"Sophia." Mark shook her gently. "How dare you compare me to Lord Harry? He joined his regiment because
he had no other choice. *I* joined because I wished to do
something with my life, as you wish to do something with
yours. I wished to rid Spain of France's tyranny. Your father only wished for excitement. He was selfish and reckless, he got himself killed, after all. I may take risks, but I
am never reckless. I am not even being reckless now. I
think I have loved you forever, since the moment I saw
you sketching landscapes in the middle of a war."

Still she hesitated. She longed to believe him, but she did
not want to be what her mother had been once. She did
not want her happiness to depend on another person, even
if that meant being alone for the rest of her life.

"Please, sweetheart, trust your instincts. In your heart
you know the sort of man I am. You drew that man once.
The man you drew later was a man who had been duped
by another woman and then forced to live without you
for months. With your help I can be the man I want to
be, the man you want me to be. And I think I can help
you be the woman you want to be. Trust your instincts,
Sophia, as I trust your instincts, as I have always trusted
your instincts . . . with my life."

She wavered, tormented by years of doubt and mistrust.
She looked up into the eyes smiling down into hers, loving
and true. How could she not believe in him? And what did
it matter anyway? She could not let her head deny her

heart. After all, it was the heart that had produced all her pictures, and her pictures had always spoken the truth. "I love you, Mark. I want to be with you, too, the rest of my life."

"My darling love." He pulled her back into his arms and held her as though he would never let her go, never again risk their chance at happiness.

PENGUIN PUTNAM INC.
Online

Your Internet gateway to a virtual environment with hundreds of entertaining and enlightening books from Penguin Putnam Inc.

While you're there, get the latest buzz on the best authors and books around—

Tom Clancy, Patricia Cornwell, W.E.B. Griffin, Nora Roberts, William Gibson, Robin Cook, Brian Jacques, Catherine Coulter, Stephen King, Jacquelyn Mitchard, and many more!

**Penguin Putnam Online is located at
http://www.penguinputnam.com**

PENGUIN PUTNAM NEWS

Every month you'll get an inside look at our upcoming books and new features on our site. This is an ongoing effort to provide you with the most up-to-date information about our books and authors.

**Subscribe to Penguin Putnam News at
http://www.penguinputnam.com/ClubPPI**